A Scientific Approach to
Healing through Faith and Prayer

40 Minutes With GOD

Spiritual Journey of a Surgeon

DR. VINOD KUMAR NIGAM
MBBS, MS, FICS, FIAGES
Consultant, General and Laparoscopic Surgery
drnigamvk@gmail.com

with

DR. SIDDHARTH NIGAM
MBBS, MS
General and Laparoscopic Surgeon
drsiddharthnigam@gmail.com

AF657809

Viva Books
New Delhi | Mumbai | Chennai | Kolkata | Bengaluru | Hyderabad | Kochi | Guwahati

Publisher's note

Every possible effort has been made to ensure that the information contained in this book accurate at the time of going to press, and the publisher and author cannot accept responsib for any errors or omissions, however caused. No responsibility for loss or damage occasioned any person acting, or refraining from action, as a result of the material in this publication be accepted by the editor, the publisher or the author.

All rights reserved. No part of this book may be reproduced, stored in a retrieval system, transmitted in any form or by any means, electronic, mechanical, photocopying, recorded or otherwise, without the written permission of the publisher.

Copyright © Viva Books Private Limited, 2010

First Published 2010
Revised and Updated Edition 2011, Reprinted 2013, 2015, 2018, 2019, 2023

VIVA BOOKS PRIVATE LIMITED

- 4737/23, Ansari Road, Daryaganj, New Delhi 110 002
  Tel. 42242200, 23258325, 23283121, E-mail: vivadelhi@vivagroupindia.net
- 76, Service Industries, Shirvane, Sector 1, Nerul, Navi Mumbai 400 706
  Tel. 27721273, 27721274, E-mail: vivamumbai@vivagroupindia.net
- Megh Towers, Old No. 307, New No. 165, Poonamallee High Road, Maduravoyal
  Chennai 600 095, Tel. 23780991, 23780992, E-mail: vivachennai@vivagroupindia.net
- B-103, Jindal Towers, 21/1A/3 Darga Road, Kolkata 700 017
  Tel. 22816713, E-mail: vivakolkata@vivagroupindia.net
- 7, Sovereign Park Aptts., 56-58, K. R. Road, Basavanagudi, Bengaluru 560 004
  Tel. 26607409, E-mail: vivabangalore@vivagroupindia.net
- 101-102, Moghal Marc Apartments, 3-4-637 to 641, Narayanguda, Hyderabad 500 029
  Tel. 27564481, E-mail: vivahyderabad@vivagroupindia.net
- First Floor, Beevi Towers, SRM Road, Kaloor, Kochi 682 018
  Tel. 0484-2403055, 2403056, E-mail: vivakochi@vivagroupindia.net
- 232 GNB Road, Beside UCO Bank, Silpukhuri, Guwahati 781 003
  Tel. 0361-2666386, E-mail: vivaguwahati@vivagroupindia.net
  www.vivagroupindia.com

ISBN: 978-81-309-1721-4

Published by Vinod Vasishtha for Viva Books Private Limited, 4737/23 Ansari Road, Daryaganj, New Delhi 110 002. Printed & bound by Replika Press, Kundli.

CONTENTS

PART II – Dr. Nigam's Technique for Health and Healing

"This book is dedicated to my wife Kumud,
whose spiritual strength and company made my job easy, to my son Kunal,
whose unending enthusiasm,
love and affection kept me working untiringly, and to my daughter-in law,
Dr. Madhur for her constructive discussions."

Dr. Vinod Kumar Nigam

ACKNOWLEDGEMENTS

We wish to thank each person who has contributed directly or indirectly to this book. The subject within may seem at odds in the context of medicine but, as surgeons, we recognise that God and spirituality are an important part of our lives.

At the start, we would like to thank Mukul Sharma, former consulting editor of The Times of India, for his help in primary editing. We are grateful that he shared his understanding of the subject and for his patience, even though sometimes at odd hours. Without him, this book would not have seen the light of day. Mukul is a man of both spirituality and science (he contributes a bi-weekly column in *The Economic Times* on science and spirituality). This book, in fact, was impossible without God, Mukul and our patients.

We are thankful to Mr. Sudama Chand, who helped us in typing and related activities for the book. We are also obliged to Mrs. Vijay Arora for her suggestions and linguistic advice.

We are indebted to all our patients, who have allowed us to share their case histories here for the benefit of readers.

We also thank Anuradha Varma for final copy editing of the manuscript.

Finally, we are grateful to Binita Mohanty for putting up with us as we burnt the midnight oil with Mukul, and for supplying us with endless cups of tea, coffee and, often, lots of beer.

Dr. Vinod Kumar Nigam
Dr. Siddharth Nigam

FOREWORD

I am impressed by this book and especially by the author Dr. V.K. Nigam, who is a laparoscopic surgeon practicing in Gurgaon, India. He is the author of a professional book on surgery, "*The Essentials of Abdominal Wall Hernias*" and two new techniques for surgical treatments of hydrocele and inguinal hernias. His career spans 35 years of clinical practice, teaching and academic activity. Between 1983 and 2000, Dr. Nigam worked as Chief Surgeon in Aden Refinery Company Hospital in the Republic of Yemen. During two civil wars in that country, he operated on literally thousands of patients. During the first war, he operated on 729 patients suffering from a wide variety of war-related traumas. Only two of these patients died due to post-operative complications. This is in a difficult setting, extremely hot and without a very high standard of general hygiene. How was this extremely low surgical complication rate (less then 0.3%) possible?

In this book, which is well written, and informative, he tells us why. First, were the kinds of patients he treated: "People of Yemen are very simple, God-fearing and they tend to lead easy, uncomplicated lives." They would tell me, "Doc, operate upon my child; Allah Kareem, nothing will happen to him. And God be with you." Second, was the kind of doctor he is: "I used to regularly pray for my patients before, during and after surgery, The prayers came genuinely from the heart".

Treat yourself to a marvelous adventure and inspirational experience by reading this book. Prayer and a strong faith in God are the keys to our healing in this world and the next. *40 Minutes With God* will help you with both.

Harold G. Koenig, MD
Professor of Psychiatry & Behavioral Sciences
Associate Professor of Medicine;
Director
Duke University Medical Center
Durham, North Carolina
USA

PREFACE

This is really a how-to book that goes beyond talking about spirituality and prayer and tells you how to make science and spirituality a part of your life. The two concepts are not at war, but actually complement each other. Mankind can truly progress only when spirituality and science learn to co-exist. Science and spirituality are both essential for one's well being.

Examples mentioned in the course of this book are real case histories, but names of those involved have been changed to keep their identities confidential. These are meant to open the connecting door between spirituality and science for the reader.

We have used guided imagery or guided visualization as an effective tool in the process of therapy. Our minds are known to respond first to images and later to words or sounds. Guided imagery helps one reach within to communicate a certain positive thought or affirmation, which urges a spiritual or mental victory during a potential encounter or situation. The process is not as difficult as one may imagine and does not necessarily require a specialist's intervention.

Prayer is a universal phenomenon and advocated across religions as a means of communicating with God, the Supreme Power or creative force. It is prevalent in all cultures. Prayer has healing powers.

Currently, in the era of body-mind medicine, doctors have begun to prescribe meditation along with drugs. This is a trend that is here to stay and, as the benefits become more and more visible, it will only become increasingly popular in the years to come. This belief forms a basis for this book.

Most people that we spoke to, and this includes doctors, believe spirituality and surgery are at complete variance. In fact, in our discussions with surgeons and others in the profession, we found that they believed there was little or no place for spirituality in surgery.

Surgery is a field where the stakes are high, and the success or failure of an operation is usually credited with the advanced technology used or a surgeon's expertise. Spirituality rarely fits into the scheme of things. But, how do you explain the success or failure of an operation, despite all these factors remaining a constant? As a patient's life hangs by a thread, despite the best medical equipment and doctors, we would like to believe that it's God who tilts the balance.

Or when we say, "Dr. John is a gifted surgeon; success is sure when he operates", what do we really mean? Are we talking of his talent and nothing else?

There are things we can't explain—on some days, surgery may seem effortless and the outcome is in the patient's favour, but on other days, things go the other way.

Spirituality and science have to hold a dialogue and understand each other; the psychic space in the mind exists, but is one that remains invisible and indecipherable to science.

An examination of the brain may show blood oozing, but not the thoughts, memory or emotions it contains. However, there is constant progress and things that were in the realm of the unknown a decade ago are now being understood with the help of PET scans and functional MRIs. Thus, something that may seem an alien concept today may be completely credible in the future.

It has been observed that even a marginal improvement in the immune system's functioning through prayer, meditation and relaxation techniques makes a difference to one's health for decades.

We have for ourselves that prayer and meditation help a person approaching surgery. Dr. Andrew Weil, MD, Faculty Member of University of Arizona College of Medicine, Arizona, USA Founder of the Center of Integrative Medicine, Tucson, Arizona, author of "Healthy Aging" a best seller, has said in support, "Meditation has also proved quite valuable in preparing patients for surgery."

We have seen witnessed people praying from the core of their heart during a medical emergency or grave illness, where death is imminent. We have experienced the power of prayer in our own and our patient's lives. We have written this book to share our experiences about healing the body and soul through an inner power. The book shows the reader how to emerge from misery, confusion and sickness to achieve health, happiness and peace.

The healing technique is explained in the book for different illnesses. We have explained the cause of sickness and the healing path. First part of the book deals with prayers, their technique, effectiveness and role of the body, mind and spirit in health and sickness. Prayer, meditation and visualization can help one regain health during sickness and after surgery. When a master surgeon fails and an ordinary surgeon triumphs, is it God or a superpower who is responsible? The mystery is analyzed scientifically. The question of how and why prayer and spirituality affect one during health and sickness is addressed scientifically.

The second part of the book deals with the technique developed by Dr. Nigam to treat certain acute, chronic diseases, which have been given little hope. The book includes interviews with renowned surgeons and other medical specialists about God, spirituality, health and medicine, on topics ranging from constipation to cancer. Read on to find answers to questions like how one can cure oneself, the role of spirituality and to understand the connection between the body, mind and spirit in sickness and in health.

Dr. Vinod Kumar Nigam
drnigamvk@gmail.com

Dr. Siddharth Nigam
drsiddharthnigam@gmail.com

PART I

40 Minutes With God

"Let us be silent, that we may hear,
the whispers of God"

Ralph Waldo Emerson

40 Minutes With God

Every dark cloud has a silver lining,
there is light at the end of every tunnel,
every barren land can experience harvest,
If tried, choice is yours.

Anonymous

"My comprehension of God comes from the deeply felt conviction of a superior intelligence that reveals itself in the knowable world"

Albert Einstein,
In answer to the question, What is
your understanding of God?

"Human beings, vegetables, or cosmic dust, we all dance to a mysterious tune, intoned in the distance by an invisible piper"

Albert Einstein

"There is no incompatibility between science and religion...Science shows that God exists"

Derek Barton,
Shared 1969 Nobel Prize for Chemistry

"The principle of (divine) purpose...... stares the biologist in the face wherever he looks ....The probability for such an event as the origin of DNA molecules to have occurred by sheer chance is just too small to be seriously considered."

Ernst Boris Chain,
1945 Nobel Prize for Medicine

1

INTRODUCTION

People are generally ignorant about the power they hold within themselves and the power of God.

Faith is the fulcrum of all relationships, whether it's between lovers, spouses, parents and children or with God. Once you put your trust in God, you will be witness to incredible developments, usually labelled miracles. Yes, miracles do occur and quite frequently at that.

We all plan our lives to the last detail, but it doesn't compare to what the Super Planner has in store for us. Haven't we often found ourselves miraculously rescued from situations that we considered hopeless? Yet, when unforeseen events throw a spanner in the works, we are quick to throw our hands up in despair, cursing "fate" or "destiny".

Blaise Pascal, French mathematician, gave us the theory "Pascal's No lose philosophy", which says, "Believe in God; if you are right, you stand to gain eternal bliss and if you are wrong it won't make any difference."

I (Dr. V. K. Nigam) worked in the Republic of Yemen as Chief Surgeon in the Aden Refinery Company Hospital and was its director from 1983 to 2000, during which time I operated on thousands of patients. I observed an extremely low incidence of post-operative complications in spite of low hygiene standards and the heat.

The people of Yemen are simple, God-fearing and lead uncomplicated lives. They would tell me, "Doc, operate upon my child; Allah Kareem (God willing), nothing will happen to him. And God be with you."

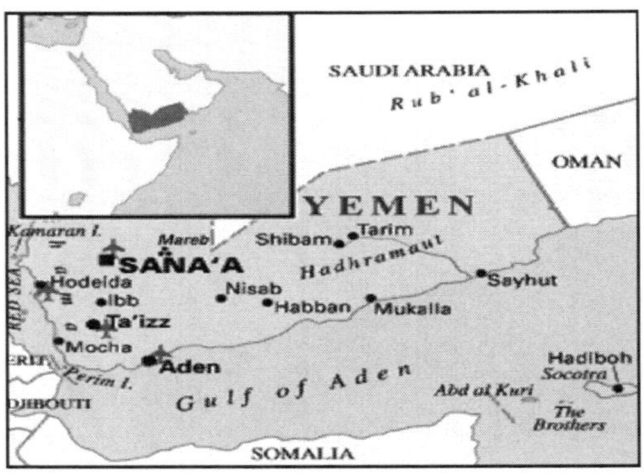

Map of Yemen

During my stay there, I witnessed two civil wars in 1986 and 1994. As the Head of the department of surgery and trauma care, casualties and deaths were routinely brought to my notice. During the first war, I operated upon 729 patients suffering different varieties of trauma, ranging from head to toe, during the course of which I witnessed horrific injuries caused by direct bomb blasts, mine detonation injuries, shrapnel related wounds and gunshot damage to bodies. In fact, some patients were even brought to me with evisceration injuries.

Injuries from blasts, penetrating missiles and burns are the main warfare injuries of the modern era. Missile wounds are caused by bullets, mines, bombs or fragments of exploding shells. Surviving casualties usually have limb injuries rather than of the trunk and head, which indicates the lethal nature of the latter.

A reason for my patient's survival, I believe, was because I prayed regularly for them—before, during and after surgery. The prayers came from the heart because I was not only praying for my patients but also out of sheer fear for my life too!

On the evening of January 13, 1986, I received an emergency call from the hospital for a trauma patient. Little did I realise that this call would change my life. As I reached the hospital, I found out that war had broken out between North and South Yemen. I stayed in hospital from January 13 to February 28 and my family had to be evacuated to India during this period.

That was when I met Mr. Ahmed bin Ahmed, a 20-year-old, who was brought in with severe blast injuries. His abdomen lay open, the intestines hanging out. Several pieces of large and small shrapnel had entered the left side of his abdomen and chest. A big piece had passed through his chest, diaphragm and lung, coming to rest just above his heart (without injuring it). Another, almost as large, had shattered a kidney.

Yemen Civil War

I operated on him for more than four hours. His left kidney had to be removed along with part of the intestines, and the "lucky" heart shrapnel taken out. As I had expected, the young man developed serious post-operative infection, mainly because of the lack of antibiotics available. However, he did have an unlimited supply of prayer. After a few days, his condition began to improve and within six weeks, he was discharged.

More and more people have started believing in God and an increasing number openly acknowledge it. Surprisingly, even doctors are turning towards spirituality and religion. A recent survey conducted by the University of Chicago in the United States has revealed that up to 76 per cent of doctors believe in God and 45 per cent feel that a religious conviction influences their medical practice.[1]

Religion, spirituality and health are now part of the curriculum of more than half of the medical schools in the USA. In November 2005, the North Dakota School of Medicine and Health Sciences arranged a lecture titled "Faith, Prayer and Miracles: The role of spirituality in the modern practice of medicine". The next month, in December 2005, Harvard Medical School arranged a CME (Continuing Medical Education) course on "Spirituality and Healing in Medicine". These trends show the emergence of research on spirituality and health in a big way. "Neurotheology", a new field, studies the neurobiological basis of religion and spirituality.

Dr. Dale Mathews physician at Georgetown University, USA, routinely enquires about the faith and religious interest of patient and has declared that the future of medicine is "Prayer and Prozac" (Prozac is an anti-depressant).[2]

God communicates with us in various languages—through silence, thoughts, reminders, responses, words, physical feelings, spiritual feelings and, ultimately, in the language of miracles. Theologian Ole Hallesby says, "Whether prayer takes the form of words or not does not mean anything to God, only to ourselves."[3]

"Those who say that the study of science makes a man an atheist must be rather silly people."

Max Born

Dr. S. Singh, 74 years old, a healthy, retired army officer working in a private hospital of Gurgaon as Medical Director, developed pain in his chest at 11 p.m. on 11th June, 2007. He walked into the ICU of a Gurgaon hospital with his son.

Five minutes later, he suffered a massive heart attack. He was resuscitated and an urgent coronary angiography (showing two severe blocks) was performed, followed by an angioplasty (PTCA=Percutaneous Transluminal Coronary Angioplasty) which saved his life. Later, he told me how he had purchased some aspirin and sorbitrate tablets the same afternoon as these were absent from his first aid-cum-doctor's kit. He had been putting this off for a few days. He developed chest pain that very night. He was informed by cardiologists that the aspirin and sorbitrate he consumed allowed him to reach the hospital safely for treatment. I call this a silent communication from God.

Warfare injuries

"God talks incessantly. But, as it turns out, mankind is deaf."

Don Wiliams Jr

Herbert Benson, physician at Harvard Medical School, writes that faith in God has health boosting effects. Dr. Harold Koenig, a psychiatrist at Duke University and Director of the Duke Centre for Spirituality, tells us that more than half the scientific papers on the topic of religion, spirituality and health show that it is advantageous to be religiously active.

Paul Mueller and his colleagues at Mayo Clinic wrote, "A majority of studies have found that religious involvement and spirituality are associated with better health outcomes". Internal Medicine Specialist at Georgetown University, Dr. Dale Mathews, states that 80 per cent of published studies report a positive association between religious commitment and better health.[4]

The more one is involved in prayer, the more a communion with God becomes visible. The field has been neglected by science since scientists look for empirical proof and it is difficult to investigate spirituality and the power of faith scientifically. Unfortunately, people who need evidence of God's existence don't try to feel His grace. I remember George Bernard Shaw for his statement, "We have not lost faith, but have shifted from God to the medical profession." Benjamin Franklin jokingly wrote the truth, "God heals and the doctor takes the fee."

The East has a lot to teach the West about spirituality; just like the West has a lot to teach the East about material matters. In other words, while the West sees science in God, the East sees God in science. However, both East and West have to live together, complementing the other's existence.

Religion may have a placebo effect that reduces stress and heals. Some believe that the idea of God is necessary for us to stay on the right path. Oxford theologian Richard Swinburne feels that God answers prayers only if they are offered for good reasons.[5]

Bob Barth, the Spiritual Director of the Missouri Prayer Ministry said, "A person of faith would say that this study is interesting. We have been praying for a long time and we have seen prayers work, we know it works. The research on prayer and spirituality is just getting started."[6]

Belief and hope, together with a few minutes of experiencing the presence of God around and within you, can significantly change your life and destiny. Your quest for answers to questions such as "What next?", "Why am I here?" can be easily found when you allow your soul to communicate with you. This approach makes for a peaceful and happy life. Knowledge is the essence, true, but knowledge with experience gives purpose to life. Peter Mere Latham, a renowned physician, said that "faith and knowledge lean largely upon each other in the practice of medicine". Our responsibilities do not end here though. We have to inculcate these basic values in the next generation too so that they can reap the benefits.

Ageing is a mental process. While the physical aspects of the body is controlled by the brain, if one provides a healthy diet to the body and soul, with adequate periods of rest and rejuvenation, it can definitely slow down the process of ageing. "Intense Yoga" and "Intense Meditation", both calling for deep focus, can also contribute positively to one's health and slow down the ageing process.

A CEO of a multinational company, Sanjay Kulkarni, walked into my chamber at Apollo Clinic in Gurgaon for a health check-up. During the course of a preliminary examination, I chatted with him, hoping to help him relax and talk about his problem. He began to tell me about his work related stress, which he feared was beginning to affect his health. I discovered he was obviously in search of something that would soothe him and give him a sense of peace.

From our conversation, I had gathered that he had a definite spiritual dimension to his being. This made my job a lot easier. Over a period of time, I gradually introduced him to my "40 Minutes With God" technique. He promised to follow it. The next time he visited me was after about four months.

Today, he is a happy man, no longer bogged down by the stress he faced earlier. He is, in fact, enjoying a happier and more peaceful life.

I have observed that 20 years ago, only one in 20 young people suffered from lifestyle related health problems. The trend has reversed now and I find an increased need for faith, prayer and spirituality in day-to-day life. The "40 Minutes With God" technique is particularly applicable for CEOs, top and middle management persons, busy businessmen, bureaucrats, politicians, housewives and busy professionals. It is not difficult to achieve something if you want it with your whole heart. All you need is trust and faith in God. Richard Swinburne, an Oxford professor of Theology, Britain, says in his book *"Is there a God?*, "A God capable of continuously monitoring and controlling the individual status of every particle in the universe cannot be simple." [7]

"If God answered most prayers for a relative to recover from cancer, then cancer would no longer be a problem for humans to solve."[8] It is a real question and the answer lies in faith, trust and the fruits of karma.

Steven Weinberg, Nobel Prize winning physicist and atheist, says "If you want to say that God is energy, then you can find it in a lump of coal." Yes, Mr. Steven Weinberg, God is everywhere and in a lump of coal too, only you require faith to see him and not an auto analyzer.[9]

It is important to first trust your belief in God; the prayer must then come from the core of your heart to be effective.

"It is neither wise nor brave to question God. It is the folly of a prideful heart."

Anonymous

It is not all that difficult to feel the presence of God, if one tries from the heart. Here, I plan to show how you too can develop a personal and sincere rapport with the master of the universe.

I have successfully practiced it and do so on a daily basis for 40 minutes comprising physical, mental as well as spiritual communion with Him.

I spend 40 minutes on a treadmill almost every morning and practice the technique during this period. As a result, I am now totally addicted to it and, therefore, recommend the same to several of my patients for their well-being. They, in turn (at least those who are serious about it), have developed a similar addiction. This addiction, however, is a positive one and not to be confused with substance abuse. One can divide these 40 minutes into various stages. You do not necessarily need to practice this on a treadmill and can either relax on the floor or remain seated through it.

Once you learn it well, you can even reduce it to half the original duration without compromising on its efficacy. And, if you dont have the time, you could do it on alternate days too.

However, you have to believe in the power of the brain, which is almost infinite in nature with nearly endless scope for development. Increasingly, doctors are coming around to accept the connection between physical health and mental state. Meditation, faith in God and specialised forms of yoga as mentioned earlier, readily result in the release of stress and reduction of depression.

For your ready reference I have divided the programme into seven parts.

1. Aawahan: Welcoming the arrival of God
2. Prayer
   For self
   For family and friends
   For an unknown person
   For an adversary or a person you don't like
   (And last but definitely not the least)
   For a sick person
3. Meditation in motion
4. Visualisation in motion
   For health of the soul
   For health of the body
5. Self-retrospection of the last 24 hours
6. Daily awakening
7. Thanksgiving

"We do not walk to God with the feet of our body but we go to him, by the affection of our soul."

St. Augustine

2

AAWAHAN

"Reach out with your faith—touch him; He will not ask, who touches me? He will know."

Peter Marshall

"When confronted with other marvels of life and the universe, one must ask why the only possible answers are religious… I find a need for God in the universe and in my own life"

Arthur L. Schalow,
Shared the 1981 Nobel Prize for Physics

Make yourself comfortable—in any posture you prefer—and close your eyes in prayer. You may open your eyes as you move along different levels in the programme or if you cannot keep them closed, for whatever reason. In the beginning, you may experience some difficulty in keeping your eyes continuously shut but a desire to do so, along with regular practice, will make it extremely easy over time.

You are going to request God to appear, listen to you and respond to your requests. However, remember that your mind will try to distract you with stray thoughts. You have to be strong-willed and bring back the focus so that you gradually learn to control the mind. As expounded in the Bhagawad Gita, the human body is like a chariot, the senses are like horses and the mind is the rein. The intellect is the charioteer and the soul is the master of this chariot. So, rein in your horses and steer them back on the right path again.

Try this technique, for instance. Visualise yourself squatting on your knees with your hands folded in any secluded place of your choice—on a large rocky surface, on a beach or in a garden. It doesn't matter as long as you are comfortable and the time is a little before sunrise when it is still dark outside. Now try to feel the silence and darkness. For a few moments, be aware of the total experience. Try to ignore noise and all movements around you.

Yes, this will take some time, practice and a lot of concentration... but a time will come when you will not be aware of your surroundings any longer.

Finally, request God to appear. In the beginning, you may have to make repeated requests for Him to do so. But, let Him know you will not discontinue your practice till He appears.

Then, begin by creating in your mind's eye an image of a tiny speck of light appearing out of the shadows at the very edge of infinity and as far out into the dark as you can possibly imagine. This light should be very bright and gradually increasing in size and intensity as it comes closer. There must also be a halo around it. Feel the happiness now that you are finally able to welcome Him into your presence. As the light approaches, it will give off a gentle warmth accompanied by an extremely elevating feeling. Suddenly, the light will be all over you and around you, engulfing your whole being, bathing your entire world.

Feel its shine. You are in the presence of God.

There is an ever growing interest among people in studies concerning health, religion or spirituality in this era of stressful and fast-paced lifestyles, so much so that if any reputed magazine reports on the subject, the sales of that issue go up. The Archives of Internal Medicine reported that when they quoted the results of the Dr. William Harris study in 1999 that a "prayer group had a better course of recovery in CCU and prayer may be an effective adjunct to standard medical care", the number of queries they received were unmatched in the history of the Journal.[10]

Keeping the eyes only halfway closed keeps the practitioner away from visual distractions, but still allows the light coming in to keep him or her awake.

Now try to open the eyelids... but don't open them. Just stretch them outwards, extended lightly. You will see a red-orange light which will make you realise that you are in the presence of God. This same light will then engulf your whole universe. Become aware of the warmth and affection of God. Linger a few moments in silence and devotion.

Next, imagine a ray of light, like a very sharp and focussed laser beam, falling on you. It bathes your whole body and gradually centres on your heart. Initially, this area is a dark one. But as the light starts falling on it, it brightens to the point of incandescence as the darkness gets dispelled. Picture this to perfection in the mind's eye.

This ball of light in your heart will then also start emitting its own internal light gradually illuminating the different parts of your body in the same way as God's light illuminates different parts of the universe. Feel this illumination in your chest, neck and head first, then the upper and lower limbs and, after that, all the internal organs. Finally, the whole body should be illuminated from the inside, leaving no dark spot anywhere. Thank Him for appearing in your vision and blessing you thus.

It reminds me of a story. A poor daily wages manual labourer routinely passed a temple of Lord Krishna after finishing his work. He would hurry home as his wife and children waited for him to bring vegetables, etc. for cooking. He would stop in front of temple daily, bow his head and say in his heart, "Krishna, I am Keshav here", and continue walking. He never went inside the temple due to paucity of time and never asked for anything as he believed that God knew everything. One day, he met with an accident and was admitted to the civil hospital. In the evening, he felt restless as he was unable to visit the temple. Not knowing what to do, he closed his eyes in deep thought. Suddenly, he heard a voice, "Keshav, I am Krishna here."

Arjuna, too, had seen this form of God once when Lord Krishna gave him the opportunity to do so and was initially fearful. You, however, will not be scared because you will be meeting Him like a child meets a parent not as a manifestation of His awesome powers.

Happy, not scared. That's because you know Him as the Creator, Preserver and Destroyer, all in one.

Thereafter, day by day, this moment will touch your heart with the feeling of utmost happiness, joy and peace. You will forget all your worries and miseries. Now you can talk to God, open your heart to him and offer your queries. Keep in mind that all this will not transpire in a day or two, the duration for it depends on the degree of your keenness, attention and concentration.

If you begin praying from the very core of your soul it will be quicker and easier. Joachim Jeremias says that "Jesus talks to his father as naturally, intimately and with the same sense of security as a child talks to his father... so is intimate prayer."[11]

I got a call from a hospital in Gurgaon to attend a serious surgical condition in a 56 years old female patient, Neelam Gupta, complaining of abdominal pain. On preliminary examination, I found she had an acute intestinal obstruction of the colon. Later, after ultrasound, CT scan, and endoscopy, I discovered the cause was most probably a malignant tumour.

The patient would not agree to surgery. Her condition started deteriorating. I remembered a saying by Surgeon Fredrick Treves, "It is less dangerous to leap from Cliffton Suspension Bridge than to suffer from acute intestinal obstruction and decline the operation."

However, after getting her consent, I operated on her and removed the cancerous tumour, including a part of the colon. On the fourth day following surgery, Neelam wanted to know the exact status of her illness and its possible outcome. As candidly as I could, I told her she was suffering from advanced cancer, which had spread to the liver and could ultimately limit her productive lifespan.

She was actually relieved to know the truth and thanked me for taking her into confidence. More importantly, however, she wanted me to give her some sort of diagrammatic representation of where her cancer sites had been. The reason? She was planning to pray, asking God to heal the affected areas. I did as she asked and she must have prayed. So did I, of course.

As I write these lines, it has been 40 months since her operation and she has been calling me once a month just to tell me that she is still alive. Medical science would have given her no more than a few months to live.

Our successful patients teach us, the doctors, how to heal and reawaken ourselves and our patients and to become better healers.

"Pathological Anatomy, the medical school text book, says that the link between development of tumours and the central nervous system has so far been very little studied...It happens rarely, but there are cases of self-induced healing...Due to some reason, the tumour starts in the opposite direction, gets smaller, resolves and finally disappears."

Aleksander Solzhenitsyn,
Cancer ward

3

PRAYER

"Prayer is more than words. It is listening, seeing, feeling as well."

Norman Vincent Peale

"Sometimes when I stand in some corner of the camp, my feet planted on your earth, my eyes raised towards your Heaven, tears sometimes run down my face, tears of deep emotion and gratitude...for once you have begun to walk with God, you need only keep on walking with God and all life becomes one long stroll, a marvellous feeling"

Esther "Etty" Hillesum,
Jewish girl who maintained a diary
while in concentration camp in Auschwitz.[12]

Prayer is the only way to be in touch with God and feel His presence. You could, for instance, pray while working out. The process will purify both your soul and the body. [13] It is the only way to talk to God and be with Him. But prayer should be intense, sincere and, more importantly, from the core of one's heart. As a child pesters his parents to get candy or toys, you must do the same with God. Pester Him. Tell Him what you want and that unless you get it you are not going to let go of Him.

There is, for instance, the famous example of a young child, who was instructed by his father, who was going out of town, to make a daily offering of food to the idol of Lord Krishna. The boy dutifully carried out his bidding but, of course, the Lord's statue wasn't eating the food. So, the boy threatened the Lord with a cane and said that if He did not appear and eat it, he would beat Him. Lord Krishna appeared and not only took the offering but also fed the boy the "prasad" (In Hinduism, a material substance that is first offered to a deity and then consumed.) with his own hands. When the father returned, his son informed him that not only did he do as he was asked to but the Lord was feeding him prasad as well. The father decided to check for himself surreptitiously. What he saw overwhelmed him and he realised that he had not been conducting the ritual from the core of his heart.

Trish, a holistic councillor in Middleton, USA, believes, "At the root of everything lies our relationship with God. We find him wherever we look, even when we look into our bodily self. We can be in denial of the existence of God or of truth, but that doesn't diminish the existence of either."[14]

According to a report in *Newsweek* magazine (17 November 2003), a poll found that 84 per cent Americans believe in the positive effects of praying for patients who are recovering from various illnesses.

It has also been found in studies conducted by Dr. Andrew Newberg, MD, Neurologist at the University of Pennsylvania, USA, that spirituality promotes longevity and that church-goers live longer than those who don't attend mass. Also, a recent survey studying 150 investigations into the effect of religion on health showed significant scientific evidence that prayer and religion protect against cardiovascular diseases, improve recovery from acute illnesses and may even slow the progress of cancer.

Prayer can be defined as a "conscious relationship with God or whatever one recognises as the creative and organising force of the universe". Prayer is the psychological boost of knowing that God or a supernatural power is on your side. Intercessory prayer is one which is done for another's benefit.

Sir Francis Galton, English Anthropologist, argued that prayers are effective and can be proved scientifically. The landmark study of Randolf C. Byrd, performed at San Francisco General Hospital, and a randomised controlled trial by William S. Harris proved the efficacy of intercessory prayer, though due to certain flaws, it was later deemed as "failing to show a significant benefit of intercessory prayer". It was seen that these contradictory studies were performed by persons performing intercessory prayer as a routine part of their jobs rather than from the core of their hearts. People forget that prayer is serious business. One has to do it with total concentration as prayer is a conversation with God.

Studying the phenomenon scientifically is difficult as both prayer and science operate at different levels. Richard Sloan, Professor of Behavioural medicine, Columbia University, USA, calls the scientific testing of the efficacy of prayer as "violence to the phenomenon of prayer". People sarcastically say that "when you talk to God it is called prayer and when God talks to you it is called "psychosis", but Mother Teresa said "Prayer is simply talking to God. He speaks to us, we listen; we speak to Him, He listens. A two-way process: speaking and listening".[15]

Reema, 50 years old, an obese lady weighing 80 kg, attended my clinic. She had gall stones along with hypertension and obesity. The hypertension was under control with drugs. She had an attack of acute pancreatitis in December, 2002, from which she recovered after six weeks without any permanent complication, except that she developed diabetes mellitus. She underwent a laparoscopic cholecystectomy in April 2004. The operation was smooth without any complication. The post-operative period was uneventful. She was discharged on the second day after the operation. While getting discharged from hospital she developed breathlessness and was taken to the ICU. She developed pulmonary embolism. As she was obese, we took preventive measures for DVT including low molecular weight heparin injections.

She, however, suffered a lot but survived with lung complications after a stormy recovery period of five days in ICU. Probably the answer to prayers were partially denied due to reasons known to Him

The CERN Laboratory in Switzerland has succeeded in producing the first particles of antimatter as a way of studying the origin of the universe. Antimatter is composed of antiparticles as matter is composed of particles. If a particle and antiparticle get too close they destroy each other and cause an explosion and both disappear, leaving behind energy. Physicists suggest that all particles had no mass after the 'Big Bang'. Every particle swims in the universe through the "Higgs Field". This field prevails throughout the cosmos and any particle that interacts with it is assigned a mass via a particle called "Higgs Boson". It is called a "God particle". After one second of the Big Bang, matter and antimatter disappeared leaving a minute amount of matter or God particle, which formed everything from the stars and galaxies to the earth and the life it supports. While science explores the God particle externally, spirituality looks inward in its search of God.

A study on the power of intercessory prayer conducted in 1988 at San Francisco General Hospital showed that such patients are discharged early from hospital.

Bob Boulton, Chief Superintendent of police, Bournemouth requested churches to hold prayers to reduce the crime rate in Bournemouth after reading about the "power of prayer"; 15 churches participated.

The High House women and children's "Mission in Oxnard" runs a substance abuse programme, which has courses such as "How to pray". One of the patients says, "I once was lost but now I am found."[16]

A study at St. Luke's Hospital, Kansas City, shows that patients, for whom prayer was conducted, exhibited 11 per cent better results than the rest. This study was published in *"Archives of Internal Medicine"* on 25th Oct 1999.

I can accept the definition of God given by Richard Dawkins in his book The God Delusion—there exists a superhuman, supernatural intelligence, who deliberately designed and created the universe and everything in it. [17] According to a poll conducted by Newsweek magazine, 72 per cent Americans believed that praying to God can cure someone—even if science says the person doesn't stand a chance. Trust and belief are powerful tools in medical therapy, and trust in your clinician causes faster healing.[18]

Koeing, H G wrote in "*Religion, Spirituality and Medicine*" that spirituality promotes longevity of life, diminishes blood pressure and reduces anxiety.[19]

When I initially began praying for patients, I did so only for those operated upon by me. The outcome of any surgery is, of course, very important for a surgeon; if the patient recovers without any complication the surgeon is considered to be good but, if not, he is regarded as somewhat less than competent.

Though healing and development of complications during and after a surgical procedure are not under the direct control of a surgeon, if anything untoward happens to the patient after he or she goes under the scalpel, the blame falls on the surgeon. So, naturally, I was concerned. It was an act of selfishness, but then it's not very easy to turn selfless overnight. The longing for fame and a flourishing practice puts a lot of pressure on a young 28-year-old doctor, as I was at the time, when he has just started on his career path.

Whenever I operated on a seriously ill patient, or performed any major life-threatening surgery, I would pray more earnestly and for longer periods. This was because I felt that success or failure here could bring fame or shame at once. Today, however, being older and more spiritually mature, I have realised that prayer is a different ball game and calls for a pure heart and mind to get God to listen. Here, selfishness has no place. A prayer with some direct or indirect personal benefits may not be very effective.

Prayer is serious business and should be from the heart, with all concentration, as chanting words or shlokas does not matter to God. He knows what you are asking for without you having to speak. Ole Hallesby, a theologian, believes, "Whether prayer takes the form of words or not does not mean anything to God, only to ourselves."[20]

So, now I pray for patients irrespective of whether or not I have operated upon them. It gives a feeling of selfless prayer. It is a satisfying process, which also helps in concentration as there is no residual guilt involved. As the great American Surgeon, J B Murphy, a pioneer in surgery, put it: "The patient is the centre of the medical universe around which all our works revolve and towards which all our efforts trend."

As mentioned earlier, I pray for my patients and have seen how it affects them. I have noticed and felt that during the course of my daily morning prayers (my own 40 Minutes With God), I can get a message from God that no harm will come to my patient. It is a feeling. I have seen patients in serious, life-threatening and terminal illnesses improving after my morning prayer. Some may call this coincidental but it happens quite often.

Dr. Herbert Benson, Cardiologist, Mind Body Medical Institute, Boston, USA, has done studies about the efficacy of intercessory prayers, which were published in the *American Heart Journal*, where he cited no difference between the patients who were prayed for and those who were not. I don't think the efficacy of prayer can be studied in this manner as the effort must come from a genuine feeling and not done as a chore to help a study.[21 & 22]

Research on the efficacy of prayer and visualisation did not happen earlier but nowadays researchers are keen to prove or disprove it. I believe that though we're unable to explain the solid scientific basis to the phenomenon in the present, we will be able to do so with further studies, as with atherosclerosis that was once considered an irreversible process but has now been proved that it can be backtracked through lifestyle changes.[23]

Science is of the belief that God cannot be seen but spirituality has a different view. Abraham Joshua Herschel says, "We cannot make Him visible to us but we can make ourselves visible to Him."[24]

"Spirituality means the ability to find peace and happiness in an imperfect world. Acceptance, faith, forgiveness, peace and love are the traits that define spirituality for me. These characteristics always appear in those who achieve unexpected healing of serious illness. Most physicians won't 'try God' until the patient is near death. Then they may prescribe a hope and a prayer. I believe it is far better to make a connection with patient's spiritual beliefs earlier. A person who believes in a benevolent higher power has a potent reason for hope and hope is physiologic."[25]

The history of stomach ulcers is similar. Earlier, it was believed that ulcers in the stomach occurred due to lifestyle related issues, but after it was proved that these are caused due to a bacteria called Helicobacter pylori by two Australian dedicated doctors, Warren and Marshall (they got the Nobel Prize for the research), the line of treatment has completely changed. The bacteria produce urease which produces ammonia, neutralises the stomach acid and affects the protective mucus covering on the stomach wall. The bacteria are shaped like corkscrew and easily burrows, by twisting through the protecting mucus lining of the stomach, causing ulcers. Earlier, a person affected with a stomach ulcer would suffer for years, but now he can be relieved from the pain after two weeks of treatment. Earlier belief are getting now explained, so is the case with spirituality.

On the other side are atheists who declare there is "no God" as there is no need for one when science can explain everything. A study conducted by Byrd R, Baylor University, Waco, Texas, USA, proves them wrong.[26] It showed that 55 per cent people believed that they are protected by a guardian angel, 67 per cent were absolutely sure that heaven exists, 75 per cent believed in hell and 4 per cent said they don't believe in God.[27]

Rashmi, a young construction worker, was brought to the casualty department of a Gurgaon hospital. A brick had fallen on her head from a height of 10 metres. As a result, she was bleeding and unconscious. A CT (Computerised Tomography) scan of her brain showed a large contusion (an injury usually caused by blunt impact in which the blood vessels are damaged, allowing blood to seep into the surrounding tissues), laceration and generalised trauma.

After showing no significant improvement in her condition for 24 hours, she was transferred to the All India Institute of Medical Sciences (AIIMS), New Delhi, where she developed seizures. At this point, the doctors at AIIMS began to fear for her life and told her family that there was nothing further they could do to help her and if they wished to take her elsewhere for treatment, they were free to do so.

Medical practice is very clear about the treatment of head injury. "No head injury is so serious that a life should be despaired off and no head injury is so trivial that you neglect the treatment".

After two days, Rashmi was brought back to the Gurgaon hospital. At this point, I began treating her along the same lines as at AIIMS. However, along with the treatment, I included prayers for her recovery. Gradually, after about a week, Rashmi began showing signs of improvement and, to everyone's surprise, her level of consciousness improved.

After another week or so, she became significantly more conscious and, after six weeks, was discharged without any physical defect or deficiency. If this is not a miracle, what is?

"*The Saline Solution*", a publication of the Christian Medical and Dental Association, feels that "the family which prays together stays together". It even teaches how to take a spiritual history from a patient. Dr. Walter Larimore, Physician from "Focus on the Family" and Dr. William Peel, Physician, feel that spiritual history must be taken like other personal histories and the patient too should be free to choose or to reject the medical care they receive. The Association of American Medical Colleges and Medical Schools states that the physician must seek to understand the patient's stories in the context of the latter's beliefs. Dr. Peel feels that excluding God from medical consultation is a form of malpractice.

Dr. Christian Puchalski, Director, George Washington Institute on Spirituality and Health, favours taking a patient's spiritual history and says, "By inquiring about a patient's beliefs the physician can assess whether the beliefs are helpful or harmful to a patient's health and medical care."[28]

Dr. Walter Larimore says "positive spirituality" involves honesty, love, peace, forgiveness and compassion and feels it must be encouraged to achieve better mental and physical health. According to Dr. Harold

Koenig, 43 per cent of the population of the United States regularly attends religious services and 96 per cent believes in God or a higher power. As shown by Dr. Herbert Benson, 76 per cent of Americans pray on a regular basis. Levin writes in his book *God, Faith and Health* that 90 per cent of Americans affiliate themselves with a religion.

D. E. King and Bruce Bushwik found in a study of 203 hospitalised patients that 79 per cent feel that their spiritual needs are considered by doctors and 37 per cent feel the need for more frequent discussion on their beliefs and 48 per cent wanted their doctors to pray with them.[29]

At the Columbia Presbyterian Medical Center, New York, patients going for heart surgery are prepared with the help of meditation.

"Turning the face towards God brings healing to the body, the mind and the soul."

Abdul Ulbaha

4

HOW PRAYER WORKS – SCIENCE OF PRAYER

"Those who say that the study of science makes a man an atheist must be rather silly people."

Max Born,
Winner of the 1954 Nobel Prize for Physics

"My patients taught me that there is more to medicine than pills and incisions... Remember that one generation's miracle may be another's scientific fact. Do not close your eyes to acts or events that are not always measurable."

Bernie S. Siegel, MD,
Paediatric and General Surgeon, USA

When a doctoral student at Princeton asked, "What is there left in the world for original dissertation research?" Albert Einstein replied, "Find out about prayer. Somebody must find out about prayer."

The word prayer came to English from Old French, "preier" which means "to request". Ninety per cent of the population prays regularly and 75 per cent pray daily. We must peep into the science of such a common ritual. Prayer may be a waste of time for atheists but for believers it is the best use of time. Gerald C. May says, "I am convinced that human beings have an inborn desire for God. Whether we are consciously religious or not, this desire is our deepest longing."[30]

The brain contains some billions of nerve cells and 150,000 to 180,000 kilometres of nerve fibres. The brain weighs only 1.5 to 2 per cent of the human body, but consumes 15-20 per cent of its oxygen supply. The largest brain in the animal kingdom belongs to the sperm whale, weighing about 8.5 kg, and is much bigger than the human brain. The latter, though, is much bigger than the brain of any animal in proportion to the body.

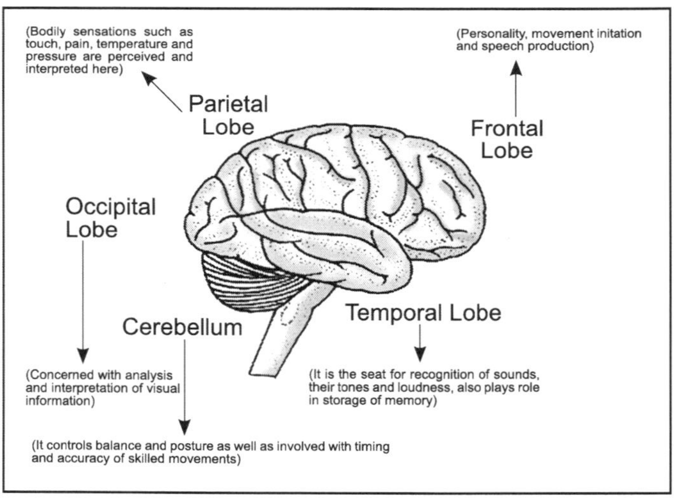

Fig: Functional parts of the brain

The seat of action for prayer and higher functions is the cerebral cortex. The anterior half of the cerebral cortex executes functions, while its posterior half is responsible for our perception of the environment.

Both parts are involved in the chemistry of prayer. The brain's functioning is based on a dual process:

1. Generation of the action potential and its conduction down to the axons.

2. Synaptic transmission of impulses between neurons.

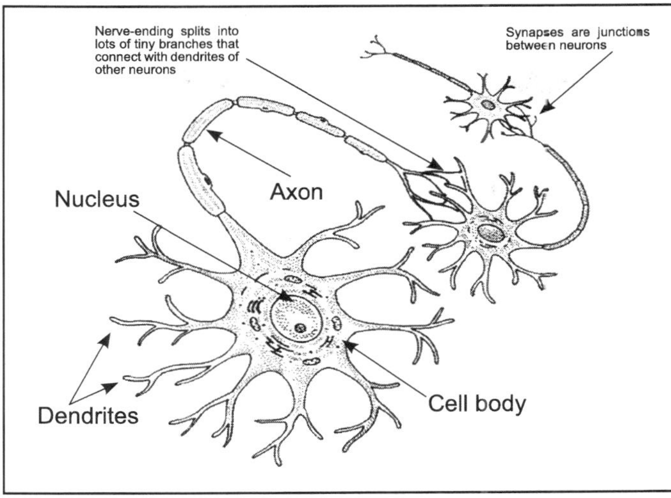

Fig: Neuron or nerve cell

More than 40 known chemicals or neurotransmitters act on different sites in the nervous system, like acetyl choline, noradrenaline, adrenaline, dopamine, serotonin, histamine, endorphins, etc.

The brain can bring about physical changes through the central nervous system and its neurotransmitters, the immune system's blood cells and antibodies, and the hormones in the endocrine system. Feelings of relaxation, peace and satisfaction send brain signals that trigger healing through these three systems. Lane Strat Hearn, from Texas Children's Hospital, studied 28 first-time mothers and their babies aged 5 to 10 months. He discovered that just seeing the baby's smile the feel good area of the mother's brain was stimulated. This was confirmed by an MRI (Magnetic Resonance Imaging). This response stimulates dopamine, the brain chemical which causes a feeling of happiness.[31]

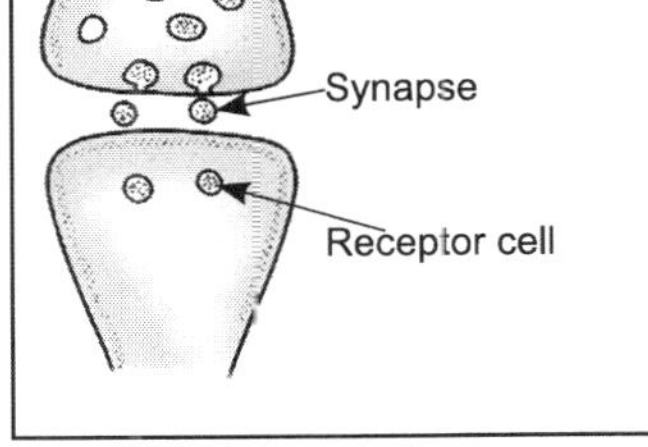

Neurotransmitters at synapse

Mueller, P.S. et al stressed in the paper "Religious Involvement, Spirituality and

Medicine" that spirituality improves the body's immunity and decreases the risk of suicide.[32]

Various researchers have tried to explain the mechanisms of distance healing through intercessory prayer. The most accepted theory of distance healing is that focussed thought has a significant impact. Researchers are of the opinion that prayers should be treated as seriously as several well-known treatments were initially subjected to scepticism.[33]

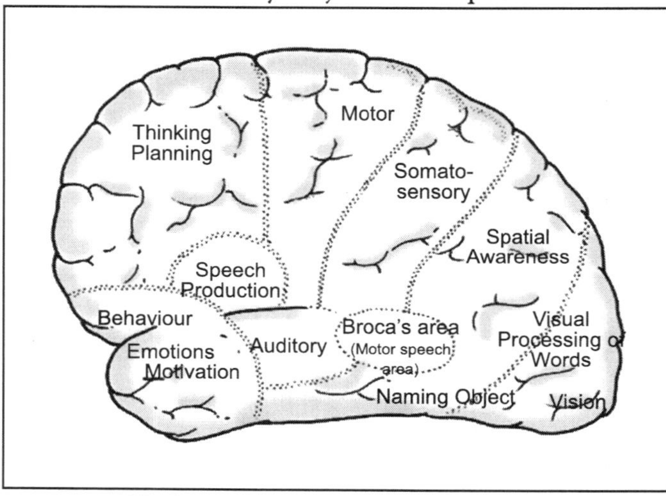

Fig: Sites of higher mental functions of brain

The landmark study on the efficacy of intercessory prayer by Dr. Randolph Byrd, Cardiologist, San Francisco, USA, and published in 1988 in the "*Southern Medical Journal*", showed that the prayer group fared better in cases of congestive heart failure, cardiac arrest, pneumonia and breathing complications.[34]

Some researchers maintain if psychokinesis (using mind power to move objects) can be accepted as effective, why not intercessory prayer? Larry Dossey, MD, says, "There is evidence that neither telepathy nor psychokinesis is nonsense." [35] The Cerebral cortex is divided into two hemispheres. Each cerebral hemisphere has four specialised lobes.

Right hemisphere:

This controls the left side of the body, deals with creative activities such as music and art, emotions and imagination.

Left hemisphere:

This controls the right side of the body and deals with logical and scientific thinking, written and spoken language and numerical skills.

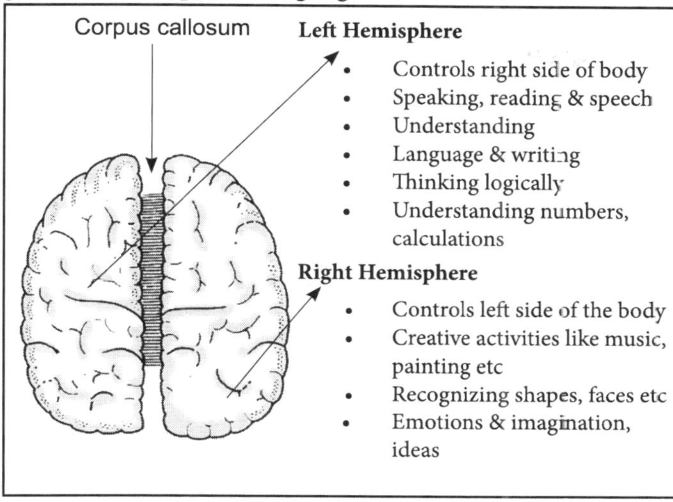

Fig: Functions of two cerebral hemispheres

In every human being, one of the cerebral hemispheres is dominant, usually the left.

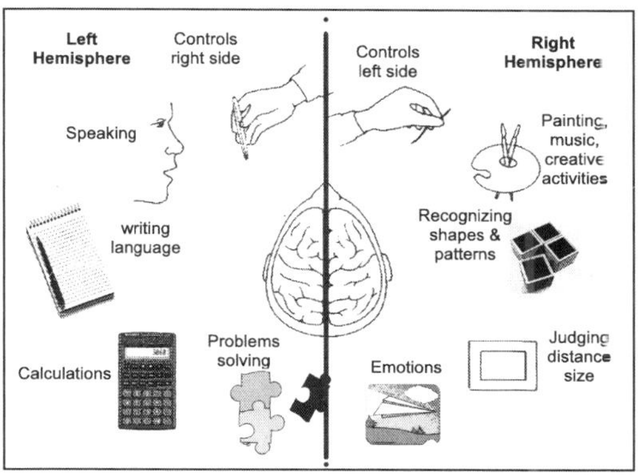

Fig: Functioning of hemispheres

"Laterality" or "Hemispheric asymmetry" is a characteristic of the human brain, in which certain functions like language comprehension are contained on one side. The right hemisphere controls the left side of the body and vice versa, which means right-handed people are left-dominant in respect to motor, visual and language comprehension.

Functions involving logical and sequential analysis generally reside in the left hemisphere while the right hemisphere controls the processing of spatio-visual information and musical understanding.

Whether laterality is genetically transmitted is yet to be confirmed.

Frontal lobes:

These are concerned with behaviour, planning, emotions, reasoning, self-conscious awareness, movements (motor area) and speech (Broca's area), etc.

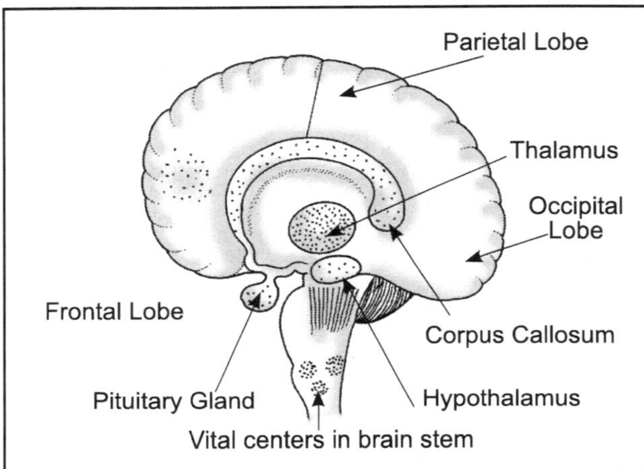

Fig: Cut surface of brain & brain stem

Studies have proved that prayer influences real changes by increasing activity in certain areas of the brain meant for concentration and decreasing activity in those related to the sense of self.

I have noticed that if a patient leans towards spirituality, this belief can translate into faster recovery, probably by providing a boost to the immune system. Similarly, Dr. David Servan Schreiber[36], Clinical Professor of Psychiatry, University of Pittsburgh Medical Center, has observed that "spirituality plays an essential role and prayer produces a state of calm, love and a sense of belonging that has a positive correlation to our health."

Parietal lobes:

These lobes are concerned with sensory and spatial perception and numerical function.

Researches show that an age-related thinning of the cerebral cortex cannot be totally avoided but can be slowed down through meditation and prayer, which help in sharpening focus and improving memory. Dr. Gregg Jacobs, Professor of Psychiatry at Harvard Medical School, wrote that meditation lowers the activity in the parietal lobes, reducing one's sense of awareness in space and time and making one feel "at one" with the universe.[37]

Temporal lobes:

They contain: Primary auditory cortex (hearing); primary vestibular cortex (space); olfactory cortex (smell); parahippocampal cortex – involved in the memory function and limbic system, including hippocampus and amygdala—which are involved in processing memory and emotions.

The dominant temporal lobe also participates in language, particularly verbal comprehension, named Wernicke's area after Karl Wernicke, German Neurologist.

A relationship between spirituality, religious inclination and serotonin is indicated by the Karolinska Institute of Stockholm, and published in the "*American Journal of Psychiatry*". They feel that the serotonin connection may be the biological basis of spiritual experiences.[38]

Andrew Newberg and Dr. Eugene d' Aquile, University of Pennsylvania, used the Single Photon Emission Computed Tomography to detect activity in different areas of the brain. They showed increased activity in certain areas of the brain during meditation and found that regular meditation increases the thickness of the cerebral cortex. They said, "Profound spiritual experiences can also be attributed to brain activities."[39 & 40]

Sara Lazar, Research scientist, Massachusetts General Hospital, found increased thickening of grey matter in sections of the cerebral cortex dealing with memory, emotions and decision making among 20 individuals who meditated for 40 minutes daily.

Occipital lobes:

These lobes are concerned with visual processing:

There are certain areas in the depth of cerebral hemispheres that have a collection of cells.

1. **Basal ganglia (Caudate and Lenticular nuclei):** Concerned with modulation of muscular movements so that they are not coarse and clumsy.
2. **Thalamus:** An egg-shaped mass of nerve cells and a sensory relay station transmitting impulses from the spinal cord and cerebellum to the cerebrum for sensory stimulation. It selects and sorts out sensory impulses which have to reach the cerebral

cortex such as sensations of severe heat, cold and pain. It may also increase or suppress information.

3. **Limbic System:** Seat of emotion and memory.

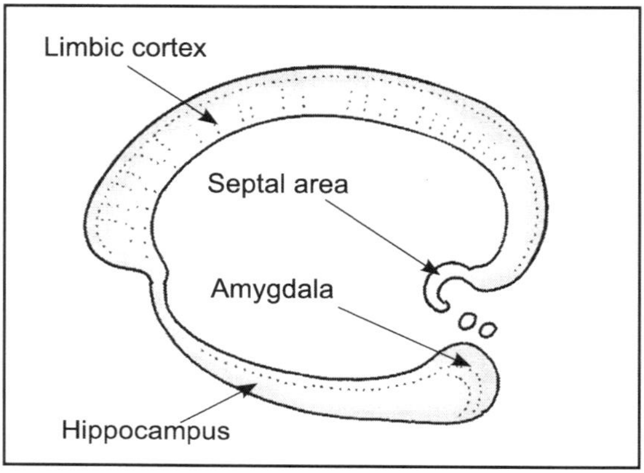

Fig: Limbic system

Limbic means "link' as it links with the cortical areas, midbrain and lower centres. The limbic system is made up of the amygdaloid bodies associated with aggressive behaviour; the hippocampus located above the hippocampal gyrus, which is involved in memory; the transparent septum, associated with pleasure; the cingulated gyrus, the fornix and the anterior commisure, which play a major role in internal communication. The mamillary bodies play an important role in memory.

Researchers have explained a form of "dwarfism" in children—"psychosocial dwarfism"—caused by emotional and intellectual stress when a child is caught in a cross-fire of hostility and feels rejected by parents and grows up with little self-esteem. The brain's emotional centre or limbic system acts upon the hypothalamus to stunt the pituitary gland's production of the growth hormone.[41]

Cognitive neuroscience is developing fast and studies have proved that certain practices can improve the brain's functioning. R. Keith Sawyer, Psychologist, Washington University, says, "We can enhance our creativity not just in art, science or business but in everyday life."[42]

4. **Hypothalamus:** A small central area of nerve cells just below the thalamus. It controls internal body functions and is regarded as an endocrine organ secreting hormones which pass down to the pituitary gland. It has the following functions:

Regulation of temperature; control of water-balance; regulation of appetite and thirst; regulation of sleep; production of some emotional reactions such as feelings of pleasure, relaxation, fear, aggression and rage; prayer and meditation probably bring a harmonious functioning of the hypothalamus and both hemispheres of the brain; coordinates fight or flight response and triggers sexual arousal.

The output of the pituitary hormones is controlled by the hypothalamus, which also controls heartbeat, blood pressure, etc. The thymus and spleen are connected by nerves to the hypothalamus, which means the latter also affects the production and response of immune cells, B cells and T cells through positive and negative emotions. Thus, the immune system is controlled by the brain through hormones, neurochemicals and nerves.[43] B cells make antibodies and T-cells attack other cells infected by microorganisms. "A 2003 survey reported 500 clinical studies documenting co-relation between religious practices, including prayer, and better health. Eight in 10 Americans believed in miracles, and more than half of all doctors reported observing miracles in their patients that defied medical explanation."[44]

5. **Cerebellum:** It is also termed the lesser brain. It lies at the back of the brain, below the occipital lobe of the cerebral cortex. It has various important functions:
   Maintaining muscular tone, coordination of muscular movements, maintaining balance and equilibrium and it is also essential in cognitive processing.
6. **Reticular formation:** It acts as a sentry to the brain. It receives incoming stimuli and prepares the brain to be alert and ready to respond.

WHAT OCCURS DURING PRAYER

When you are silently focussed on praying from the core of your heart, it is a form of meditation. During such prayers, the following changes can be noticed in the brain with the help of ECG, PET and Functional MRIs:

Alpha waves/rhythms occur in an inattentive state or when a person feels drowsy or during light sleep. In the wakeful and alert state, when the eyes are open, these waves disappear due to visual and mental stimuli.

Beta waves/rhythms are recorded during mental tension or when a person wakes up from sleep. During prayer, beta waves decrease as the cortex starts reducing the processing of information.

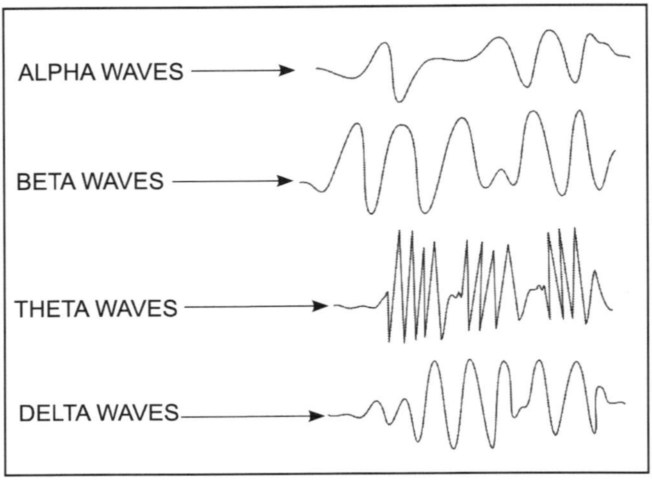

Fig: Brain waves

Delta waves/rhythms occur mostly during sleep. These occur usually in children below five years of age, during deep sleep and serious brain disorders.

Theta waves/rhythms are produced in children and during a state of deep relaxation in adults. During prayer, theta waves increase. The activity of the parietal lobes and frontal lobes diminish. They don't shut down the brain but block information to the parietal lobes. The thalamus starts suppressing information to the cerebral cortex to keep the mind at peace.

When prayer is intense, it turns into serious meditation and the brain's alpha-waves change to theta-waves, shifting from a state of arousal to one of deep relaxation.

Prayer, if combined with meditation and deep abdominal breathing, relaxes the body and mind. This triggers a positive parasympathetic response by the body through decreased metabolism, rate of breathing, blood pressure, muscle tension and heart rate. The function of the viscera improves with a sense of relaxation and sleep becomes deeper and more sustained. Fatigue levels come down. The findings during meditative states have pointed to a deeper level of relaxation at a physical level and to a more reduced arousal state. The oxygen intake and carbon dioxide output are minimal as is seen during deep sleep, but the EEG pattern is one of complete alertness.

Research using biofeedback machines shows that you can use power of thought to increase blood circlulation and temprature upto 5 to 10 degrees and it can help to lower blood pressure and tension headache.... you can watch your pulse rate fall as you meditate... blood pressure reduces by 15.3/17.8 mm/Hg. [45, 46, 47, 48]

"Scientific prayer is the harmonious interaction of the conscious and subconscious levels of mind scientifically directed towards a specific purpose"

Dr. Joseph Murphy

Neuroscientist Andrew Newberg of the University of Pennsylvania School of Medicine has used several imaging systems to observe the brains of subjects as they meditate or pray. He found that the deeper people descend into meditation or prayer, the more active the frontal lobe and the limbic system gets. The frontal lobe is the seat of concentration and attention; the limbic system is where positive feelings, including ecstasy, are processed.

When these regions flash to life, another important region—the parietal lobe at the back of the brain—dims. This lobe orients the individual in time and space. Take it away, and the boundaries of the self fall away, inducing a feeling of being at one with the universe. Combine that with what is going on in the other two lobes and you can put together a profound religious experience.

Believers, who acknowledge the idea of a 'God gene' being at work, should have little trouble in accepting that it is necessary to our survival.

A New Zealand study published in *Psychosomatic Medicine* found that patients who were worried before undergoing hernia surgery reported 48 percent slower, more painful recoveries than those who were less worried.[49& 50]

I prepare my patients for hernia surgery with visualisation and meditation, leading to faster and smoother recovery and reduced intake of painkillers after surgery.

Peter Albright, MD and past president of the American Holistic Medical Association, writes in his book "*Complimentary Therapies*" that "mainstream medicine doesn't have all the answers. A growing number of people are turning to complementary therapies natural, often ancient for health and healing. A great majority of people acknowledge God or an equivalent concept, as a real part of their lives and their consciousness. One has to appreciate that prayer has healing power."[51]

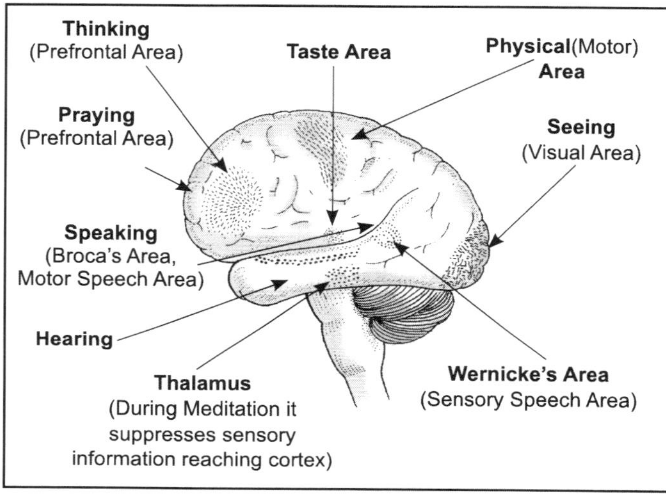

Fig: PET (Computerized positron emission tomography)

It has been reported in *Nature Neuroscience* that areas of the brain associated with navigational ability and special memory became enlarged among London cab drivers. It is similar to the changes seen in the brains of those practicing regular meditation, such as Buddhist monks, as shown by a functional MRI. Studies conducted on children found a positive effect of meditation, with less pain reported post-surgery.[52]

A *Newsweek* article noted that 57 per cent of the population regularly attends church or religious services and 80 per cent of baby boomers consider themselves religious and believe in life after death. When parents display a belief in God, children learn that faith provides a firm foundation for the future."[53]

Scientists believe the world runs on natural laws, which can be influenced by prayer for health gains. Physicians believe that supernatural healing occurs through auto suggestion and by combining the power of the body, mind and spirit.[54]

Belief in spirituality, religion and God has strong roots in India, with 95 per cent of Indians believing that their prayers will be answered.[55]

"The principle (divine) purpose stares the biologist in the face wherever he looks. The probability for such an event as the origin of DNA molecules to have occurred by sheer chance is just too small to be seriously considered"

Ernst Boris Chain,
Winner of the 1945 Nobel Prize for Medicine

Einstein died at Princeton Hospital on April 18, 1955. A pathologist, Dr. Thomas Harvey, performed the autopsy and, without permission, removed the brain and kept it.

It was Einstein's wish that his body be cremated, and his friends considered the removal of organs a violation of his wishes.

After the cremation, the Einstein family learnt about the brain and agreed to let Dr. Harvey keep it if he did not use it for commercial purposes but only for scientific study.

In 1985, an article in Experimental Neurology, reported that Einstein's brain had an above-average number of glial cells (these nourish neurons) in those areas of the left hemisphere that are thought to control mathematical and linguistic skills.

Sanda Witelson, a neuroscientist at McMaster University in Ontario, Canada, published some research results on the brain in June 1999, in the British medical journal Lancet. They discovered that in Einstein's case, the part of the brain thought to be related to mathematical reasoning—the inferior parietal lobe—was 15 per cent wider than normal on both sides. Furthermore, they found that the Sylvian fissure, the groove that normally runs from the front of the brain to the back, did not extend all the way in Einstein's case. Witelson theorises that this latter feature could be the key to Einstein's intelligence, because the absence of a full groove may have allowed more neurons to establish connections among one another and work together more easily.

It has been recently proved by several studies done by functional MRI that the thickness of the cerebral cortex increases in people who meditate regularly. This is an indication that one can develop the brain and, thus, intelligence.[202]

"My comprehension of God comes from the deeply felt conviction of a superior intelligence that reveals itself in the knowable world."

Albert Einstein,
in response to the question,

"What is your understanding of God?"

Deepak Chopra, best-selling author of *"Ageless Body, Timeless Mind"*, "*Quantum Healing*" wrote in his other bestseller "*How to know God: The Soul's Journey into the Mystery of Mysteries*", "Science is guilty of trying to explain it away instead of explaining it. So is prayer or hope. A striking example that there is a reachable place beyond material reality is prayer. The phenomenon of prayer is gaining sudden popularity. Prayer is a journey in consciousness, the patient is not a stranger, nor is she removed from space. It takes you to a place different from ordinary thought. In this place, the patient is not a stranger, nor is she removed in space. You and the patient are joined in a place where boundaries of the body no longer count. Your intention to make her well has an effect across the space-time boundary. Prayer is a quantum event carried out in the brain ...these are the realities. Faith in God is a way of opening the lines of communication beyond the material. So is prayer or hope. At a lower level, the thoughts behind a prayer may be too diffuse to create a result. Every prayer is answered. At the level of miracles, prayer has the power to alter untoward events."

The persons who take care of their terminally ill relatives or friends derive strength and comfort from prayer and take better care of the patient.

Deepak Ranade, Neurosurgeon, feels that the Higgs-Boson Particle, popularly called "God particle" is actually the representation of Shiva, the mass and Shakti, the energy. They are inter-convertible. To understand the entire mystery of creation, one does not need a large Hadron Collider but a large perception assimilator.

"There is no incompatibility between science and religion......Science shows that God exists."

Derek Barton,
Winner of the 1969 Nobel Prize for Chemistry

5

PRAYERS ABOUT

"There is no peace without grace of God, There's no grace of God without prayer."

Mahatma Gandhi

"To me God is psychoneuroimmunology. God is scientific. God is light. God is darkness. God is all ...Certainly, spirituality and science can come together."

Bernie Siegel, M.D
Paediatric & General Surgeon, USA

"The world does not need a new medicine, it needs doctors who know how to pray and obey God in their own lives. In such hands medicine with all its modern resources, will bring forth fruits in abundance."

Paul Tourvier,
General practitioner, Geneva, Switzerland

PRAYER ABOUT WISDOM

"Knowledge comes, But wisdom lingers."

Lord Alfred Tennyson

"Wisdom is not a product of schooling but of the lifelong attempt to acquire it."

Albert Einstein

Ask God to give you wisdom, so that you can differentiate between good and evil. With wisdom you can carry out your duties selflessly. However, do not confuse wisdom with knowledge. Wisdom makes clear in your mind the greatness and vastness of God. Philip Yancey writes in his book, *"Prayer, Does It Make Any Difference?"*, "I realise my tininess and God's vastness, and the true relation of the two. In God's presence I feel small because I am small."[56] "The sound basis for the art and science of true prayer is your knowledge and complete confidence that movement of your conscious mind will gain a definite response from your subconscious mind, which has boundless wisdom and infinite power. Your prayers will be answered."[57]

The following incident took place in 1989. Mohammed Abdul al Awadh, 43-years-old, was brought to the emergency ward of Aden Refinery Company Hospital in Aden, Yemen, suffering from severe lower abdominal pain along with vomiting and fever for about 24 hours. He narrated a typical history of migratory pain. This led to a diagnosis of acute appendicitis, which a clinical and ultrasound examination later confirmed.

Appendicectomy was performed and the appendix was found to be mildly inflamed with some fluid around it. However, the patient did not improve after surgery and continued to exhibit the same distressing symptoms as before. In fact, his condition deteriorated. Re-operation was done and, to our surprise, it was discovered that a perforated duodenal ulcer was responsible for the mild inflammation of the appendix and the fluid gathered around it. The patient recovered and was discharged in good condition.

This was an example of a lack of observation on one's part, which resulted in an unnecessary re-operation. Spirituality does not mean that we can leave an unfinished job for God to take over and finish. This is exactly what Lord Krishna told Arjuna on the battlefield of Kurukshetra. Although the battle itself had already been fought, decided and won by him, Arjuna still had to perform the rites of war to fulfill his own dharma.

It was a lesson that would remain with me throughout my life.

That one may be allowed to forget one's triumphs perhaps but not failures. Thanks to God, good sense prevailed and the patient was re-operated.

"Out of compassion I destroy the darkness of their ignorance, from within them I light the lamp of wisdom and dispel all darkness from their lives."

Bhagvad Gita

Ernest Hemingway, a Nobel Laureate, was undoubtedly an immensely knowledgeable man who enjoyed worldwide fame and following. He was also a powerful writer and achiever but, obviously, something somewhere in his life was not quite right. So, he took the decision to end it. That's because wisdom and knowledge are two different things. One may be very knowledgeable but not be very wise. It is always better to have wisdom. A wise man is able to utilise knowledge better.

METHOD

Relax in any position, anywhere. First take a few deep breaths, then concentrate on your breathing.

For some time, do deep abdominal breathing. Imagine yourself squatting in a prayer posture. Ask God to grant you wisdom, so that you may be able to differentiate between good and evil. Repeat this three times.

Imagine God's light falling on you. Then, let silence reign for a while.

Now, imagine yourself growing in confidence to tackle things in a better manner. Make a solemn promise not to use your wisdom for your own gains or to harm others. Feel yourself growing in confidence and getting ready to lead a wise life. Try to feel the satisfaction that whatever you do, you would only do after proper consideration. You will never allow the heart to rule over the brain.

Technique of Deep Abdominal Breathing:

When we are in stress we breathe from the chest and it is shallow breathing. When we breathe from the diaphragm (abdominal), it is deep breathing. Shallow or chest breathing doesn't utilise 10-15 percent of lung capacity, so there is less oxygen in the blood, and also less vitality and freshness.

- Stand or sit or lie down.
- Inhale deeply from the diaphragm, pushing out the abdomen without moving your chest and count 1, 2, 3, 4 slowly in your mind while inhaling.
- Hold your breath by counting 1 to 16 in your mind.
- Exhale by pushing the abdomen in and not moving the chest and counting from 1 to 8 in your mind.
- Repeat it five times.

PRAYER ABOUT HAPPINESS

Happiness is the ultimate goal of our lives. It gives comfort to the body and brings peace to the soul. But happiness is not found outside the body or soul, it resides within. Recognise the happiness lying deep inside you and feel it. Do not search for it in worldly possessions. Wealth and fame cannot bring lifelong happiness. That is a state of mind.

Screen goddess Marilyn Monroe was at the peak of her acting profession when something made her stumble. Suddenly, at the age of 36, she was found dead from an overdose of a cocktail of drugs and alcohol. She committed suicide midway through a successful career. She had fame and beauty, but was she happy?

Happiness also gives you the desire to live. But remember, happiness depends upon wisdom. Before doing anything, ask yourself whether the act will give you happiness. You have to be happy before you can spread happiness.

"We praise God for destroying the mighty forces of evil that over-shadow knowledge. He, the Bestower of learning and happiness, is all powerful."

Sama Veda

METHOD

Relax in any position, anywhere. First, take a few deep breaths. Then, for some time, do deep abdominal breathing. Imagine yourself squatting in a prayer posture. Ask Him to make you happy. Repeat the following prayer three times: "Lord, show me the path to be happy." Now, try to feel your happiness and empty your mind from all worries. Try to forget day-to-day worries. Concentrate and feel God's blessing. Feel your body relaxing and the pressure inside your mind disappearing; a sense of well-being is spreading over you. Make a mental picture of yourself as relaxed, smiling and in a happy mood. Continue for some time.

After a few days of practice, your concentration will definitely make you feel better.

PRAYER ABOUT PEACE

"Any doctor will agree that the absence of peace, in the form of stress, fear, tension or worry, endangers physical health as much as a disease microbe."

Peace is also brought by gratitude, which ensures physical health and recovery. Such people live a happier, more satisfied and longer life.

With peace, thinking becomes clearer and one can work better, think better and take the right decisions. Crusaders of peace like Mahatma Gandhi and Martin Luther King Jr will be remembered more than all the kings who fought wars. Pray so that your mind too can take the right decisions. The person who has peace of mind has everything and can achieve anything. Peace makes a human being humane.

Elvis "The King" Presley was only 42 when he was found dead in his bathroom in 1977, apparently due to a drug overdose. He had wealth and fame but, obviously, no inward peace. He was an extremely tormented soul. It goes to show that peace is not only a basic need of all human beings but it makes them lead lives full of contentment.

Michael Jackson, the legendary singer and dancer, met with a similar fate due to the absence of peace.

Try to become free of desires and lead an egoless existence. Desire and ego are the two most important enemies of peace. However, remember not to confuse desire with needs. Desire is the longing for non-essential possessions. Needs are the essentials you require to live.

A recent survey conducted in America by the Pew Forum revealed that one–fifth of people who say they are atheists also say they believe in God and four per cent of Americans claim to be atheists.[58]

"Thank God, I am still an atheist!"

Anonymous

METHOD

Relax in any position, anywhere, any time. First, take a few deep breaths. Now, for some time, do deep abdominal breathing.

Imagine yourself squatting in a prayer posture. Ask God to bring peace to you. Repeat earnestly three times: "Lord, confer peace upon my soul."

At this point, it would help if you tried to recall some particularly disturbing episode from the past, which had made you agitated and angry. Try to recall this episode in detail. In other words, once again try to relive the same emotions you had felt at that time.

Now, imagine God showering peace on you in the form of a white and bright light. Feel gradually that you are getting less agitated and angry, more relaxed, less perturbed. Continue for a while longer. Gradually, you will start feeling that you are more at peace and not so angry.

PRAYER ABOUT HEALTH

Dr. Christian Bernard prayed to God before the first heart transplant—"Lord, guide my hands".

A healthy soul in a healthy body is what we all want. If we have these two things, we can achieve virtually anything. In fact, it should be our duty to keep our physical form in the peak of health since it is a gift from God.

They say that the body is like a temple, and with good reason, because that is where the spirit (part of the super soul) resides. One should keep it vigorous and free from disease.

Dr. Manoj Jain, Infectious Diseases Physician, Memphis, USA, feels that, "Treatments and prayers are complementary. I firmly believe that prayers help patients recuperate faster. I believe that medical science and prayers are complementary and must be followed regularly. A few years later, we can expect praying or spirituality to be brought into the medical fold."[59]

Dr. Ramesh Sarin, Oncologist, Indraprastha Apollo Hospital, New Delhi, prays whenever he feels helpless. He takes refuge under the "supreme power" when medical science purportedly fails to deliver.

Dr. Sharat Chandra, Neurosurgeon, All India Institute of Medical Sciences, says, "Medical science doesn't have answers for everything and this is the reason I pray before I start any surgery."

Dr. Sushil Sharma, Chairman, Arthritis Foundation of India, has regular weekly Gita sessions at his home. He says, "Meditation and prayers have miraculous powers, which even medical science doesn't posses. They defuse our health problems which are due to psychological factors. It is noteworthy that almost half the ailments arise for these reasons."[60]

Dr. Brij Bhushan Agarwal, Laparoscopic surgeon, Sir Ganga Ram Hospital, New Delhi, teaches yoga to his patients before they go for surgery.

He says, "Hatha yoga or asanas help in releasing endorphins, which are natural feelgood chemicals that reduce the need for painkillers."

Dr. Ashvini Chopra, Gastroenterologist, Aashlok Hospital, Delhi, feels that it is all about faith. He helps his patients by providing healers, hypnotics and reiki masters.[61]

I was called one night to see an emergency case at about 11:30 pm in the casualty department of a hospital in Gurgaon in July, 2003.

Mr. Ram Tandon, 48, a middle aged senior executive, was a well-built gentleman with pleasant manners. He was accompanied by his wife. He was running high fever of 103 degrees Fahrenheit, his pulse was 114/min and blood pressure was maintained at 110/70 mmHg. He had a foul smelling discharge from the scrotum, which was swollen enormously and gangrene was clearly present. His RBS (Random Blood Sugar) was 340 mg/dl. He was quite toxic. He was not a known diabetic. He was diagnosed as a case of "Fournier's Gangrene" (a deadly infection with death of tissues), which is also called idiopathic gangrene of the scrotum. It is also described as Necrotizing fasciitis Type I. It is a deadly infective gangrene. Gangrene is the death of the tissue with putrefaction.

Fournier's gangrene is a deadly infection by very virulent bacteria, i.e. streptococci, staphylococci, E. coli and clostridium welchii. This infective gangrene is usually fast spreading and can destroy the whole scrotum within 1-2 days. In Mr. Tandon's case, some areas of the scrotum skin were sloughed out resulting in the oozing of a foul smelling muddy discharge. Dirty white foul-smelling discharge is a scary thing for a surgeon.

It definitely denotes gangrene. Dead tissue was grey and listless. I discussed the diagnosis, treatment and prognosis with Mr. and Mrs. Tandon and made them aware of his serious condition. His scrotum, as well as his life, was in danger. I told them that I would try to save both but couldn't promise anything. They were quite upset but agreed for an operation.

I started him on a strong antibiotic combination to cover all deadly aerobic as well as anaerobic bacteria. It was a combination of Tazobactum and Piperacillin with Amikacin and Metronidazole. All antibiotics were given intravenously.

Mr. Tandon signed the consent form. I operated upon him the same night. A thorough surgical debridement (removal of dead tissue) was done trying to remove every bit of dead tissue from the scrotum. Tissue with a grey, dead look was removed until the normal red and blood oozing tissue was seen. It took 2-1/2 hour to finish the scrotal debridement. A surgical toilet was performed with 3-4 litres of normal saline after irrigating with povidone iodine solution mixed with hydrogen peroxide to wash out dead tissues and to remove bacteria.

The grey necrotic tissue and muddy discharge are a surgeon's nightmare as he knows this gangrene can spread very fast and can resist all antibiotics.

The only thing left was to say a prayer from the core of the heart.

After he regained consciousness, I explained to Mr. Tandon what I had found and my course of action. I tried to explain the severity of infection and gangrene without making him and his wife too panicky. But, being educated people, they realised the gravity of the situation and were quite shaken. They were a God-fearing couple and I could feel that they would surrender themselves to God. I also reassured them that I would pray for him, which I did from the core of my heart. They also prayed regularly.

Fournier's gangrene has taken thousands of lives. It is a deadly disease and a man who is saved from it must thank God for his survival. Here comes the role of prayer, trust in God, in treatment and healing. All these factors improve the body's immunity and curb the process of gangrene.

The next day, I took him to the operation theatre to review the infection and a further debridement and surgical toilet was performed. The testes were exposed as the overlying skin was removed. A padded dressing was done.

This was done under general anaesthesia. The patient was dressed in the operation theatre daily. Debridement and surgical toilet were done regularly. In the second week of treatment, he became very toxic and infection increased. We felt his gangrene was spreading again to surrounding tissues and that it would be difficult to save him. The wound was still bad and further debridement was performed with a surgical toilet. The same process was repeated daily. Visible signs of healing could be seen. Gradually, his toxic symptoms started to subside, the infection came under control and the healing process began. It took eight weeks for Mr. Tandon to become fit for discharge from hospital. Skin grafting was done after the infection subsided completely.

Alexander the Great died at the age of 33 of a simple viral infection and high fever for which, at the time, there was absolutely no treatment or cure. A man who had conquered almost the whole world and had everything he could dream of, fell victim at a very early age to an ordinary illness that could affect any common person in the world. He could not defeat the disease and died.

METHOD

Relax in any position at any place and time. Take a few deep breaths. Now, do deep abdominal breathing for some time. Imagine yourself squatting in a prayer posture. Ask God for blessings of good health for the body and soul. Repeat earnestly three times: "Lord, let me live a healthy life, as free from sickness as possible." Visualise a picture of the sick organ in question as a dark spot in your body. Then, feel that He is cascading a radiant light on you, which is both soothing and strong. Imagine this light concentrated on the diseased part of your body and contemplate on that area, gradually turning it less dark and ultimately shining with the light rays falling on it. Feel relaxed, cured, comfortable, full of energy and power. It you are not sick, then let the light bathe your whole body from head to toe and visualize vibrant health.

PRAYER ABOUT BLESSINGS

We are the handiwork of our Creator. We require His blessings. If you are a blessed one, you are the one who should not do anything wrong and also try and bring others on the right path. One who is blessed cannot harm or be harmed by another. To be a blessed one, you have to be a good person too. God blesses everyone but the one who is compassionate and kind gets His blessings easily. Mahatma Gandhi, Martin Luther King, Mother Teresa, Sant Kabir, Meera Bai and other such saints were the blessed ones.

The bomber Enola Gay dropped the atom bomb on Hiroshima on 6th August, 1945. The bomb on Nagasaki, which was dropped three days later on 9th August, was actually not meant for that city but for Kokura which was the primary target. But Kokura's skies were overcast that day and, therefore, it was spared. (However, it also seems to be a blessing in disguise for the Allied powers that Germany or Japan didn't develop the bomb first!)

Three call centre employees and the driver of the cab had a miraculous escape on 17th July, 2008 when a 50-feet-long iron girder fell on their cab at a metro construction site near Ram Manohar Lohia Hospital, New Delhi. The iron girder fell on the cab crushing the bonnet, dashboard and driver's legs. The driver Manoj sustained multiple fractures in his legs. The passenger Pankaj Singh, sitting next to the driver, sustained only a few bruises. The two girls, Kanta Anand and Anju Dixit, sitting on the backseat, escaped unhurt. Even the difference of a fraction of a second could have proved fatal to all the four occupants of the vehicle. Is this not a miracle or did not the "Hand of God" protect them?[62]

METHOD

Relax in any position, any time and anywhere. First, take a few deep breaths and now do deep abdominal breathing. Imagine yourself squatting in a prayer posture. Ask God to bless you with all his affection and mercy. Repeat earnestly three times: "Lord, bless me." Feel that God is giving His blessings in the form of rays of light falling on your whole body; feel His affectionate and fatherly presence and a sense of humbleness and confidence inside you. Feel you are becoming fearless and blessed. Ultimately, feel a sense of satisfaction.

German citizen Kirchen Horst was admitted to a hospital in Gurgaon in July 2002 with a rare perforation of the large intestine called "caecal blow out". A CT scan revealed a tumour of the large intestine. I immediately operated and found the tumour obstructing the left side of the colon.

The pressure in the proximal colon went up so much that the caecum literally blew open, not a very common occurrence. A major part of the colon was then removed and the remaining ends joined. The patient's condition started to improve. On the third day, however, he developed a sudden and severe pain in the abdomen and started deteriorating fast.

A second operation was hurriedly performed the same day and I was surprised to discover a spontaneous rupture of the gall bladder, another rarity with a very high mortality rate. The patient again began improving but developed faecal fistula (opening of the colon outside with faecal matter coming out) this time. So, a third operation and an ileostomy were performed. But his wounds refused to heal. He developed a "burst abdomen" (which was subsequently repaired) and became very weak and emaciated.

I treated him with medicines and nursing care, in conjunction with my daily personal attention, advice about nutrition and, of course, prayer. After four days of hovering between life and death, he came out of septicaemia and was discharged after two months.

The reason I mention this case is because Kirchen was also a man of deep spiritual beliefs and inquisitive about Hinduism, which is why he had come to India in the first place. By the time I met him, he already possessed a collection of various stone Shiv lingams collected from all over India. In the evenings, in his hospital room, we would often sit together and offer silent prayers together for a few minutes for his recovery. That, I think, was sufficient.

How much truth is there in the words of the great surgeon John Hunter, who is regarded as the Father of modern surgery. "The last part of surgery, namely operations, is a reflection on healing art. It is a tacit acknowledgement of the insufficiency of surgery. It is like an armed salvage who attempts to get that by force which a civilised man would by stratagem."

"Our power to heal people and their lives seems to have diminished as dramatically as our power to cure diseases has increased. In the maze of scientific advances, we have lost human dimensions."

Bernie Siegel, MD,
Paediatric and General Surgeon,
USA

"Nothing in life is more wonderful than faith. The one great moving force which we can neither weigh in the balance nor test in the crucible."

Sir William Osler,MD,
Father of Modern Medicine

6

PRAYERS FOR

"Pray, for all men need the aid of the gods."

Homer

PRAYER FOR SELF

First pray for yourself. This is not an act of selfishness because only if you are in proper physical and mental health can you help others and persuade them to try and become physically and mentally healthy too. You can also spread the benefits of prayer and trust in God. One has to carry the torch to guide others and, in due course, others too will become torch-bearers who spread the light.

Dr. Herbert Benson, MD,[43] co-founder of the Mind/Body Clinic of Harvard Medical School, mentions in his book, "*The Relaxation Response*" that "stress raises blood pressure, increases heart rate and makes breathing rapid while lowering the body's immune response." The opposite, however, he says can be achieved by repeating a prayer, a word, sound, phrase or movement and disregarding other thoughts. Meditating, in short.

According to Dr. Benson, "The relaxation response is a great longevity tool, since deep relaxation promotes greater oxygenation of blood and tissues and causes the adrenal glands to switch their production of age accelerating hormones, adrenaline and cortisol, to life-enhancing DHEA (dehydroepiandrosterone, a steroid hormone reduces the risk of heart disease, increases well being, fights serious infections and may prolong life)."[63]

METHOD

Relax in any position at any time and in any place. First take a few deep breaths. Now, do deep abdominal breathing. Imagine yourself squatting in a prayer posture. Feel the presence of God and His light falling on you along with a sense of total peace. You should be praying for the five aspects discussed above wisdom, health, peace, happiness and blessings.

PRAYER FOR FAMILY AND FRIENDS

Frank Laubach, a missionary, wrote in his book "*Man of Prayer*" that "One need not tell God everything about the people for whom one prays, for God knows better than we what our friends need, yet our prayer releases his power, we know not how."[64]

You should memorise a list of all your family members and friends and then pray for them as you would do for yourself. You could also pray for one family member at a time on a daily basis by rotation.

Friends and relatives can add years to your life and you can also prolong their lives. Lynne C Giles, doctoral researcher and lead author of a study conducted at Flinders University in Adelaide, Australia, has found that the presence of older relatives and friends in some way seems to be a key factor in longevity. The study also indicated that people with the largest number of friends survive the longest.

It is not coincidence that God has selected your friends and relatives—for instance, your mother—but after a plan. He chose her over billions of other people to bring you to Earth. Close your eyes and ask yourself: Do you think this is merely a coincidence? Understand the importance of friends and relatives.

METHOD

Relax in any position you like, in any place and at any time. Now do deep abdominal breathing. Imagine yourself squatting in prayer posture. Recall the face of the person for whom you are praying. At the start, make a mental picture of a ray of light from God falling upon and blessing this family member. Imagine his or her body shining. Try to get involved and pray seriously. Pray for the same qualities you were praying for yourself. And, for every quality repeat three times, "God please grant him this what I pray for."

In 1991, Pat Loder, Milford, Michigan, woman, was driving with her family when a speeding motorcycle slammed into her car. Her two children, a five-year-old son and eight-year-old daughter, were rushed to hospital. She clung to the belief that God would intervene when things looked helpless. "When you are a parent and are standing over the body of your child, who may be dying ... you have to have that belief." Dr. Lenworth Jacobs, Professor, University of Connecticut, USA, did a survey in 2005 involving 774 doctors, nurses and medical workers, which showed 20 per cent of doctors and other medical workers believed that when their own relatives are gravely ill or injured, God could reverse a hopeless outcome. About 57 per cent of the general public, who were surveyed, said God's intervention could save a family member even if physicians declared treatment to be futile.[65]

PRAYER FOR AN UNKNOWN PERSON

"Purest form of love is given with no expectation of return. Measured by this standard, earnest prayer for others is a magnificent act of love."

David Hubbard

You have to choose a person you do not know. He or she could be someone who happens to be sitting next to you, or you may have just seen him or her before starting the programme. You could even select your domestic help or a neighbour. This develops in you a feeling for people you are not very familiar with. It is also a totally selfless prayer since you don't benefit from it at all. God would surely like this. It is based on the philosophy that every human being has a soul or spirit which is part of the supersoul or God. We are all the same. Like brothers; all children of God.

Dr. Mitchell Krucoff, of Duke University in the United States, studied the power of prayer in 150 cardiac patients and noticed a 50 per cent reduction in heartbeat abnormalities and a 100 per cent reduction in heart attacks and heart failures. It was a genuine eye-opener.[66]

Dr. Mitchell Krucoff and his colleagues started the MANTRA (Monitoring and Actualization of Noetic Trainings) pilot study to observe the effect of spirituality on healing. 150 patients with chest pain, while at rest, were exposed to imaging, touch therapy, stress relaxation, distance intercessory prayer and standard care while undergoing angioplasty. The MANTRA pilot study results were published in 2001 in the American Heart Journal. A 25-30 per cent reduction in adverse outcomes was seen in all except standard care group and the least adverse outcome was noticed in the prayer group. The MANTRA II study was conducted later with 748 patients, which showed that patients receiving prayers and other alternative therapies such as music, imagery and touch therapy displayed better results than patients receiving only standard care.[67]

METHOD

Relax in any position of your liking in any place and at any time. First, take a few deep breaths. Now, do deep abdominal breathing for some time. Imagine yourself squatting in prayer posture. Recall the face of the person you are praying for and imagine that he or she is kneeling before God too and God's blessing is falling upon his or her body in the form of a shaft of light. Feel Him blessing the person. Repeat all the five prayers as you did for yourself and your family.

PRAYER FOR A PERSON YOU DON'T LIKE

This is a prayer for your enemy, a person you hate or someone who has harmed you. Forgive this person, like Jesus said when he was on the cross: "Father, forgive them; for they know not what they do." Also, pray for him or her as you pray for yourself without any bad feelings in your heart. Be warned, this is not easy. It takes a lot of effort and time but it can be achieved. However, if you manage to succeed, after a few weeks you will not have anybody left on your list of enemies. This prayer cleanses your heart, reduces your anger and purifies your thoughts and this, in turn, gives you better health and peace.

"Love your enemies, bless them that curse you, do good to them that hate you, and pray for them which despitefully use you, and persecute you."

Mathew 5:44

I operated on a person for perforation of a gangrenous appendix with peritonitis. Appendicectomy was performed with lavage and cleaning of the peritoneal cavity. He improved and was discharged. Later, he developed a wound infection and, after some time, intestinal obstruction due to adhesions. He was operated upon for acute intestinal obstruction and recovered completely. I was treating him to the best of my ability. I also prayed for his recovery. Gangrenous appendicitis is a life threatening disease. I was happy that his life was saved, so was he and his family. I was astonished when, after two years, he complained that he suffered due to a wrong surgery and not because of his sickness. I was disturbed as I know his life was saved by God and that he was now enjoying normal health. How can a man be so selfish and forget the past? I had already explained the complications of the disease to him. However, I forgave him. Gradually, I forgot his behaviour and my anger and distress subsided. I felt better and my soul was unburdened and happy.

Stephen R. Covey, writes in his bestseller, *The 7 Habits of Highly Effective People*, "I believe that there are parts to human nature that cannot be reached by either legislation or education, but require the power of God to deal with."[68]

Paulo Coelho, the famous Brazilian philosopher, lyricist and novelist, once related an incident in his life: "One morning, going from Death Valley in California to Tuscon, Arizona, I made a mental list of everyone I thought I hated because they had hurt me. I went along pardoning them one by one and, six hours later, in Tuscon, my soul felt so light. My life had changed much for the better."

Dr. Andrew Weil also mentions in his book, "*Healthy Aging for Enhancement of Spiritual Health and Well-Being*", "Reach out and try to remove constraints with someone from whom you are estranged; practice forgiveness."[69]

Mrs. Sheila, 68-years-old, an obese patient of 74 kg, was admitted to a local hospital in July, 2005, as an emergency. She had a history of Diabetes type II and Hypertension, which were controlled with drugs. She was suffering from sudden abdominal pain and vomiting from the previous night. Examination and investigation revealed it as a case of acute intestinal obstruction. Ultrasonography and CT scan confirmed a diagnosis of acute intestinal obstruction, but could not explain the cause. The same day, the patient was operated on by fellow junior surgeon. I was called during the operation to help. When surgery was performed, the loops of intestine were found dilated. On exploration, I found a strangulated femoral hernia causing intestinal obstruction.

Strangulated hernia is a dangerous condition (Queen Caroline, wife of George II of England, died of a strangulated umbilical hernia at the age of 55 in 1736).

It was a case of a missed femoral hernia (by a junior surgeon, who relied more on laboratory tests and not on his examination skills) in an obese female. If a serious and thorough examination was done, proper and correct diagnosis would have been made preoperatively with adequate preparations, without any harm to the patient. Spirituality doesn't mean being less observant and watchful.

"On complicated tests we much rely, And use too little hand and ear and eye"

Zachary Cope

METHOD

Relax in any position of your liking, at any time and place. First, take a few deep breaths. Now, do deep abdominal breathing. Imagine yourself squatting in a prayer posture.

Make a mental picture of the face of the person and imagine the light from God falling upon him and blessing him. Feel that you have forgiven him, that the hatred has melted from your heart and you have also started feeling good and affectionate about this person. You don't want any harm to come to him or her. After a few weeks, you will start feeling good and enjoying it too.

PRAYER FOR A SICK PERSON

The best gift for a person who is sick is a prayer. When the person comes to know that people are praying for him, he feels stronger as he is not fighting the battle alone. A sick person is low in flesh as well as spirit, and this support helps him to overcome the weakness.

The world is full of misery, poverty and sickness. Prayers for the poorest of the poor are the best form of prayer. You should feel happy and satisfied in helping anybody who is in trouble and, generally speaking, should have no trouble finding such a person. However, in the event you are not able to find such a person on a daily basis, then just carry out prayers for the same person for a few days.

The efficacy of intercessory prayer is so far not understood by science as science wants to dissect spirituality in the laboratory. However, researchers on religion, spirituality and health believe that convincing evidence will be available in coming years. Sir John Madox wrote in *Nature*, "The most important discoveries of the next 50 years are likely to be the ones of which we cannot now even conceive."[70]

W. L. Larimore, a proponent of the use of religion and spirituality in medical treatment, boldly puts his views in the journal, *American Family Physician*, "To exclude God from a consultation is a form of maltpractice."

Dr. Harold Koenig, a psychiatrist at Duke University, states that 88 per cent of 16 studies about efficacy of spiritual and religious factors affecting health, found lower blood pressure in spiritual and religious persons. This is also indicated by studies published in *Journal of Cardiopulmonary Rehabilitation* about cardiovascular health.[70]

Various studies have been carried out to evaluate the effects of intercessory prayer. Some of these have shown ambiguous results and some apparently positive ones. Dr. Mitch Krucoff of Duke University in the US, for example, has demonstrated excellent results. My own opinion is that the methodology was faulty in all these studies. A prayer emanating from the core of one's heart – and not normal prayer – is what is always effective.

METHOD

Relax in a position of your liking in any place and time. First, take a few deep breaths. Now, do deep abdominal breathing for some time. Imagine yourself squatting in a prayer posture. Make a mental picture of the sick person's face whom you have seen, known or is unknown to you. Visualise the rays of light from God falling upon him and blessing him.

Pray for him for exactly the same things you pray for yourself. This form of prayer would obviously find God's pleasure, while, in return, you too would benefit from it.

Ashok Kumar, an 18-year-old boy and a manual labourer, was brought unconscious to the casualty department of Umkal Hospital in Gurgaon. A few people carried him and one person held his intestinal loops, which had come out of a bleeding abdominal wound. I examined him and transferred him to the operation theatre with the resuscitation process going on. His breathing was fast and shallow; his body cold and clammy and the blood pressure was not recordable as he had bled profusely. While working at a construction site, he had fallen from a height of 10 metres over a vertical 10 centimetre-diameter iron pipe which went through the left side of his abdomen and chest.

On opening him up, I found that the left kidney had been wrenched out and torn. The aorta was bruised but, fortunately, had escaped fatal trauma.

The lower lobe of the left lung was badly damaged with an air leak and four lower left ribs were fractured. The diaphragm was also ruptured and the stomach and intestines perforated at several places. The spleen was half torn. His abdominal cavity was full of blood and faeces. The left lobe of the liver was punctured at two places because the ribs had pierced it.

He also suffered a cardiac arrest while on the operation table and had to be revived.

"If a series of events can go wrong, it will do so in the worst possible sequence"

The Extended Murphy's Law[72]

He was given six units of blood during and after the operation and, on the second day, even developed DIC, which is a form of severe internal bleeding and in which mortality rates are extremely high. At this point, I began praying for him on a regular basis and in earnest, as I'm sure his family must also have done. True, the boy had got timely intervention, medication, attention and care and the best possible medical facilities. But he had also got our prayers. He recovered completely in about six weeks despite his horrific injuries.

It is difficult to scientifically prove the percentage of the contribution of prayer, his faith and trust in God and family support in his total recovery other than timely and just treatment.

Most of us feel that God should cure a person when somebody prays for a cure. But if God does that, nurses and doctors would not be doing what they are meant to do. I remember a story written by Bernie Siegel in his bestseller, *Love, Medicine and Miracles*, "A man with cancer was told by his doctor that he will die within an hour. He prayed, 'God save me'.[73] A voice came, 'Don't worry, my son. I will save you'. The man went back to his bed reassured. A surgeon called him to say, 'I can operate and save you'. The man said, 'God will save me'. Then, an oncologist and radiotherapist called to say, 'We can save you'. The man replied, 'No, God will save me'. After an hour, the man died, walked to God and said, 'You said you'd save me, and here I am, dead.' God replied, 'You dumbbell. I sent you a surgeon, an oncologist and radio therapist'.

The hidden power of the following lines is understood by me very well after this case.

"Natural forces within us are the true healers of the disease"

"Thou shalt behave and act without arrogance and with undistracted mind, humility and constant reflection, Thou shalt pray for the welfare of all creatures (not only your own patients)...."

Hippocrates of Cos,
460 – 375 B.C. The Father of Medicine

"Prayer is the most powerful form of energy we can generate"

Alexis Carrel

7

MEDITATION IN MOTION

"With meditation, one can harness the powers of the mind."

Bhagwad Gita

"I admit that thoughts influence the body."

Albert Einstein

"Even a minute of meditation has value... you continue to meditate subconsciously throughout the day."

Dean Ornish, MD

WHAT IS MEDITATION?

I studied at the G S V M Medical College in Kanpur, India, from 1966 to 1974. I got to know Swami Harinanda, a saint, teacher, writer and humanitarian. He would ask me about the structure and functioning of the human body while, at the same time, teaching me yoga and meditation. This experience helped me take my first steps towards spirituality and meditation.

The word "meditation" comes from the Latin "meditari", which means to contemplate. Meditation can, in fact, be called "the science of healing" in its broadest sense. It consists of emptying one's mind to focus on one thought, sound or picture for a certain period. As a result, it diminishes stress, anxiety, tension, heart rate, blood pressure, oxygen consumption and makes one relaxed and calm.

It is also said that unless you suffer from hypertension, stress and anxiety, you do not see the requirement of meditation.

"There is only one road to true human greatness: The road through suffering."

Albert Einstein,

Mind-body masters in India were able to slow their heart rates by way of self-regulating yoga techniques. During the 1960s and 1970s, college students around the world learned a variety of consciousness expanding meditation techniques and began reporting beneficial changes in their minds and bodies. It was discovered through investigations that people have the ability to alter their physiology in ways that had not been believed possible. Through simple shifts in attention and intention, meditators are able to slow their heart rates, reduce their breathing patterns and lower their blood pressure.[74]

Meditation is a safe and simple way to balance a person's physical, emotional and mental states. It is easy to learn and can be useful for treating stress and pain. It keeps the attention focussed on the present. It is neither about reacting to past events or being preoccupied with future places.[75]

Interest in meditation has increased phenomenally worldwide due to its health benefits. At the Maharishi University School in Iowa, USA, students are required to regularly meditate twice a day. Celebrities like Goldie Hawn, Shania Twain, Heather Graham, Richard Gere and Al Gore have, at some time or the other, practiced meditation regularly. Being role models, they encourage friends and fans to take up the practice too.

Meditation is for everybody. Age or sex is no bar. One can meditate from childhood to old age. It is not a religion-based practice since people of all faiths can do it. Moreover, meditation can be achieved through speech, by listening to the sounds of speech, breathing, concentrating on breathing or on sight.

"Meditation, not medication, cures."

Author

Peter Harrison, a teacher and psychotherapeutic counsellor, who has been running meditation and sound and voice workshops since 1970, states in his book, *A Complete Guide to Discovering Meditation:* "When the natural composure and rest is lost, it gives rise to discontent, unhappiness and misery. It affects our immune system as it is well connected to our sense of well-being; health begins to suffer. For this, we need meditation".[76 & 77]

PHYSIOLOGY OF MEDITATION

Healthy, successful and contented people have a well-balanced activity of both the right and left hemispheres of the brain. Meditation also encourages a balanced activity of these two lobes. It improves the link between the body and mind too.

Richard J Davidson, PhD, Professor of Psychology and Psychiatry at the University of Wisconsin at Madison, USA, also the Director of Laboratory for Affective Neuroscience at the University of Wisconsin, has worked with the Dalai Lama since 1992 and studied the brains of Tibetan monks. He has shown that regular meditation shifts the activity in the prefrontal cortex—

the part of the brain implicated in planning complex cognitive behaviours, personality expression and moderating correct social behaviour—from the right hemisphere to the left.

People who have a negative disposition tend to be right prefrontal oriented, while the left prefrontal-oriented have more enthusiasm and more interests, are more relaxed and are generally happier.[78]

Dopamine, serotonin and noradrenalin are three "body-friendly" neurotransmitter substances secreted in our bodies. Dopamine is a substance invariably linked to states of well-being. Its reduction causes the perception of pain to be heightened. Serotonin is an extremely important chemical in the brain as it is involved in suppressing pain, maintaining high moods and possibly sleep. Some antidepressant drugs work by maintaining it at high levels in the brain.[79] Serotonin brings sleep and relieves the symptoms of stress. If its secretion is reduced, it causes mood disturbances. Noradrenalin is found primarily in areas of the brain involved in governing the involuntary autonomic nervous system. All three—noradrenalin, serotonin and dopamine—achieve a balance during the process of correct meditation, inducing a sense of well-being and satisfaction.

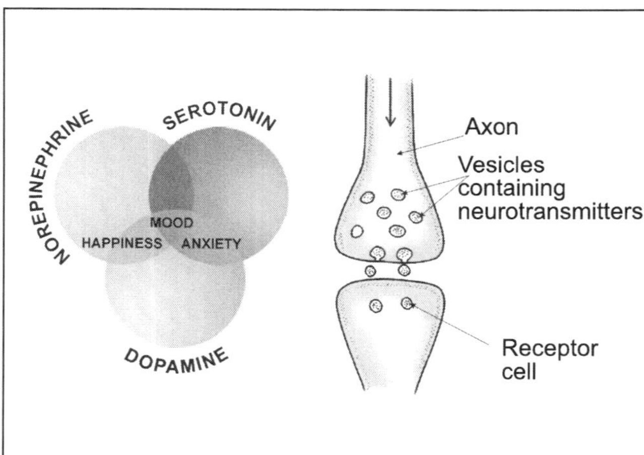

Fig: Neurotransmission of neurotransmitters

During meditation, the brain generates alpha waves or theta and delta waves. Alpha waves are associated with an individual in the waking state and are characterised by low-voltage activity of mixed frequency. Slightly slower in frequency, theta waves are strong during internal focus, meditation, prayer and spiritual awareness. It reflects the state between wakefulness and sleep. Delta waves are of the lowest frequencies. These occur in deep sleep and influences our ability to integrate and let gc. It reflects the unconscious mind.

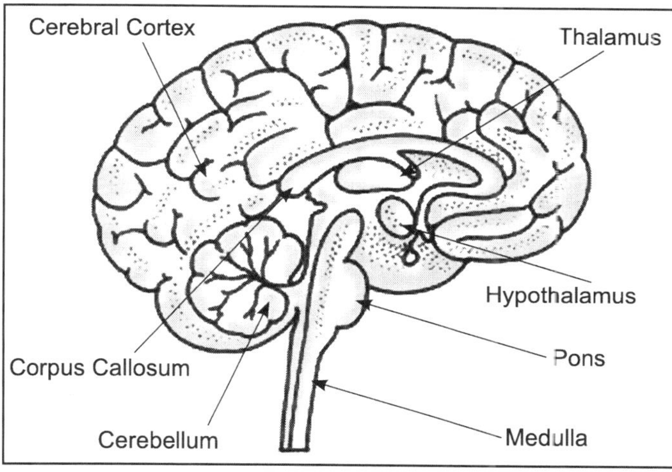

Fig: Functional parts of the brain

In addition, the frontal lobe of the brain, which is the seat for reasoning, planning, emotions and conscious awareness, gets attenuated during meditation. The parietal lobe processes sensory information about our surroundings, orienting us in time and space. During meditation, it slows down. The thalamus is a gatekeeper, which allows some sensory information to reach the vital structures of the brain and stops others. Again, during meditation, it reduces incoming information. The reticular formation is the brain's additional guard which receives information and puts the brain on alert, enabling it to respond accordingly. Meditation does not allow this to happen.

Additionally, in recent studies reported in the November 2005 issue of *Neuro Report and New Scientist*, researchers are now saying that although meditation is known to alter resting brain patterns, suggesting long-lasting brain changes, a new study by researchers from Yale, Harvard, Massachusetts General Hospital and MIT (Massachusetts Institute of Technology) shows that meditation is also associated with increased cortical thickness. Structural changes were found in areas of the brain that are important for sensory, cognitive and emotional processing.

A University of Kentucky research found that meditation boosts performances in tests that measure attention. People taught to meditate did better on tests compared with their earlier performance. Meditation also improved performance after the subjects had lost a night's sleep.

I have observed an increase in research on spirituality, religion and health since 1990. More and more papers are published about the efficacy of spiritual involvement and distance healing.

The healing power of faith is attracting the attention of scientists in a big way as a link develops between beliefs, faith, spirituality, religion and health. This is a welcome sign, as earlier this bond was disregarded by some researchers, without any study having been conducted. All over the world, an increasing number of people are beginning to believe in the association between spirituality and health and its contribution towards enhancing comfort and peace during sickness. I feel that a higher percentage of people are interested in exploring the connection between God and health. In various studies, more than 75 per cent of people showed that spiritual faith helps in fighting a disease and recovering from it. Many reputed magazines such as *Newsweek, Time, USA Today, Prevention, Reader's Digest,* etc., are publishing more and more articles and devoting their editions to faith, power of prayer and spirituality, which shows that people like to read such articles.

There is also a growing number of physicians interested in such topics and even supporting them. Some of these physicians are Dr. Christina Puchalski of George Washington Institute of Spiritual Health, Dr. Herbert Benson of Harvard Medical School, Dr. Dale Mathews of Georgetown University, Dr. Harold Koenig, Dr. William Harris, Dr. David Larson, Dr. Jeffrey Lewin, Dr. Walter Larimore, Dr. Michel NC Gellough, Dr. Deepak Chopra, New Age Guru, Dr. Mitchell Krucoff, Duke University, etc.

On the other hand, some researchers such as Dr. Richard Dawkins, Zoologist, Oxford University, Dr. Neilscheurich, Psychiatrist, University of Kentucky, and Steven Weinberg, Nobel laureate physicist, University of Texas, believe that religion, spirituality and medicine should not be linked without significant scientific evidence. Books like *The Seven Spiritual Laws of Success* by Dr. Deepak Chopra and *Spontaneous Healing* by Andrew Weil are bestsellers, which shows the growing public interest.

In spite of extraordinary advancements in various fields of medicine, people are turning towards spirituality and the spiritual aspects of health and treatment of illness.

These are some shifts that show that the inclination of people towards spirituality during illness is growing:

1. Dissatisfaction with the way medicine is practiced today.
2. The callous attitude of the medical fraternity, probably due to their busy schedules.
3. Doctors spend less time with patients and more time with administrative and paperwork, investigative reports and research.
4. Waiting time in OPD is increasing and most people feel that going to the hospital means losing a full day, especially in government-run hospitals.
5. Cleanliness levels are not up to hygienic standards in most government-run and some corporate hospitals.
6. The spiralling cost of medical care.
7. The nursing staff does not display kindness or compassion.

(I remember a male nurse, Rajiv, in my OPD at Apollo clinic, Gurgaon, who was very polite and hardworking. Patients used to flock to him for checking their BP, dressings and other small procedures. The insensitive behaviour of hospital staff makes the patient feel like a bundle of illnesses rather than a human being.)

8. Nowadays, medicine has also turned into a market commodity. Everything revolves round finance and this gives a bad impression of the medical profession. Some patients feel that certain decisions are taken more for the money than the disease. As worldwide research proves, 50 per cent of coronary artery bypass grafts were not required.
9. Technology has advanced but not our human approach to the patient. We don't feel other's pain.
10. Unethical practices in today's healthcare, such as demanding unnecessary tests, have increased.

MEDICAL BENEFITS OF MEDITATION

Meditation allows you to identify your inner self first and then a higher self or higher truth. It makes you understand that the soul is a part of the super soul. It changes your views and attitude towards life and fellow human beings. Meditation also leads to relaxation, peace and happiness. Along with faith in God, it brings mental peace, self-control, mental and physical health, happiness and can, in certain cases, even ultimately pave the way to nirvana or moksha.

The benefits of meditation are due to its calming effect on the brain. Dr. Herbert Benson, Professor of Medicine at Harvard Medical School, USA, has found that meditation decreases oxygen consumption by up to 17 per cent, reduces heart rate by three beats per minute and increases theta brainwaves.

Free radicals are produced in most cells of the body as a byproduct of metabolism. The most important free radicals found in humans are of the oxygen group. Once formed, they oxidise the molecules used inside cells, causing cell death and injury. The body has of course developed various mechanisms to protect itself from the damaging effects of free radicals but we can further help our bodies by lessening the amount of oxygen present to do the damage in the first place. And this, as we have just seen, is precisely what meditation accomplishes.

Other than the general overall benefits that meditation can deliver, there are also some specific medical benefits that can be derived from meditation. *Davidson's Principles and Practice of Medicine,* a standard prescribed textbook in medical schools all over the world, for instance, puts it this way: "Formal relaxation classes, meditation and biofeedback have all been shown to reduce blood pressure... Their efficacy is usually proportional to the enthusiasm of the teacher and the commitment of the participant."

Let us see what some of these benefits can be:

1. It provides rest and relief to the body and mind.
2. It reduces heart rate and blood pressure, thus preventing hypertension.
3. Meditation can stop the advancement of atherosclerosis. World famous cardiologist, Dr. Dean Ornish, has proved that severely blocked arteries can be opened up without surgery with regular meditation, yoga, diet and aerobic exercises.[57]
4. It assists the onset of normal sleep and therefore overcomes insomnia.
5. It reduces the metabolism of the body and therefore its oxygen consumption by tissues so they can have a period of rest and a chance to rejuvenate the body and mind. I call it "inner cooling" or "meditation at the cellular level".
6. It helps in the de-addiction process from drugs, alcohol and

nicotine.

7. It relieves physical and mental stress and strain. "To heal our egos, we need to believe in something much greater than ourselves. We realise that the Divine Mystery is willing to offer us great abundance, yet we often cut off the very source that can supply us with the things that we so desperately want in our lives." [79] Or as Deepak Chopra in his book "*Creating Affluence: Wealth Consciousness in the Field of All Possibilities*" puts it: "When we transcend, we obtain knowledge directly free from the distracting intervention of spoken language. This is the value of meditation, which gives us the experience of pure being, which is in itself an expression of pure bliss and pure joy."
8. It balances the activities of the two brain hemispheres, which brings coordination, calm, relaxation and equilibrium in life.
9. It cures depression and anxiety and helps in ameliorating panic attacks. Ruth Stafford Peale, author of *Secrets of Staying in Love* and chairman of the Peale Centre of Christians Living, remembers that, in 1938, her husband Norman Vincent Peale, the famous writer, philosopher and proponent of positive thinking, was discouraged during the Great Depression and became very pessimistic. One day, she told Norman, "Now look, Norman, you talk about positive thinking and now all you are doing is thinking negatively. I think what you need is to practice what you preach about faith and positive thinking." The good life is one in which you are at peace with your inner soul.[80]
10. Meditation helps patients to prepare themselves for surgery. If a patient is taught how to prepare for surgery, then a calm state of mind helps during surgery and in post-operative recovery.
11. Meditation reduces the negative effects that the body's stress response can build up, thus protecting, even improving the immune system.
12. Meditation increases the level of tolerance, which helps people who suffer from chronic pain. (For more on pain and pain management via meditation see Notes.)
13. It is a scientific fact that meditation slows down the ageing process. Dr. Dean Ornish, Head of Preventive Medicine Research Institute in Sausalito, California, USA, recently published his study in *Lancet Oncology*, recommending lifestyle changes, such as a diet rich in fibre, vegetables, whole grains, legumes and soy

> products, moderate exercise like walking for half an hour a day and an hour of stress management methods like meditation. [81] These increase the body's level of telomerase, an enzyme which further enhances the length of telomeres, which are part of chromosomes and control the longevity and maintenance of immune system cells. A shortening of telomeres causes premature death by sickness like cancers of the breast, colon and lung and other diseases. Lengthening of the telomeres aids longevity, supported by regular meditation. Jon Kabat-Zinn, founder of the Stress Reduction Clinic at University Mass Medical School, treats patients of cancer, AIDS and chronic pain without medication but with meditation. He injected flu vaccines in individuals who meditated and those who did not, while measuring brain activity with functional MRI. He found more antibodies and shift of activity from the right brain to the left in the former group.

Meditation is being increasingly recommended by physicians to relieve pain of chronic heart disease (such as angina), AIDS related complications, cancer and painful infertility conditions like endometriosis. Meditation is also being used to restore the balance in the face of psychiatric disturbances like depression, hyperactivity and attention deficit disorder syndrome.

It has now been confirmed that meditation strengthens the immune system. In a research conducted by Dr. David Cresswell, University of California, USA, 67 HIV patients were studied, where 48 patients practiced regular meditation. The study included male, African, American, homosexuals, unemployed and those not on ARV (Anti Retro Viral) medication. They followed a stress lowering program called "Mindfulness Based Stress Redection Meditation". The more frequently volunteers meditated, the higher was their CD4T-cell count. The CD4T-cell count was measured before and after the two-month programme. Results showed that meditation may sometimes be able to slow down the advancement of AIDS.[82]

CD4-T-lymphocytes are called generals that direct the immune system cells. As the power of CD4-T-lymphocytes diminishes, susceptibility to infection increases. It is not clear whether meditation boosts CD4T-cell level or suppresses the virus.

Cancer is an uncontrolled growth of tissue, which occurs due to cellular multiplication, probably due to the body's suppressed immune response.

Relaxation techniques like prayer, meditation and guided imagery can improve the body's immune system, thus controlling cellular multiplication and preventing cancer. It is debatable whether healing depends on one's sainthood or holiness, but it definitely has a lot to do with the concentration with which you practice relaxation techniques [83]

Larry Dossey, MD, feels that immunity enhancing practices such as prayer, meditation and guided visualisation should be a part of the treatment strategy of all prognostically poor and chronic diseases.[84]

Dr. Brent, MD, Director, Mayo Clinic, is doing research on complementary and alternative care. The mind body connection treatments are based on the idea that the two function as a unified field. The principle of meditation works on the premise that stress is the outcome of a restless mind. Meditation observes the flow of thoughts without judging them, a process that helps the mind to slow down naturally. He says, "In our study, people who used yoga and relaxation techniques in addition to a wrist splint experienced more relief from the carpal tunnel syndrome than those who used splints alone."[85]

Dr. Dean Ornish is of the view that meditation may slow the advance of prostate cancer and, in April 2003, announced his findings in a meeting of the American Urology Association.

Dr. Harold Koenig, Psychiatrist and Director of the Centre for the Study of Religion/Spirituality and Health, Duke University, reports in his book "*The Healing Power of Faith*" that religious people have stronger marriages, healthier lifestyles, cope better with stress, live longer, may have strong immune systems, use fewer expensive hospital services, remain protected from serious cardiovascular diseases, are less depressed and recover quickly when afflicted.[86]

I have observed in my 35 years of surgical practice that when a patient, who has to undergo surgery, is trained beforehand in deep abdominal breathing exercises—along with meditation—the oxygen saturation level in his or her blood increases by two to three per cent, specially if the oxygen saturation is less than 100 per cent without additional oxygen supply. This may seem like a small percentage but is very helpful both during and after surgery in the recovery period. It has a direct positive effect on operative and post-operative complications and healing.

I am also treating patients suffering from irritable bowel syndrome with meditation but, of course, along with the usual drug therapy. Another important step in controlling this syndrome is learning how to relax and how to benefit from massage, yoga and meditation.[87]

BENEFITS OF MEDITATION IN CHILDREN

Several studies have shown that meditation among children improves their performance in examinations, sports as well as other extracurricular activities. If we guide young people to look within, they will develop a sense of calm, peace and self-esteem.

Plato, the Greek philosopher, believed that a nation cannot be strong unless it believes in God. It will do us no harm to believe and it may do us and our children immeasurable good. The more you focus on your body, the more you switch off from the world.[88]

The authors of "*Teaching Meditation to Children*", David Fontana and Ingrid Slack, who are fellows of the British Psychological Society and specialise in working with children, suggest that children should be taught to meditate because, "The more we can help children to be at peace with their own bodies, the better chance we have of helping them to avoid these killers in later life." The benefits, however, are not just for the future.

Teachers in the USA are faced with mistrust when they attempt to teach students the concept that faith, religion and science complement each other and are not contradictory forces. David Lampbill, a biology teacher at Ridgeview School, Jacksonville, Orange Park, Florida, USA, wonders if the new generation of Americans will embrace scientific evidence alongside religious belief. He says, "It may jeopardise their belief in the basic power of science to explain the natural world."[86] Dr. Harold Koenig feels religious belief makes people to cope better with stress.[89] It is true with children also.

Meditation gives even very young children power over their thinking and their emotions, not by repressive self-control, but by an enhanced understanding of themselves and self-acceptance. Fontana and Slack advocate meditation as a gentle and effective means of overcoming a wide variety of psychological and behavioural problems, such as anxiety, hyperactivity and aggression, and have backed this up with case histories. They also see meditation as a much more general tool, applicable to all children and bringing about the following benefits:

Physical relaxation
Improved concentration
Increased tranquility and ability to deal with stress
Improved awareness
Improved creativity
Improved memory

I can recall many benefits from meditation in my own life. My younger son, Kunal, who is now a doctor, was in class X and was to appear for his final board examinations after two months. He was studying at Kanpur's Methodist High School, Uttar Pradesh, India. I was working at Aden, Yemen, and he was living with my parents. He started neglecting his studies and his grades went down badly, to the extent that he was not permitted to appear in his board examination. I was called from Yemen. I met Mrs Brown, the Principal, who advised that Kunal skip the examination that year and prepare for the coming year.

I pleaded with her to re-assess Kunal after two weeks and to allow him to appear for the exams if he scored over 50 per cent marks. After a lot of persuasion, she agreed. I sat with Kunal the same day and he apologised and agreed to do his best. I forgave him and we charted out a plan. It was a study plan with two breaks of 15 minutes each for meditation and visualisation. Everything went smoothly and he appeared in the test after two weeks and secured 55 per cent aggregate marks. He was allowed to sit in the board exams after six weeks. The preparation went on as planned. He would meditate and visualise for half an hour before the scheduled time and then do the same in the examination hall for two minutes after receiving the question paper. Eventually, he secured 86 per cent aggregate marks in the results. We gave due credit to his hard work, but I believed that the meditation also helped.

Among other tangible benefits of meditation for a child is an overall improvement in performance, besides a lowering of negative behaviour such as hyperactivity, disobedience and violent or abusive behaviour as well as a reduced risk of developing coronary artery disease in later life. Meditation should start at an early age to prevent diseases that make their first appearance during childhood. Children should be taught a simple form of meditation such as concentration on breathing from the age of 10. They should do it for five to 10 minutes everyday, if possible after school or at any convenient hour.

Deborah Rozman, an American psychologist and holistic educator and author of *Meditating With Children: The Art of Concentrating and Centering,* shares her proven techniques for teaching the art of concentration and centering to children. It adds balance and self-esteem and improves decision making, while putting children in touch with their deeper core values, she says.

Rozman teaches children to centre in the heart, which puts them in touch with the depth of their own being. By using the heart as the primary focus for centering and concentration, children balance their mental, physical, and emotional natures. Self-esteem goes up, decision-making skills improve and the ability to concentrate increases.

Guided imagery, yoga, creative fantasy, movement, psychology and love are used to give form to the inner spiritual qualities inherent in youth, resulting in happier, more caring children who may communicate the truth of their hearts.

THE MEDITATION TECHNIQUE

Fig: Meditation

Meditation requires personal tranquility, a feeling of mental solitude and a quiet, secluded spot. To begin with, sit in a comfortable position or lie supine on the floor in a silent room. Next, relax your body and try to release it of all tension so that the limbs and torso become completely limp. Alternatively, get into any posture which you find comfortable. Then, close your eyes and focus your attention on your breathing, observing the movement of air as it goes in and out of the nose. Continue this till the mind almost shuts itself out from all outside stimuli and sensations.

Gradually concentrate by gently rejecting or turning away from any thought coming to your mind. Next, concentrate on an object like a flower, or a symbol like Om ॐ*

This is what I do next: I begin by first inhaling deeply and holding that breath while I visualise the symbol Om and trace out its form in my mind's eye, starting from the top curl to the bottom and end by tracing the dot and arc under it on the top. Having done this imaging, which takes approximately 15 to 20 seconds at the most, I slowly exhale, holding the same image till the very end. Then, I repeat the same process about 10 times, the whole thing taking about six to eight minutes. My advice to beginners, therefore, would be to gradually increase the duration of holding their breath from 40 seconds to a minute.

"Those who eat too much or too little, Will not succeed in meditation.But those who are temperate in eating and sleeping, work and recreation, will come to the end of sorrow through meditation."

Bhagwad Gita

TYPES OF MEDITATION

There are several types of meditation practiced by people from all over the world. Each is a valid form and only techniques differ while the basics remain the same. For the sake of convenience the most common varieties can be classified as:

Meditation in motion

Although this form of meditation is difficult, it is nevertheless very tempting. Here, one can continue with the usual lifestyle activities while simultaneously meditating. In other words, no specific posture is required here—one can be walking, working or idling while meditating. Meditation in motion suits those who are extremely busy otherwise and cannot afford to spare much time due to professional requirements and other pre-occupations. CEOs, senior and middle-level management people, professionals, politicians and others benefit from this type of meditation.

[*Please note that the process of meditation does not belong to any religion, creed or cult. In fact, I advise people—especially beginners—to associate their practice of meditation with the form or shape of any article which might be more familiar to them to make the initial steps easier. A Christian can focus on the shape of the cross, a Muslim on the word Allah or an image of the holy Kabbah and a Hindu on the Shivalingam. Human beings are gifted with the capacity for meditation from birth, thus it is free from all social, cultural and religious influences that come later in life.]

Transcendental Meditation (TM)

Maharishi Mahesh Yogi popularised this form of meditation way back in the late 1950s. A few years later, even the Beatles, along with well-known Hollywood stars like Mia Farrow, Michael York and Uma Thurman took to TM in a big way. Proponents have claimed TM to be a simple, natural, easy-to-learn mental technique whose regular practice leads to significant, cumulative benefits on all levels, including the mind, body, behaviour and environment. TM is practiced for 15 to 20 minutes twice daily while sitting comfortably with the eyes closed. In essence, the TM technique comprises the silent mental repetition of a simple sound known as a mantra, allowing the repetition to spontaneously become quieter and quieter, until it disappears and one is left conscious, but without thoughts.

According to R. K. Wallace et al, "During T.M. Practice, the body gains a deeper state of relaxation than during ordinary rest or sleep."[90]

R. W. Cranson wrote, "Changes in brainwaves indicate a state of enhanced awareness and coherence. TM has been found to increase intelligence, creativity and perceptual ability and reduce blood pressure and rates of illnesses by 50 per cent.[91] Patients with coronary heart diseases who practiced stress reducing TM technique had a nearly 50 per cent lower rate of heart attack, stroke and death compared to patients in the non-meditation control group, according to the results of a first-ever study presented during the annual meeting of the American Heart Association in Orlando, Florida on November 16, 2009.

Transcendental Meditation (TM) has been shown to improve immune function. In TM, your mind and body experience a state of deep relaxation.

The level of rest is deeper than what you get during the deepest sleep. As a result, the body repairs itself.[92]

Vipassana

Vipassanā is a Pali word which is often translated as "insight" or "clear-seeing" and is referred to as Buddhist meditation. It is the practice of insight meditation that is very simple and depends on direct experience, observation, rather than belief. It has three parts—adherence to a moral code, controlling the mind and development of concentration and detached observation of the reality of the mind and body from moment to moment. This practice develops a deep, experiential understanding of reality and also brings to the surface and dissolves deep-seated complexes and tensions.

T'ai Chi

This is a Chinese martial art based on Tao philosophy often practiced for the purposes of health and longevity. It is considered a soft style martial art, and one applied with as complete a relaxation or "softness" in the muscles as possible, to distinguish its theory and application from that of the hard martial art styles which use a degree of tension in the muscles. T'ai Chi is well-known as one of the slow motion routines that groups of people practice every morning. In T'ai Chi classes, one is taught awareness of one's own balance and what affects it, awareness of the same in others, and appreciation of the practical value in one's ability to moderate extremes of behaviour and attitude at both mental and physical levels.

Zen Meditation or Zazen

In it, one cuts all connections with the external world, to let go of all concerns within. Sitting in absorption, Zazen is at the heart of Zen practice. Zazen is different from other meditation in that it uses no meditation object or concept to focus on. The aim of Zazen is to first still the mind. Then, after years of practice, it reaches a state of pure thought and free wakefulness so that the mind can realise its own Buddha nature. In Zen Buddhism, sitting meditation or Zazen is a meditative discipline to calm the body and mind and experience insight into the nature of existence. While the term originally referred to a sitting practice, it is now commonly used to refer to practices in any posture, such as walking.

Spider Woman Meditation

She is a native American goddess. This form of meditation explores native American spirituality. It helps you to understand the power of myth and interconnectivity. It is based on a myth that before the universe came into existence, the spider woman wove a web in which every individual on earth was entangled. One has to meditate on the spider woman myth.

Amaterasu meditation

She is the sun goddess of Japan's Shinto religion. She was abused by her brother and retreated to a cave. This meditation helps you when you are abused or wounded. One has to meditate on the Amaterasu myth.

Quaker way meditation

The "Quaker movement" was started in the seventeenth century by George Fox in England. Followers of this movement are called "Friends of Jesus".

They meditate in a group of friends by sitting together in silence. It gives peace of mind and promotes a direct relationship with God. It encourages community feeling. Quakers try to be open with God and to friends in a group.

Kabbalah meditation

It is a Jewish meditation technique and a way to experience the presence of God. It connects you with God. In this technique, the word "Shema" is repeated. "Shema" is a Hebrew word meaning "hear". As you exhale, say "shh" and while inhaling, say "mmm". Repeat this process. It is a way to get connected with God and understand the purpose of your life.

When pop superstar Madonna disassociated herself from Britney Spears as she left Kabbalah, she told her, "I can't work with her as our faiths are against each other." Madonna follows Kabbalah meditation and is becoming more tolerant gradually. Earlier, she was a more disturbed and unsatisfied soul but is gradually improving with meditation.

BEST FORM OF MEDITATION

I feel that "living in the present" is the best form of meditation. In other words, no matter what activity one may be involved in (so long as it is a morally and socially accepted activity), it should be considered an act of meditation. What do I mean by this? That if, for instance, you are driving a car, exercising at the gym, eating, studying or even bathing, it should be carried out in its totality, as if you were truly getting lost in the occupation.

Let us, for example, suppose that you are bathing. Feel the water flow over your skin, feel its movement, fluidity, temperature, touch and the sound it makes as it comes out of the tap and falls to the floor and flows away down the drain. Feel it co-mingling with your body.

One has to get so deeply involved that he or she actually forgets the surroundings.

"For me, faith begins with the realisation that a supreme intelligence brought the universe into being and created man."

Arthur Compton,
1927 Nobel Prize for Physics

8

VISUALISATION IN MOTION

"Imagination rules the world."

Napoleon

"Imagination encircles the world."

Einstein

I was attracted to the techniques of visualisation or guided imagery as a student during my association, as mentioned earlier, with Swami Harinanda. But this was solely for the purpose of achieving good grades in medical college and to get rid of my constant "wet palm syndrome" associated with examinations and interviews, especially viva tests!

The practice of visualisation gradually increased my confidence and came in handy when I was developing my 'Window Operation' technique, which required me to give talks, present slide shows and take part in professional discussions at various forums in several countries.

WHAT IS VISUALISATION?

Visualisation means "seeing with the mind" or "forming a mental image".[93] It is basically internal imagery. Visualisation has been used for centuries by various religions and cultures to heal the body and mind. It can be practiced anywhere, in any position and any dress. It does not require any special equipment or apparatus.

Fig: Seeing with the mind

A mental image generally represents something perceived by the senses. Guided visualisation is a therapeutic technique in which patients enter a relaxed state and focus on an image related to the issue being confronted. Through dialogue, the therapist helps the individual resolve the problem. The technique is also used for relaxation and stress management, behaviour modification, pain management and the treatment of life-threatening and terminal illnesses.[94]

The book "*Spontaneous Regression of Cancer*" by the former President of the American College of Surgeons details 176 cases of remission, where the patients have been prayed for.[95] Even so, this is a very small section of people. Medical literature now estimates that perhaps two or three out of every 1,000 people with cancer experience such "cures", apparently unrelated to treatment. I feel that this incidence can be increased with the help of meditation, prayer and other relaxation techniques by boosting the immune system of the body.

Visualisation is a way to achieve your goal, fulfill desires and improve self-confidence. For most beginners, visualisation usually turns out to be more difficult than meditation but once a level of competence is achieved, the whole process moves along smoothly and without much difficulty. Over time, one can plan his or her own agenda to achieve a given purpose.

Myra Huth, Assistant Vice-President of the Center for Professional Excellence Research at Cincinnati Children Hospital Medical Center, wrote in the *Journal of Paediatric Nursing* after her study on children, "Guided imagery really works. It should be used in conjunction with pain medication, but it really works. Children using guided imagery felt significantly less pain and anxiety after a surgical procedure than the control group."[96]

Fig: Imagine a walk on beach

It is our imagination which creates for us our own hell or heaven. Similarly, through visualisation, we can achieve success as well as health. Regular practice also gives a sense of happiness. With visualisation, you can groom yourself to avoid negative thoughts and become positive in life.

You can heal your body and mind by diverting the dormant energy lying within, for useful purposes.

PHYSIOLOGY OF VISUALISATION

The exact method by which visualisation works is not generally known, but in all probability, and according to experts, it acts by bringing spiritual, physiological and biochemical changes in the body. Through visualisation, one can manifest a scene in the mind's eye and carry it through to the end, terminating it in a happy ending or as ultimate success. This boosts one's confidence. This process is known as "creative visualisation". It is used to solve a problem, achieve a goal or reach success. World-class athletes, for instance, routinely visualise a whole sequence of subsequent events even before the actual advent of their track and field endeavour. Lance Armstrong, the famous cyclist, proved the power of strong will by conquering dangerous testicular cancer.

Says Wally Amos, founder of the Amos Cookie Company and author of the book "*Man With No Name*", "I believe our imagination is the source of our individuality, our capacity for glory and our own peerless talent. I use the creative power of my mind to confront and shape my unique reality. I construct mental pictures of the steps leading to the goal. Prayer and visualisation call up your limitless spiritual resources to move you towards your vision."[97]

Visualisation activates the cerebral cortex and reaches the sensory centres, in turn creating a reality to which the body responds. The cerebral cortex gets activated depending on the sense—touch, smell, sight or hearing—receptor that is stimulated. Jean Achterberg, PhD, President of the Association for Transpersonal Psychology, says that imagery can affect immune functions, blood flow and heart rate.[98]

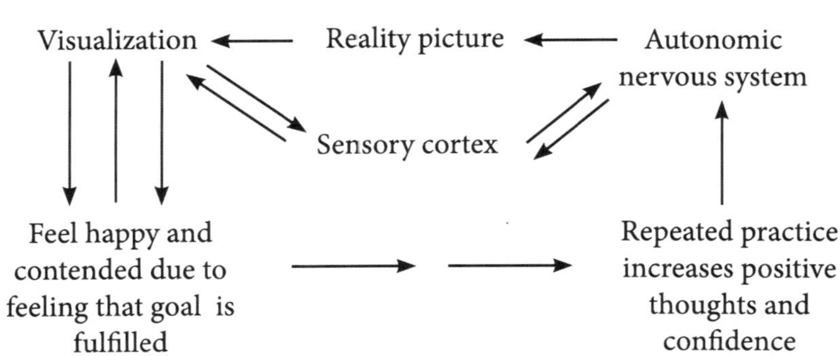

The seat of the conscious mind is in voluntary nervous system, the brain and spinal cord, with its control centre being the cerebral cortex.

The seat of the subconscious mind lies in the involuntary nervous system, which is the autonomic nervous system, so it's centres are in the brain stem, cerebellum, hypothalamus and amygdala.

When the conscious mind grasps an idea, it sends electrical impulses to your voluntary nervous system, which in turn shares it with the involuntary nervous system or subconscious mind, a creative medium that turns thought into a perception of reality.[99]

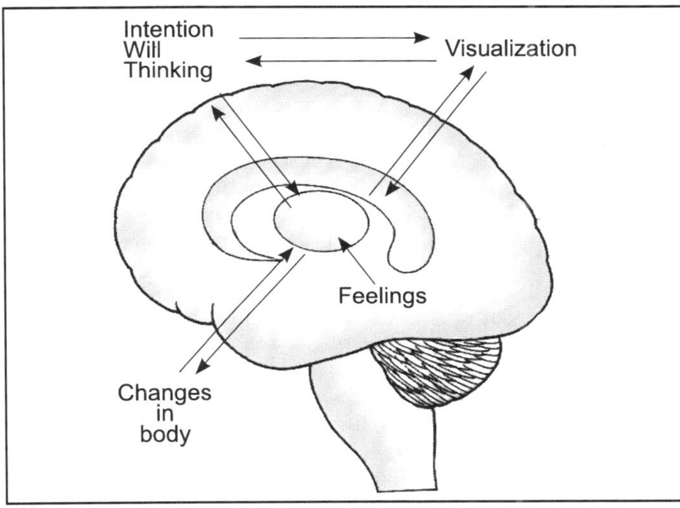

Fig: Physiology of visualization

In *Kabbalah and the Power of Dreaming: Awakening the Visionary Life,* author Catherine Shainberg writes: "The images may be 'fantasy,' but their effect is real. Imagination affects the physical and vice-versa. The two worlds interact through the body. The way a great band of nerve fibers, the corpus callosum, connects your right and left brain hemispheres, your body also connects your inner dream world with the outside physical world. Your body is the boundary and the link. Being securely grounded in your body, with a strong habit of paying attention to the messages your senses give you, maintains your access to both worlds, while at the same time safeguarding you from the danger of losing yourself in either."[100]

Martin L Rossman, MD, Academy for Guided Imagery, Mill Valley, California, USA, believes that imagery is simply a flow of thoughts that one can see, hear, feel, smell, taste or experience. The sensations in the body that imagery creates are a very real phenomenon that can be measured with laboratory devices. Research using brain scans indicates that imagery activates parts of the cerebral cortex and sensory centres of the brain. During visualisation, the visual (optic) cortex is active, and when sounds are imagined, the auditory cortex gets active. It appears that the cortex can create imaginary realities and the lower centre (and perhaps every cell in the body) responds to this information. The internal process involved in "worrying yourself sick" and "imagining yourself well" are quite similar."[101]

I always prepare my patients for surgery with the help of this visualisation technique so that they can visualise for themselves the act of surgery and also emerge from it in good health, conscious and happy, without excessive pain or discomfort.

What they actually visualise is a hundred per cent successful operation. Later, in the post-operative period, while they may experience a certain amount of weakness, they are able to carry on a conversation with friends and relatives who visit, without much effort. Most adult patients do not require too many painkillers in the post-operative period as compared to those who do not undergo visualisation. In fact, some patients did not need a single shot or tablet of an analgesic.

If you visualise a cheerful event or a pleasant experience from your life, it can give you the same amount of joy and happiness in the present moment.

BASIC TECHNIQUE OF VISUALISATION

1. You can practice visualisation in any comfortable clothes.
2. Choose a quiet and restful place where there are fewer chances of being distracted.
3. Once again, sit, kneel, lie or take up any comfortable position. Incidentally, some people find that during this period the lighting of perfumed candles or incense is conducive to the practice. This is totally up to you.
4. Begin by closing your eyes.
5. Concentrate on regular breathing.

6. Focus on your abdominal breathing.
7. Open your eyes and look around the room and select an object. Observe this object, concentrate on it, scrutinise it in detail, without straining your eyes.
8. Close your eyes, try to visualise the same object in its original detail.
9. Gradually, the image of the object will fade away.
10. Open your eyes and repeat the process.

SELF-INTROSPECTIVE SPIRITUAL VISUALISATION (SSV)

This is an experiment, which has many beneficial effects.

1. Choose a night when you are relatively free and relaxed. This experiment is conducted late at night when the environment is peaceful and most people in the house have retired.
2. Sit comfortably on a chair in front of a big mirror, which should not be more than 12 inches (30 centimetres) away from your eyes.
3. Look at your face in the mirror, observe it carefully, starting from the hair region to the forehead, down to the right ear, right cheek and chin, progressing upwards to the mouth and nose before going to the left cheek, left ear, forehead and settling finally on the eyes.
4. Close your eyes and try to visualise your face in the same sequence.
5. Now open your eyes and look into your eyes in the reflection. Try to gaze into the blacks of your pupils as if looking inside them. After some practice and with some concentration, you will start feeling that the person you are looking at is someone different from your body. This inner view of yourself is the real you—the spirit within, the soul.
6. Now, close your eyes and visualise those powerful staring eyes. Feel that deep gaze. Feel your spiritual self. This is the moment when you recognise the Godhead that resides in you at all times. Remember you are an important incarnation as a human being. Remind yourself that you have been brought to Earth not merely by some random accident but as part of a divine plan.

You have a mission. You have to fulfill this undertaking without getting lost along the way by your weaknesses, distractions and undue desires. Try to remember throughout the day that your real self—the gaze—is observing you, so that you do no wrong.

This is the soul about which Lord Krishna had told Arjun on the battlefield of Kurukshetra. As narrated in the "*Bhagwad Gita*", he said: "The soul has no birth or death. It has no being and, hence, will never cease to be. Birthless, deathless and without any beginning or end, the soul is not destroyed when the body is destroyed. The self cannot be wounded by weapons, burned by fire, moistened by water or blown away by wind. The soul cannot be divided, burnt, dissolved or dried up. It is eternal, all pervading, unalterable, unmoving and without a beginning."

SSV improves one's will-power, the ability to overcome problems and also one's general lifestyle. It enables you to manage anger better, become aware of your duties and become more humane. It develops your powers of forgiveness and gives you peace, health and happiness.

ADVANCED VISUALISATION TECHNIQUE

Relax in a sitting or lying position and feel comfortable. Take a few deep breaths. Now, create a mental picture of yourself lying or sitting and try to visualise yourself as another body. Then, as if your body is actually emerging out of itself, feel yourself getting up, putting your feet on the ground and getting into your slippers, feeling the touch of the slippers on your feet.

Next, picture yourself walking towards the refrigerator till you are standing in front of it. Visualise the refrigerator; hold its handle and feel the cold touch of the metal and open the door. Cool air is blowing out and touching your face. Feel that coolness.

Take out a lemon and hold it in the palm of your hand. Close the door. Become aware of the sound of the door closing. Now, bunch your palm into a fist and feel the coolness of the lemon inside it. Squeeze it a little and feel the roundness and firmness of the fruit. Now, open the palm into the form of a cup and feel the weight of the lemon by letting your cupped palm droop down slightly. Toss the lemon into the air and catch it again.

Now, imagine the soothing colour of the fruit. Its colour is lighter on the side where it catches the light. Also, the lemon's skin is not uniformly yellow; there are tiny dark dimples or pockets on the surface. The spot where the lemon was attached to the tree is visible as a small, round, off-white patch. Visualise all these things in sequence.

Next, take the lemon to the sink and wash it. Hear the sound of water splashing in the sink. Move towards the dining table and draw the chair towards you; listen to the sound of it dragging against the floor. Sit on the chair holding the lemon. Feel yourself seated on the chair with its pressure against your buttocks and under your thighs and knees. Smell the lemon.

After a little practice, you should be able to smell the fragrance. Lift the lemon and cut it with a knife and try to see the juice-filled fibers and seeds. Take one half of the lemon and as you lick the surface gently, savouring it, your mouth will fill with saliva. The point is to experience all the senses during the course of this exercise. Do it sincerely and then open your eyes. You should feel relaxed and fresh.

Visualisation—A Mind-Sharpener:

The left hemisphere of the brain is responsible for logical thinking while the right hemisphere is linked to creativity and artistic expression. Start by visualising a sick man, using your left brain and right eye since, as mentioned, the left hemisphere controls the right part of the body and vice versa. (To make the right hemisphere more dominant during this exercise, it will help to keep your left eye closed.) Simultaneously, visualise a healthy man with your right brain and left eye. (To get the left brain to work dominantly, keep your right eye closed.) Now, try to combine both pictures in your mind with both eyes closed. This technique improves the process of thinking, planning, concentration, reasoning and creativity.

"When confronted with marvels of life and the universe, one must ask why the only possible answers are religious. I find a need for God in the universe and in my own life."

Arthur L. Schalow,
Shared the 1981 Nobel Prize in physics

GUIDED VISUALISATION IN MOTION FOR THE BODY

"This is supposed to be a professional secret but I will tell you anyway. We doctors do nothing, we only help and encourage the doctor within."

Albert Schwietzer, MD,

"The more I study nature, the more I am amazed at the creator."

Louis Pasteur,
Father of Antisepsis

Visualisation is a variety of mind-body therapy that induces physical and mental relaxation, which benefits health. Dr. Andrew Weil treats his patients with guided imagery for better clinical results.[102]

Martin E. P. Seligman, Professor of Psychology, University of Pennsylvania, mentions in his book "*Learned Optimism*" that optimists do better than pessimists in almost every aspect of life, including the functioning of their immune system. Optimism can be learned. Images can influence behaviour and thus prompt a cure, which is why visualisation is being used by psychotherapists to treat their patients.[103]

Focus on the five vital organs of your body—brain, heart, lungs, liver and kidneys—during visualisation, to be healthy and free of disease.

Visualisation can be performed even when the body is in motion, when you are travelling, exercising on a treadmill or walking in the park.

Brain

"We are not human beings having a spiritual experience. We are spiritual beings having a human experience."

Teilhard de Chardin

"There is nothing so disobedient as an undisciplined mind, and there is nothing so obedient as a disciplined mind."

Gautam Buddha

Imagine a ray of light from some very distant source showering radiance on your whole body. Then, imagine its focus on your brain. Bathed in this light, the brain then begins to gradually outshine the rest of the body which then dims and finally recedes into the background. You can now view the outer structure of the brain, including its intricate convolutions and valley-like fissures on the surface.

The whole brain is now shining, and there is no black spot or haziness on it. Now feel fresh, stress-free and happy with clear thoughts. R Killner et al mentioned that "guided imagery can decrease chronic nightmares, reduce substance abuse, and alleviate many other psychological and physiological problems."[104]

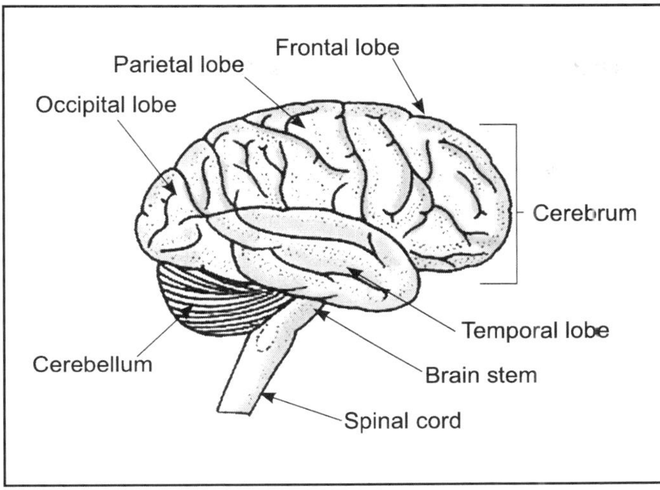

Fig: The Brain

A number of conditions may be worth treating with psychological therapies alone, such as fibromyalgia (chronic muscular pain) and irritable bowel syndrome (IBS). Psychological therapies include stress management, relaxation and imagery.[105]

HEART

Form a picture of your heart in the mind, including all the coronary arteries. Feel a shower of light bathing your heart and your heart emerging from this as a shining organ. Feel your blood flowing freely in these arteries without any obstruction. Feel the whole heart beating comfortably, slowly and regularly. Then, feel the warmth and freshness spreading from your heart to all parts of the body, making the entire body healthy.

Jeanne Achterburg, Ph D, President, Association for Transpersonal Psychology, wrote, "Every mental image a person has can affect such important body processes as the immune system, blood flow and heart rate."[106]

Meditation and visualisation are powerful tools to help you become aware of your true needs and then make them happen. Seeing what you want in your mind's eye creates an atmosphere of hope in your unconscious self.[107]

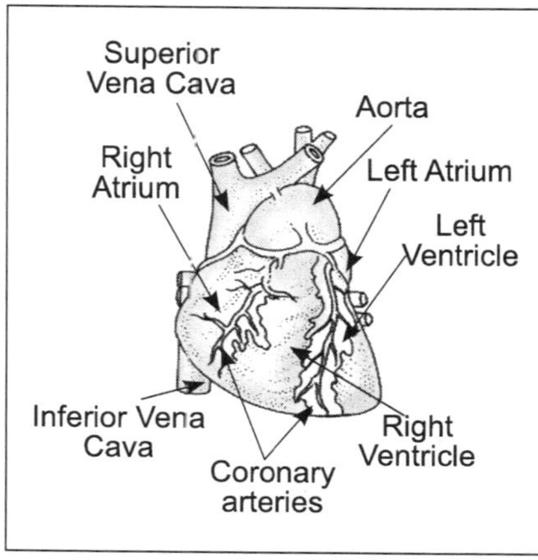

Fig: Parts of the Heart

LUNGS

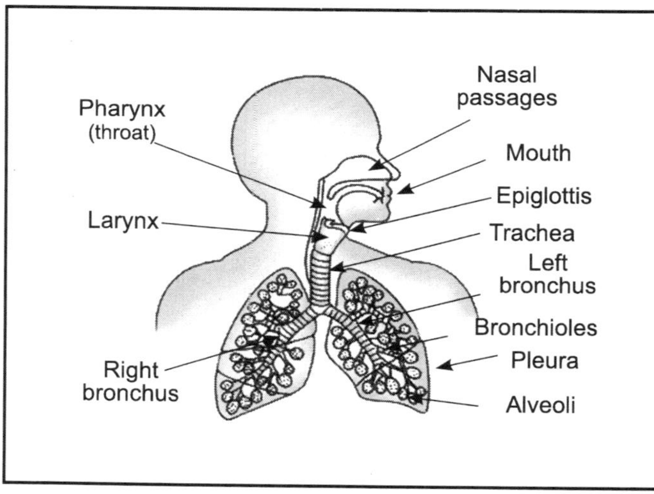

Fig: Parts of the Lungs

Visualise the lungs. Imagine that you are breathing in the light falling on it. Feel the tubules inside the lungs getting relaxed and dilated with large amounts of fresh bright light falling on them. Feel the freshness in your chest, which is now getting oxygen rich air and light. Your lungs emerge from this shower of radiance as glowing organs. Feel the same freshness in your breath. The air/light you are breathing now is full of oxygen and light, rejuvenating your whole body.

LIVER

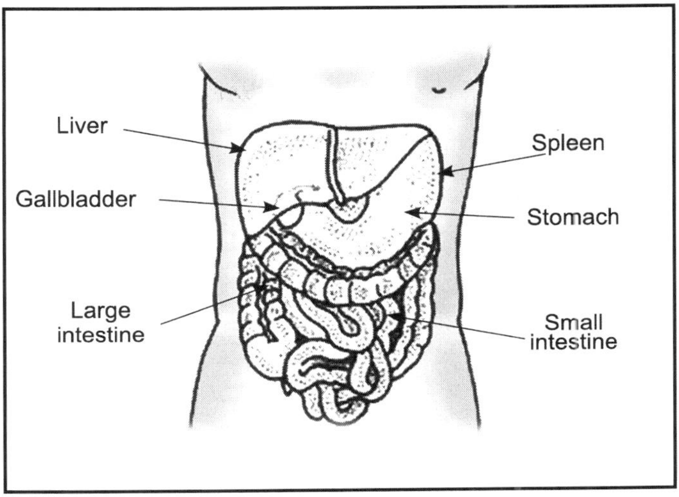

Fig: The Liver

Make a mental picture of your liver in your mind. Now, feel that shower of light bathing your liver. Gradually, the light makes the organ fresh and bright. Your liver emerges from this shower of light as a shining and healthy organ. Imagine you are feeling light, alert and fresh; visualise yourself as energetic, free from toxins and pollutants. Feel your appetite improving and picture yourself healthier.

KIDNEYS

Visualise the kidneys. Now feel the shower of light bathing them. Gradually, the light gets concentrated. The two kidneys are becoming brighter and cleaner and emerging from this shower of light as glowing and healthy organs. Feel your body rejuvenated by this process as lots of toxic substances leave your body through the kidneys. Your body is becoming younger and healthier. Feel this health.

One must develop the ability to change a negative image to a positive one by regular practice of imagery. The surgical patient, who is headed for surgery, can improve his emotions and get a feeling of happiness by changing the negative image of a painful operation to a positive one of comfort and success. It is good practice to teach patients guided imagery. I train my patients in guided imagery before surgery and prepare them to deal better with postoperative pain, discomfort and emotions.

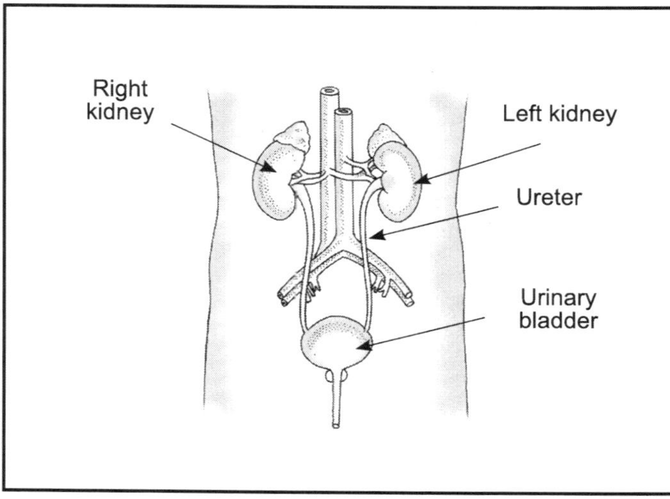

Fig: The Kidneys

Mr. Ahmed Hussain, 45 years old, was suffering from a discomfort in his chest, GERD (Gastro Esophageal Reflux Disease), and was a heavy smoker. He attended my surgical clinic in Apollo Clinic, Gurgaon in July, 2008. His wife was accompanying him for Upper Gastrointestinal Endoscopy. She told me that he had suddenly developed a feeling of claustroptrobia in small or dark rooms. He would not agree to endoscopy as he was scared of a tube going down his throat. I trained him with visualisation for a few days. He felt better and agreed to undergo endoscopy, which was successfully done under 5mg of Diazepam delivered intravenously. This is an example of how relaxation techniques can help one in even avoiding anaesthesia in such cases.

VISUALISATION IN MOTION FOR THE SOUL

"Our nervous system is not just a fiction, It is a part of our physical body, and our soul exists in space and is inside us, Like the teeth in our mouth. It can't be forever violated with impunity."

Boris Pasternak, Nobel Laureate
Doctor Zhivago.

Relax in a comfortable position, The can do your workout on a treadmill machine holding it's bar or spot jogging in a room. Imagine God in the form of a huge source of light like the sun. Imagine a drop of light from this source getting detached and disappearing into your heart. Now imagine a drop of light coming out of your heart and gradually moving up and uniting with the huge source of light or God.

A soul is immortal because a soul is nonphysical and not subject to death.

9

SURGERY, MEDITATION AND VISUALISATION

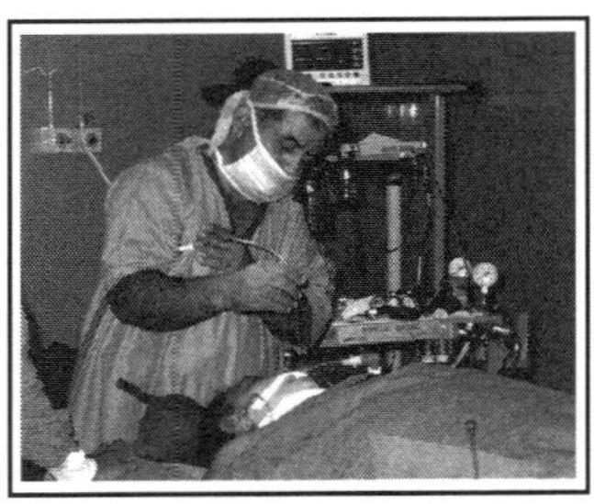

"Take time to pray. It is the greatest power on earth."

Anonymous

- I obeserve in my surgical practice that when a person who has to undergo surgery is trained beforehand in deep abdominal breathing exercises along with meditation, his or her oxygen saturation of the blood increases by two to three per cent. This may seem small but is very helpful both during and after surgery in the recovery period in relation to complications and healing.

Such people require less painkillers in post-operative period.

- Dr. Alice Domar, Psychologist, at Harvard University, has observed that patients who did two minutes of deep breathing and meditation in the operation theatre before going in for surgery had lower blood pressure, bled less during surgery and took less time.
- Meditation helps to prepare patients for surgery and may improve the outcome and lead to speedy and uneventful recovery.
- It relaxes the mind and body, reduces anxiety, brings peace and strengthens the immune system thereby inducing an improved immune response from the body for healing after surgery.
- Start practicing meditation daily a few days before surgery.

How to prepare yourself for surgery

- Meditation for surgery begins with deep abdominal breathing
- Take a comfortable position in a sitting or lying posture.
- Visualise your whole body
- Concentrate on the diseased area of your body and visualise yourself in the operation theatre and on the operation table
- Visualise your surgeon standing next to you in the operation theatre.
- Imagine a laser-like bright light falling from your surgeons hand on to the diseased part of your body.
- Imagine the sickness gradually disappearing under the light.
- A wound is left, which is also gradually healing till it is completely healed.
- Now, your body is again healthy and glowing with health and strength.
- Repeat this process three times.

Nathan Schmulewitz from University of Cincinnati, Cincinnati, USA, studied the effect of "Healing Touch" therapy. He reported in *Science Daily* that a light touch on the face, neck and head along with with mild sedative relaxes the patient and prepares them well for surgical procedures. The healing touch harmonises the energies in the person's body, mind and soul.[108]

It has been proved by many studies that those who do regular meditation have 40 per cent to 50 per cent lower brain response to pain than others who never did meditation.

I have observed that while doing Upper Gastrointestinal Endoscopy, if the patient feels nauseated, just rub the tip of the nose with a finger and request the patient to feel the touch and concentrate on it, it stops nausea or retching.

"You cannot live a perfect day without doing something for someone who will never be able to repay you."

John Wooden

10

RETROSPECTION OF THE LAST 24 HOURS

"He who knows others is wise, He who knows himself is enlightened."

Lao Tzu

Once a day, you should review the events of the past 24 hours of your life. It is best done in the morning, along with your normal exercises.

Close your eyes. Try to recall the past 24 hours and analyse the mistakes or wrongs you may have commited. For instance, it could have been a bout of anger, binge eating, skipping exercises, etc. You have to tell yourself not to do this again. Repeat three times: "I will not make the same mistake again; God will help me."

Everyone needs to introspect to examine one's thoughts and feelings from time to time. One has to survey, analyse and review the past course of events over a fixed period of time.

Introspection has the power to provide an intimate understanding of where the fault lies. One can then take corrective steps.

I wanted to lose weight but was unable to, no matter how hard I tried. I avoided lunch but my weight continued to increase. I began introspecting every morning for a few minutes to discover the reason. After a few days, I realised the problem and, perhaps, its possible solution. Although I was skipping lunch, I was munching on high-calorie snacks several times during the day. I told myself that I would only have regular meals, with no munching in between.

Introspection answers the what, where and why. But retrospection also gives a person a point of reference for avoiding the mistake in future. It is a daily process of awakening and I recommend it once every 24 hours. The ideal time is in the morning, before one starts the day. Gradually, this should turn into a habit.

"Transform your thinking, and you transform your life."

Rex Johnson

11

DAILY AWAKENING

"I heard a voice cry, Sleep no more."

William Shakespeare

At the end of your 40 Minutes With God, you must remind yourself you are now awake and it is clear in your thoughts that you are a part of God. You should never forget this. And, if God has made you, he cares for you too.

You can ask for anything because you are an element of God and God is with you.

Promise yourself you will not do anything wrong and give a bad name to your Creator. In case of any wrong done unknowingly, ask for his forgiveness. Remind yourself of your confidence in God and your own self-control.

Repeat three times with confidence: "I am a part of God, I will not do anything wrong; I am capable of doing anything and everything with his blessings. I will help others and will not cause harm to others physically or emotionally. I am confident that I can do it and I will do it."

"O supreme Lord!
Thou art ever existent,
Ever conscious, ever blissful
We meditate on thy most adorable glory.
May Thou guide and inspire our intellect on the path of highest divinity!
May we be able to discriminate between truth and falsehood."

Rig Veda

You have to awaken yourself daily to bring your life under control.

Julie Redstone, Founder of the "Light Omega", a Spiritual Centre for healing and transformation, believes that an awakened person feels connected with God. There is a wakefulness that comes from a clear mind, unobscured by want, erring thought and preoccupation, and there is desire to be awakened that comes from a clear heart, willingness to engage with life as a gift and as an ever unfolding revelation of the purpose of creation. Such an awakened heart cannot respond indifferently to life because it sees the outstretched hands of the Creator at every turn and in every particle of the experience.

"If everyday is an awakening, you will never grow old, you will just keep growing."

Gail Sheeby

12

THANKSGIVING

"If the only prayer you ever say in your entire life is thank you, it will be enough."

Meister Eckhart

The last thing in "40 Minutes With God" is not the least; you have to also thank God for being with you the whole time. Be thankful to him for his blessings and for listening to your prayers. By giving thanks to God, we also improve our habits for daily living. Always be thankful to God whenever a problem you have prayed for, is resolved. Do not forget Him once your job is done.

When you pray to God and put your trust in him, don't doubt that he will answer. Neale Donald Walsch, writes in his bestseller *Conversations With God*, "The correct prayer is, therefore, never a prayer of supplication, but a prayer of gratitude, especially when you thank God in advance for that which you choose to experience in your reality. You, in effect, acknowledge that it is there already in effect. Thankfulness is thus the most powerful statement to God."

Mr. Hasib Alam, 20 years old, a manual worker, was admitted in a hospital with severe abdominal pain and high fever. He also vomited once. He had fever for three days, but the pain in the abdomen developed only on the 24th evening. He was treated by a local General Practioner who referred him after three days of treatment to Sri Ram Hospital, Gurgaon.

Being a case of high fever, the duty doctor referred him to the physician on call, who diagnosed it as enteric fever and started appropriate treatment. The patient was referred to me due to abdominal pain. There was no history of trauma. He passed normal stool.

He was toxic, his temperature was 103 degree Fahrenheit, pulse 118 / min, BP 110/70, the blood count was normal, haemoglobin 7.8. The chest x-ray was also normal. There was no gas under the diaphragm. An ultrasound revealed splenomegaly and some free fluid in the peritoneal cavity.

However, high fever, pain in the left side of the abdomen, anemia, mild distension of the abdomen, tenderness in the left upper abdomen and low blood pressure at the time of admission were puzzling.

The patient was a poor man, so advanced imaging investigations like CT scan and MRI were out of question.

The physician was of the opinion that his low hemoglobin was due to his poor nutritional state and thus not unusual symptom.The combination of a low level of Hb and pain in the abdomen with some free fluid in the peritoneal cavity would not allow me to pursue conservative treatment.

I remembered Hugh Dudley's words, "It is as much an intellectual exercise to tackle the problem of belly ache as to work on a human genome." Now, I understood this phrase better and decided to open up the abdomen. The patient and his relatives were not prepared for this, as they believed his condition was improving and the pain decreasing.

I've always valued the advice of Sir Vincent Zachary Cope, Surgeon, England, that, "In doubtful cases, do not wait too long before exploring, for it is quite wrong to get upon the slogan 'wait and see', when looking may provide the remedy."

I arranged three bottles of blood. The operation began and I made a small midline mini incision to peep inside the abdomen, which revealed the tip of the iceberg, haemoperitoneum (blood in peritoneal cavity). I enlarged the incision, saw a mixture of fresh and old clotted blood filling the peritoneal cavity. The blood pressure of the patient suddenly dropped to 60/40 from 130/80. A hurried exploration revealed a rupture of the enlarged spleen. There was a big 13 cm long deep fissure in the spleen on the outer surface and another small fissure over the inner surface near the hilum (centre of the spleen). Fresh blood oozed from both fissures. I had to do an urgent splenectomy (removal of spleen) to save the patient's life and the BP began to improve after the splenectomy. The anaesthetist was relieved and told me there was no hurry as the vital signs of patient had improved.

This was a case of rupture of the diseased and enlarged spleen due to a trivial trauma. Later, I sat with the patient and inquired in detail about the onset of pain and what occurred before the pain started. He then remembered that he was patted on the left side of his abdomen by a friend with some enthusiasm and force to get well soon.

Here was an example of severe damage done by a well-wisher. Thank God, the patient was operated upon.

It is unfortunate that human beings have a short memory. We usually end up forgetting our worries and stresses of a short while ago once a problem is finally resolved. So, it is correct to thank God for keeping one away from wrong paths and deeds. Saying "Thank you, God" is not time consuming as it takes only a few seconds. Repeat this from your heart three times: "God, I thank you very much for what you have given to me, including what you have not given to me, for only you know best what to give. I now wait to meet you again tomorrow."

"When you look at others with smiling, kind and caring eyes, the act of looking becomes a prayer, a meditation and a way of healing."

Anonymous.

13

WHEN AND WHY PRAYERS FAIL

"Shallow men believe in luck, believe in circumstance. Strong men believe in cause and effect."

Ralph Waldo Emerson

All prayers are not answered. A study conducted by Newsweek magazine of the USA, in the 80s, indicated that 80 per cent of Americans feel that their prayers are answered about 80 per cent of the time. What happens to the remaining 20 per cent of the prayers? Why are these prayers not answered? In Oscar Wilde's opinion, "When the Gods wish to punish as, they answer our prayers."

We are not aware of the percentage, but a lot more people than we imagine, when faced with this situation, get depressed and lose hope of their prayers ever being answered.

Spiritual writer Philip Yancey writes in his book *"Prayer – Does it Make Any Difference?"* that some prayers go unanswered because they are simply frivolous. The Bible also makes it clear that a prayer may go unanswered because of a flaw in the person praying, not because of the prayer itself. Sometimes, sin disrupts communication with God. If a man shuts his ears to the cry of the poor, he too will cry out and not be heard. Prayer involves more than bowing the head a few times a day; it pervades all of life and vice versa. We ask, why does God not answer my prayer as he answered that man's prayer? We should ask instead about where our life failed to match up to the other man's. Some prayers are impossible to answer, such as opposite sides praying for victory in a match. Just because he doesn't answer, doesn't mean he doesn't care. Some of God's greatest gifts are unanswered prayers.[109]

A Times –TNS India Survey, conducted across 10 major cities of India, showed that 95 per cent of Indians believed that God answered prayers, while 5 per cent didn't. 54 per cent believed that all their prayers were answered and 41 per cent felt that some of their prayers were answered. 90 per cent of the population believed in going for pilgrimages and 83 per cent prayed at home.[110]

C. S. Lewis says that all prayers are heard, though not all prayers are granted. Only faith vouches for the connection, no empirical proof can establish the reason. We believe that a prayer has been answered not because of any scientific criteria proving cause and effect, but as a result of faith.[111]

Philosophically, a "No" from God is also taken as an answer to a prayer, which may be a "Yes" or "No". A "No" may be due to a deficiency in the prayer, it may not be from the core of the heart or maybe it was performed merely as a ritual, as in various medical studies, disclaiming the positive effects of prayer on illness. Sometimes, it is difficult to find answers for those who really prayed from the core of their hearts and got "No" for an answer as seen on 11th September, 2001, during the World Trade Centre attack. Only a few survived as their prayers were answered, while 3,500 died even as they prayed from the core of their hearts.

On 25 September, 2005, Mrs. Kiran Singh, a 66-year-old obese female, a resident of Gurgaon, was admitted with acute appendicitis to a local hospital. She was operated under spinal anaesthesia. It was difficult and could not be done even after two attempts by the anaesthetist. So a light general anaesthesia was administered as the operation was crucial for saving her life. The operation was conducted without any problems. An open appendicectomy was performed. The appendix was inflamed with an impending perforation. As the patient recovered from anaesthesia, she developed paraplegia (paralysis of both lower limbs) as a rare complication of the anaesthesia. She developed haemorrhage in the spinal canal, which created pressure on the spinal cord. She was operated upon to remove haematoma from the spinal canal to relieve pressure on the spinal cord. She improved, but could not become normal. I continuously prayed for this lady, but recovery was not complete, probably the prayers were not powerful.

Some prayers reduce the importance of prayer, such as "God! Please bring rain so that I can skip school." Sometimes, the man who prays is not in the right, like an alcoholic who prays to prevent cirrhosis, but does not stop consuming alcohol.

People sometimes ask for something which is not fulfilled, but this does not mean God does not listen.

Perhaps, God has created troubles to teach us to pray. When you pray, you must believe that he can solve every problem and bring about miracles. Only then your prayer will be answered.

Prayer is a difficult phenomenon to understand. It is impossible to fully understand God's way of working. There must be many reasons for a prayer not being fulfilled. Sometimes, perhaps, God wishes to teach a lesson or allow the person to develop himself in a particular area, which may not happen if his prayer is instantly answered. Sometimes, the person may not have faith in God and his prayer.

The intensity of prayer is directly proportionate to the magnitude of the problem. An honest prayer done for someone else, even if not done correctly but from heart, is answered often.

There is another reason why prayers are sometimes not answered. For instance, according to some eastern religions, human beings accumulate bad karma from their past life and are given a fresh opportunity to correct the mistakes in their new lifetime. God will not change this magnificent system by granting a prayer instantly, but instead would want the person to work towards changing himself.

If someone has committed a crime, like causing a cowry death, and prays for his malignancy to go into remission, a positive answer would defeat the whole purpose of the Dharmic Code.

Sometimes, our prayers fail, because of the following reasons:

- Lack of confidence and trust, which moves the subconscious mind to utilise its mental and spiritual resources give poor response.
- Doubts about efficacy of our prayer makes the prayer itself weak.
- "No" should be taken as an answer too.

"A man stands in his own shadows and wonders why it is dark."

Zen saying

14

NOTES

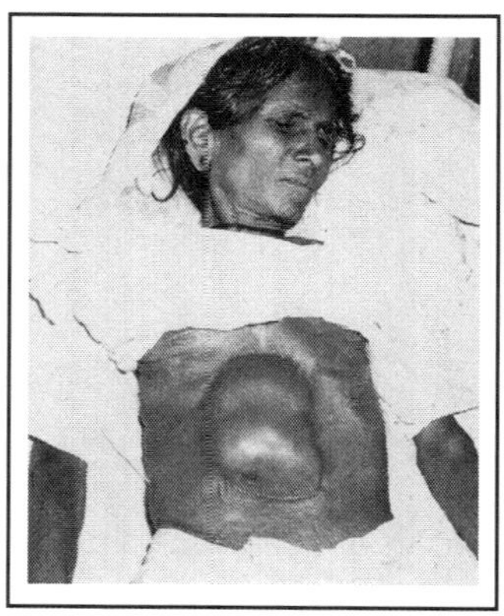

"Pain is perfect misery, the worst of all evils, And, if excessive, overturns all patience."

John Milton, 'Paradise Lost'

If pain is so bad and useless, then why has God created it in the first place? Pain is not as bad as we make it out to be, and has several beneficial aspects. It is a protective phenomenon and reminds us that somewhere, something in the body is not quite right or functioning optimally. In many cases, it could be a forewarning of a serious and potentially lethal sickness or injury.

Think for a moment of life without pain. Any sickness can strike suddenly without warning. Sometimes, a baby is born with a poorly developed nervous system so that he or she lacks the ability to feel pain. It can be an alarming situation as the child could be suffering from an unnoticed injury or illness and not be aware of it till it is too late.

Pain is usually caused by the firing of nerve endings caused by external or internal stimuli, which is then received by pain receptors that cause an electrochemical impulse to travel to the spinal cord via peripheral nerves and then to the pain centres in the brain.

Surgical or other trauma damaged tissues which cause the release of pain causing substances like prostaglandins, histamines, substance P, etc., at the site of the trauma, which initiates the pain impulse.

Ronald Melzack, who developed the famous "Gate-control Theory of Pain" in 1965, indicated in the theory that a gate—particularly for pain impulses exists at the level of the spinal cord in the dorsal horn (rear of the spinal cord). This acts like an entry gate that allows some impulses to pass through while stopping others, thus explaining the different intensities of pain felt by different individuals receiving the same type of stimuli like a needle prick at the time of blood sampling.

However, Melzack himself modified his theory in the early 1990s saying that the seat of pain is in the brain. A person without a spinal cord would be able to feel pain even without any injury. When emotional turmoil and negative thoughts can cause pain without any physical stimuli, why can't the process be reversed using meditation?[112]

The regular practice of meditation can blunt pain perception through the mediation of the brain. In fact, regular meditation, along with relaxation techniques, can also reduce migraine by decreasing the accompanying stress, a factor that stimulates migraine. Lowering one's response to stress through yoga, meditation, hypnosis and biofeedback is helpful for many patients of migraine.[113]

I also teach my patients the technique of meditation and visualisation during the pre-operative period to help them make a smoother transition from surgery to the post-operative period. During the post-operative period, meditation reduces the number of doses of analgesics and sedatives required. Through meditation, patients are able to cope better with their pain and distress symptoms.

This is especially useful in people suffering from gastritis, hyperacidity and peptic ulcers, where nonsteroidal antiinflammatory drugs can trigger pain and even lead to gastric bleeding. It is also beneficial for people who are hypersensitive to such drugs. Or, as the *Oxford Handbook of Clinical Surgery* says: "Psychological preparation of patients can reduce narcotic requirements by 50 per cent in post-operative pain."[114]

When I dress patients with large and painful open wounds or burns, I find they are almost always terrified of the concomitant pain involved and plead to be given strong sedatives or analgesics. Hence, I train them in deep abdominal breathing and meditation during the course of the dressing as this considerably reduces the need for such pain suppressants.

The Harvard Medical School Family Health Guide, for instance, says that "chronic pain is one that lasts at least for six months and does not respond well to medical treatment. On the other hand, relaxation and meditation therapies teach individuals how to relax muscles, relieve anxiety and disrupt the cycle of pain, anxiety and tension."[115, 116]

Paul Roland describes in his book *How to Meditate* that researchers at Stanford University, USA, compared 144 methods of relaxation and concluded that transcendental meditation was more than twice as effective as compared to any other technique in reducing stress."[117]

If you feel somebody's pain and suffering then you are better equipped to help him sympathetically. Some people can in reality feel other's pain. This phenomenon is known as "Mirror Touch Synthesis". Michael Banissy, Department of Psychology, University College of London studied 10 such people.[118]

"Divine is the task to relieve pain."

Hippocrates

PART II

Dr. Nigam's Technique for Health and Healing

"Can we afford to ignore the role of emotions, hope, the will to live, the power of human warmth and contact just because they are so difficult to investigate scientifically and our ignorance is so overwhelming?"

David Felten

"Institutions that ignore the spiritual dimension increase their chances of becoming only biological garages where dysfunctional human parts are repaired or replaced; such prisons of technique merely obscure the integrity *and scope of persons."*

Thomas Berry

"Health is the greatest of all possessions. "

Ali ibn Abi Talib (r.a)

"O Lord of mankind! Take away this pain, and give health; for Thou art the giver of health: there is no health bu Thine, that health which leaveth no sickness."

Prophet Muhammad

1

INTRODUCTION

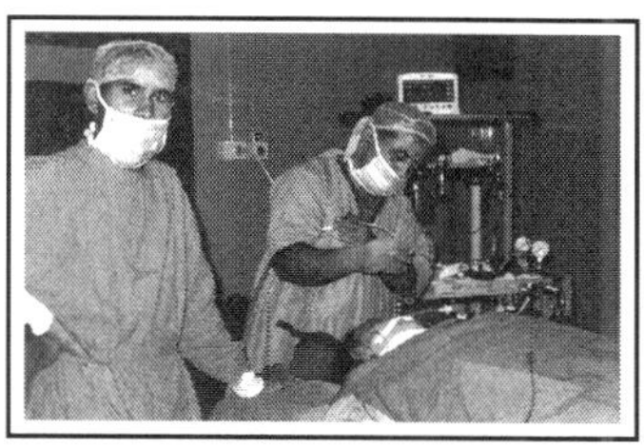

"Natural forces within us are the true healers of the disease."

Hippocrates
The Father of Medicine (460- 375 BC),
who wrote The Hippocratic Oath.

Health is defined as "a state of optimal physical, mental and social wellbeing" The popular idea that it is merely an absence of disease and infirmity is not complete. Healing is a process of cure or restoring wounded parts or to become well or healthy whereas spiritual healing is the cure or improvement of an illness through spiritual practices like prayer.[119]

Dr. Alexis Carrel, French physician, winner of the Nobel Prize in Medicine, wrote in his book *Prayer and Modern Man,* "Pray regularly and you will find your life improved. The bodily posture itself—relaxing, joining hands, bending knees—has health benefits."[120]

The only thing that can prevent the healing of sicknesses with my technique is your mistrust in its healing. My technique is based on the fact that every sickness has two aspects, the physical (body) and the spiritual (mind). Unless both aspects of sickness are handled well, there is no way one can heal completely.

Studies have shown that women who meditate and use guided imagery have higher levels of immune cells that are known to combat breast tumours. Dr. Dale Mathews and Dr. David Larson hope that the wall separating medicine and religion will be soon removed.[121]

Healing is usually a tissue response to a wound, inflammatory process or cell necrosis. Healing of body tissues is a spontaneous process, which starts immediately after injury. The injured area heals by either regeneration or scar tissue formation. Regeneration is the replacement of lost or damaged tissue with the original tissue.[122, 123]

Regeneration happens in skin, liver and the alimentary tract lining. These organs can lose a portion and again regain the same tissue as they heal. Now we know that the liver retains its capacity to regenerate even after 80 per cent of it has been removed. The heart, brain and nerves do not regenerate. After a heart attack, a portion of its wall becomes dead and is replaced by scar tissue, which is weaker than the normal heart tissue. The scar tissue area of the heart weakens the heart. Regeneration, if possible, can make the heart as strong as it was before the attack. A similar process takes place in the brain after a brain injury or a Cerebro-vascular Accident. The scar made during this period acts as a trigger for epileptic attacks. Stem cell therapy is trying to induce regeneration.

I was called on the night of 6th Aug, 2008, to see Mrs. Binita Mohanty, a 51-year-old cheerful lady, the wife of a friend. She was restless and experienced palpitations without chest pain suddenly while watching a thriller on television. She was conscious, with a heart rate of 180 per minute and BP 160/100 mm Hg. I know that this is an abnormal form of tachycardia (faster heart rate than normal). I shifted her to Artemis Hospital, Gurgaon, without losing time, fearing a cardiac arrest. Cardiologist Dr. B. Kalra was in casualty then at the state-of-the-art hospital. Immediately, 3 ml xylocard was given intravenously and the heart rate began to come down, reducing within two minutes to 110 per minute. The next day, echocardiography, coronary angiography and a thalium scan were done, which revealed an old myocardial infarction (MI) in the apex of the left ventricle. She gave a history of heart attack at the age of 28. Now, this scar tissue was creating trouble and had reduced her normal ejection fraction to 19 per cent from 65 per cent. It was sending exciting electric signals to the heart to beat fast. The condition is known as ventricular tachycardia. This could happen to her anytime without warning symptoms and the galloping heart could stop due to fatigue. We decided to introduce an ICD (Implantable Cavdioverter-Defibrillator), a sophisticated and expensive device that automatically senses and terminates the life threatening arrhythmias with energy shocks.

Binita is an atheist and when I reached her home that night, her heart rate was 180 beats per minute. On our way to the hospital in the car, it went up to approximately 200 beats per minute. I requested her to keep calm on the way to the hospital by deep abdaminal breathing, which she did as she was quite scared. I believe that it was because of this that her heart rate did not increase further and recorded 184 beats per minutes when we reached the casualty department. She has promised me to learn and practice meditation and visualisation for healing and regeneration of her cardiac injury which, unfortunately, she has not done till now.

Dr. Josephine P. Briggs, Director of the National Centre for Complimentary and Alternative Medicine, National Institute of Health, USA, said there are more than 80 million adults in the US who are using some form of alternative medicine, from herbs to yoga. [124]

I am sure further research in the field of healing and regeneration will unfold more secrets. So far, we do not know enough about the scientific basis of the healing effects of relaxation techniques, spirituality and the response of these factors on cellular and sub-cellular levels.

Dr. Dean Ornish has established that "a comprehensive lifestyle programme can lower cholesterol and blood pressure more than has ever been reported without drugs and can even begin to reverse severe coronary heart disease."[125]

This technique treats the illnesses through visualisation or guided imagery. I call it therapeutic visualisation as it treats diseases. A combination of guided imagery and self-hypnosis works best, and helps stop the process of sickness, bringing it back to being healthy. The actual chemistry is not clear, but it ultimately provides relief. Why we feel good after a workout was not known earlier, but now we know that it is due to the release of certain chemicals called endorphins from the brain cells.

The chemistry of my cleansing process and healing is a matter for further research. The technique can be combined with "Forty Minutes With God" for best results.

You can see with the naked eyes only what already exists in the external world. In a similar way, that which you can visualise in your mind's eye already exists in the invisible realms of your mind. What you form in your imagination is as real as any part of your body. The idea and the thought are real and will one day appear in your objective world if you are faithful to your mental image. This process of thinking forms impressions in your mind. These impressions, in turn, manifest as facts, adding experiences to your life. [126]

"Thy name is my healing, O my God."

Baha Ullah

2

NEUROPHYSIOLOGY OF THIS TECHNIQUE

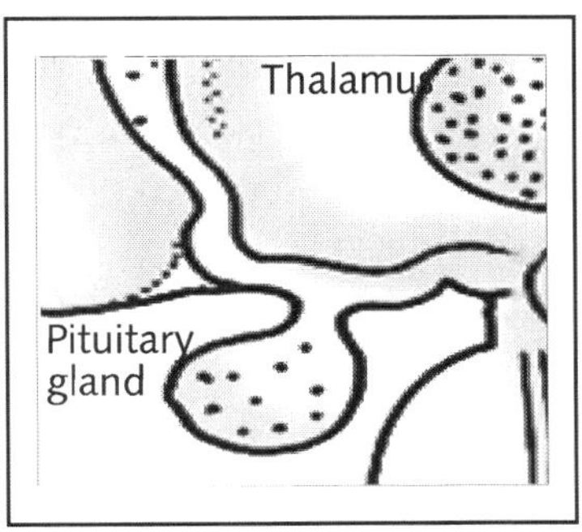

"O God, If on the day of battle, I forget you, You do not forget me."

William King

Guided imagery is a therapeutic technique. It is designed to help people gain access to their inner world of imagery and to use it for their benefit.[127]

Therapeutic visualisation requires deep concentration and regular practice. When we perform therapeutic visualisation, we make an image of the sickness and then a picture of health, which activates the cerebral cortex.

The sensory receptor areas related to the visualised image get stimulated and the body responds to this information. The thoughts here are related to smell, taste, vision, hearing and experience. The few changes in the stimulated areas of the brain can be seen and recorded by functional MRI. When we visualise scenes, the cortex of the brain is activated and when we visualise sounds, the auditory cortex gets activated. So, the cerebral cortex creates imaginary realities and the lower centres respond to this information. What neurotransmitters and hormones are created is a matter of further research. Dr. Irving Oyle, a California physician, says, "Positive, beautiful thoughts trigger the release of beneficial hormones in the body and those in turn help the body to heal itself." It is confirmed by studies that depression, sadness and isolation lead to suppression of the immune system and positive emotions improve the functioning of the immune system.

"Our body loves us, and even while the spirit drifts dreaming, works at mending the damage that we do."

John Updike

"Start by doing what's necessary, then do what is possible and suddenly you are doing the impossible."

Saint Francis of Assissi

3

HYPOTHESIS OF DR. NIGAM'S TECHNIQUE

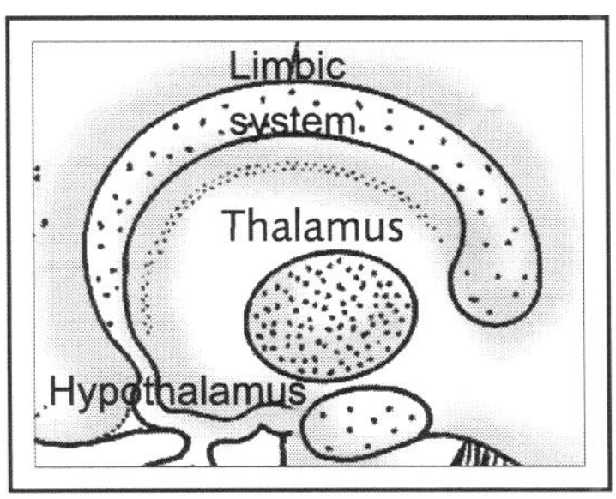

"I dressed him and God healed him."

Ambroise Paire,
Famous French Surgeon of the 16th century

Research now shows that prayer and other alternative therapies like imagery, meditation and touch therapy can improve healing, and certainly cause no harm.

Grief may suppress the function of a lymphocyte and increase the risk of cancer. Those who marry early after bereavement of spouse live relatively normal lives afterwards.[128, 129]

Dr. Dale Mathews of Georgetown University believes the future of medicine lies in "Prayer And Prozac".[130]

The following theories offer explanations of this technique:

Theory of Competitive Inhibition

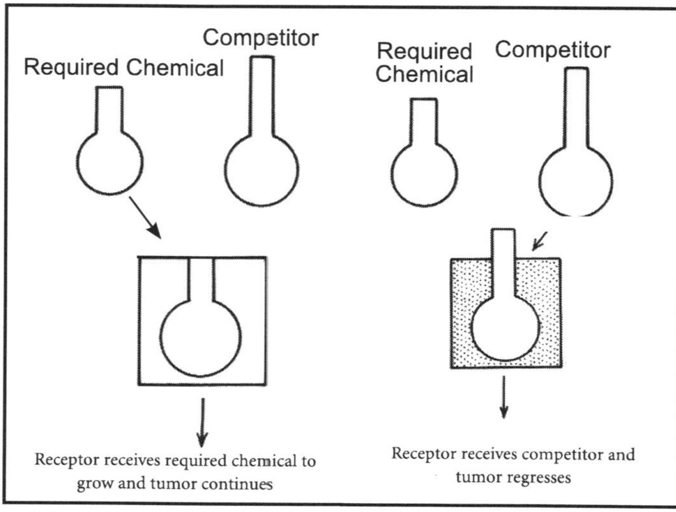

Fig: Theory of Competitive Inhibition

I feel that the effectiveness of this technique may be similar to "Competitive inhibition". Tamoxifen, a drug used to fight breast cancer, acts through competitive inhibition of the female hormone oestrogen. In the tumour, the receptor accepts drug and does not take oestrogen as it cannot differentiate between oestrogen and Tamoxifen, due to their chemical similarity. The tumor regresses as it requires oestrogen for its growth. My technique replaces the picture of sickness in the body with one of health, so that a mental image of healing develops and the sickness starts to fades away.

The brain starts sending signals to the diseased organ for improvement and it gradually starts chemical and structural changes towards healing. The chemicals and hormones required for healing the particular illness are perhaps produced by the body due to the repetitive visualization, and the brain too starts producing chemicals that heal. This is the probable explanation and it requires further research.

Theory of the Subconscious Mind

The "brain" is an anatomical entity and "mind" is a psychological entity. One can see the brain with an MRI or CT scan, but the mind is not visible. The mind works continuously throughout life.

The mind is of two forms:

1. Conscious mind
2. Subconscious mind

The conscious mind is also called the voluntary mind and the subconscious an involuntary one.

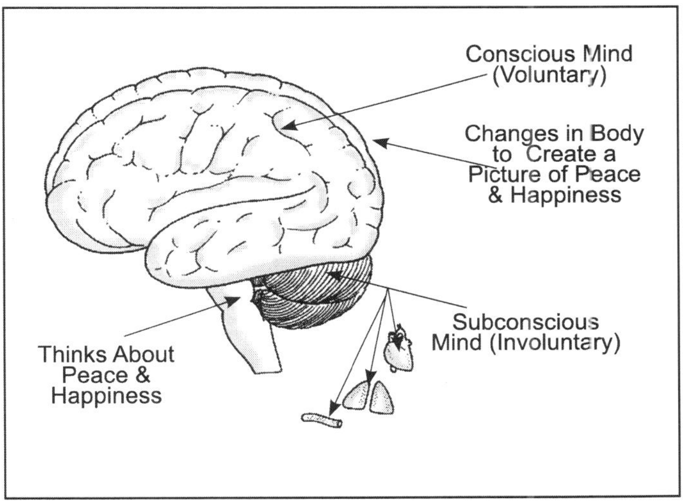

Fig: Theory of Subconscious Mind

The conscious mind is the one that reasons and takes decisions of which you are aware. It is under your voluntary control whereas the subconscious mind works involuntarily and without your control.

The subconscious mind takes care of the body's vital functions, like the heartbeat, respiration and digestion. Whatever your conscious mind reasons, whether positive or negative, the subconscious mind takes as a command.

If the conscious mind produces negative thoughts or depression, misery and confusion, they will be imprinted on the subconscious mind. If the conscious mind draws a picture of happiness, peace and harmony, the subconscious mind takes it as the truth and follows it blindly. The subconscious mind conveys the effect to various vital organs of your body to create that picture of peace, harmony and happiness. Similarly, if the conscious mind repeatedly presents a picture of health and freedom from sickness, then the subconscious mind produces the same in reality and makes your body free from sickness. It is true that, "the way you think you become" so don't create a negative picture in your mind. Always think positive because your thoughts will become reality.

Theory of Hormone Secretion

There may be secretion of some neurotransmitters like dopamine, which has a healing effect at the cellular level.

"Little by Little, through patience and repeated efforts the mind will become stilled in the self."

Bhagwad Gita

Dr. Nigam's technique, which is based on imagery, is a powerful way to heal the body and mind. It can enhance one's performance in competitions, sports and in day-to-day life as well. It heals or treats by developing a direct link between the mind, body and soul. A bridge develops between the body and the conscious and subconscious mind and a certain harmony is achieved. My technique is based on the fact that we are ignorant about the powers of the brain and underestimate its capabilities.

Dr. Harold Koenig of Duke University found that more than two-thirds of all researches and studies on spirituality and health showed a positive relationship.[131]

Paul Mueller, a physician at Mayo Clinic, USA, found that religious involvement and spirituality are associated with better health outcomes.[132]

"Health is harmony, disease is discord."

Aristotle,
Pupil of Plato and Tutor of
Alexander the Great

4

DR. NIGAM'S TECHNIQUE FOR TREATMENT OF...

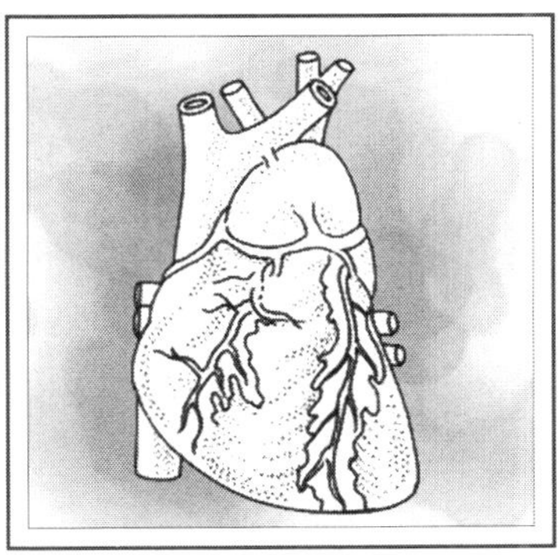

"When staying trim and exercising can have such a dramatic impact on the length and quality of life, just imagine the impact that vegetarianism, healthy nutrition, worship, stress management, visualisation, art of breathing, yoga, spirituality and altruism could have."

Sian Bryson

ATHEROSCLEROSIS AND CORONARY ARTERY DISEASE (CAD)

Dale Mathews of Georgetown University says that 80 per cent of the published studies report a positive association between religious commitment and better health.[133]

Atherosclerosis is the most common killer of man today. It, and not infectious diseases, is the leading cause of death and disability in the developing world. The number one cause of death in India is now coronary artery disease, not respiratory infections or diarrhoeal illness.[134]

Some Startling Facts

- Smoking increases the risk of CAD and heart attack by 70 per cent.
- A small dose of aspirin, if taken daily, reduces the risk of CAD by up to 44 per cent.
- Smoking, diabetes, high blood pressure, high cholesterol levels, alcohol, obesity, stress and a sedentary lifestyle are the main risk factors for CAD and heart attack.
- In the next five years, India will have more heart patients than any other country.
- Approximately, 100 Indians die of heart attacks every hour.
- 10 per cent of Indians suffer from CAD and 30 per cent are at high risk.
- Younger Indians have 10 times more chances of developing CAD than their counterparts in Europe and America.
- CAD affects Indians 10 years earlier than Europeans and Americans.
- According to a study by Dutch experts, weighing 2.2 kg over your ideal body weight may increase the risk of heart attack by 20 per cent, in spite of normal levels of cholesterol and blood pressure in a non-smoker.
- Over time, meditation can reduce the risk of hypertension and improve cardiac function in people with coronary heart disease.[135, 136]

What Is The Defect?

Atherosclerosis indicates degeneration of the arteries. The word "atherosclerosis" comes from the Greek "scleros", meaning "hardening".

Atherosclerosis is a painless and slow process of narrowing of the arteries by deposition of a lipid called atheroma or plaque, and proliferation of muscle cells, leading to narrowing of the lumen of the arteries. It blocks the arteries totally later on. This causes heart attack (MI or Myocardial Infarction), if the coronary arteries (arteries supplying blood to the wall of the heart) get blocked, and stroke, (CVA or Cerebro Vascular Accident) if the cerebral arteries (arteries of the brain) are blocked. The plaque deposition occurs after the inner lining of the arteries gets damaged. Cholesterol is the main culprit in causing atherosclerosis and CAD.

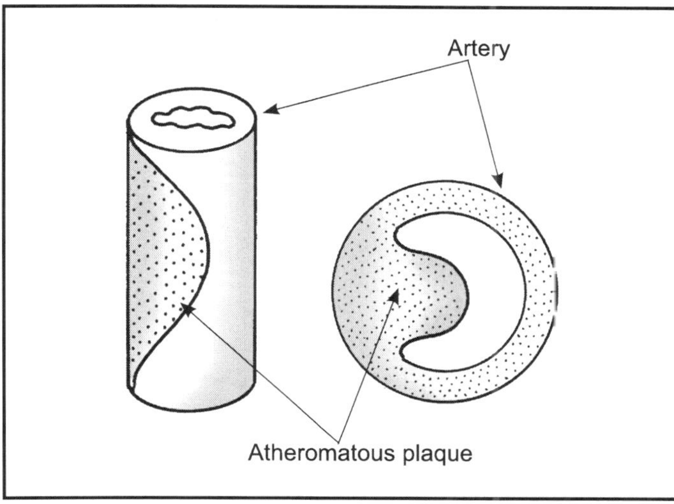

Fig: Atheroma or plaque in the wall of an artery

Atherosclerosis can occur anywhere in the body. However, plaque usually builds up at points where the arterial wall is subjected to a turbulent flow of blood, such as where the artery divides. Atherosclerosis of the coronary artery causes its narrowing and reduction in blood flow. During any activity, the heart beats faster and the requirement for oxygen by the heart muscles increases, but the extra blood required cannot pass due to narrowing of the passage, so muscles "cramps" or "angina" occurs due to the exertion. Angina is a sign that muscles of the heart wall are not receiving sufficient blood. The medicines dilate the coronary arteries, allowing more passage of blood.

Why We Eat Cholesterol

Cholesterol is a fatty and wax-like substance. It is an essential element required by our body for the following:

1. Cell membrane formation
2. Nerve insulation
3. For certain hormones, which contain cholesterol

Cholesterol circulates in our blood, attached to the protein, and we call it lipoprotein. It is of two types:

1. LDL: Low density lipoprotein or bad cholesterol. This is the cholesterol which forms plaques.
2. HDL: High density lipoprotein or good cholesterol. It acts as a scavenger and cleans the arteries of plaques.

Know Your Cholesterol

Types	Desirable(mg/dl)	Borderline	High
Total Cholesterol	Below 200	200-239	240 and above
LDL Cholesterol	Below 130	130-159	160 and above
HDL Cholesterol	Above 45	40-45	Below 40
Triglycerides	Below 150	150-199	Above 200

Causative factors

The most common factors are:

1. Hypertension (high blood pressure)
2. Smoking/Nicotine
3. High blood cholesterol
4. Stress
5. Diabetes mellitus: It accelerates the process of atherosclerosis.
6. Lipid imbalance: It is the main culprit for plaque formation.

What Happens

The damage to the lining of the artery occurs due to hypertension, high nicotine intake, high cholesterol, etc. Then, a process of repair through cholesterol and collagen deposits takes place, causing a partial block. If the plaque ruptures, for any reason, it causes a total blockage leading to M.I. and CVA.

The drugs, angioplasty or CABG (Coronary Artery Bypass Graft) alone is not a sure way to treat atherosclerosis. They are not a cure. They only treat the symptoms and not the cause. Ten to twenty per cent of the arteries will be blocked within the first post-operative year of CABG and 80 per cent will be blocked within seven years. Arteries opened by balloon angioplasty will be blocked earlier, 10-20 per cent within six months.

Andrew Weil, Director, Program in Integrative Medicine at University of Arizona, USA, writes in his bestseller book "*Spontaneous Healing*", "When I was in medical school, I was taught that atherosclerosis was irreversible. Once coronary and other arteries were stiffened and narrowed by cholesterol deposits, inflammation and calcification, they could never improve, only worsen. We now have clear evidence that atherosclerosis is reversible."[137, 138]

Dale Mathew of Georgetown University writes in his book "*The Faith Factor*" that the patient, Martha, suffering with adenoid cystic carcinoma of the ovaries, was in a terminal stage and was told that conventional cancer treatment would not help. She turned towards alternative therapy involving regular visits to the church, a macrobiotic diet and prayer. The tumour did not disappear but neither did the size increase.[139]

Imagery can do wonders for healing if combined with faith. A definite and positive attitude brings healing through the subconscious mind.

"We can easily conceive the marvellous effects which confidence and imagination can produce."

Pietro Pomponazzi,
Italian philosopher

My Technique

This process can be done anywhere, anytime and in any position, sitting or lying down. It can be done while travelling in a bus, car or train. It does not require any equipment or any special attire. It only requires a high degree of trust in yourself and God. To get hundred per cent results, you have to believe from the core of your heart that you are going to be all right, with God's blessings.

1. Relax in a comfortable position.
2. Concentrate on your regular breathing for a few minutes.
3. Make a mental image of your heart and big vessels of your body by remembering the pictures given in the text.

4. Feel happy, confident and hopeful. Visualise your arteries with blocks as shown in the text. First try to visualise the blocked arteries in your body. Imagine that a very small amount of blood is passing through the blocks in your arteries when your heart pumps out blood, coming out only in streaks and not in full flow.
5. Take a few deep breaths. Imagine you are breathing white and intense bright light, coming from the cosmos. It enters through your nostrils to your lungs and then spreads through your entire body. Your body gets a glow.
6. Concentrate and try to develop an image of the light rays passing through the blocked arteries. The light rays are not able to pass completely and only very little light passes through the blocks. Now feel the light ray like a shining laser. The rays of light are moving in circles, like grinding blades of a grinder. First, clockwise and then anti-clockwise. The light is moving very fast. Now feel the laser grinding the blocking plaques of your arteries. While this is on, you produce the sound of grinding from your mouth slowly "krrrrrrr......" "krrrrr....." krrrrrr......" and as you do this, try and feel that a real grinding is in progress. Feel the grinding of the blocks in arteries.

Concentrate and experience it. Make a mental picture of the blocked plaques melting and the blocks gradually diminishing in size as fresh red blood slowly flows through the arteries freely. Progressively, the blood flow increases through the arteries. Imagine an auto absorbable smoke rising while the grinding is on. Repeat the whole process three times with total involvement and concentration. Try to make it real and picture the artery blocks getting reduced in size, the artery and the flow of blood returning to normal.

Gradually, imagine an image of the normal flow of blood without any blocks and try to feel the blood flowing normally in the arteries through your body. Feel a sense of warmth and freshness. Feel a sense of relief, as if a burden has been taken off your chest.

With the help of the sketches, you can use this process for arteries of the heart, brain, limbs and vital organs. Visualise the arteries of the brain, heart, lungs, kidneys, liver and limbs. Feel your body becoming healthier, glowing, fresh and active. Feel all your vitals organs getting rejuvenated.

7. Now make a mental picture of your heart contracting and relaxing

to full capacity (see text for the sketch and understanding of the anatomy). When the heart contracts, the fresh red blood full of oxygen goes to the head, limbs, all vital organs and throughout your body. The body gradually glows. Feel the warmth and energy of health.

8. I advice patients to continue their medical treatment and other precautions recommended by the cardiologist and simultaneously practice my visualisation technique. Gradually, you will get its beneficial effects. Your arteries will start opening and your physician will reduce the amount of medication. A day will come when you will be drug-free and enjoy good health.
9. One can mark arterial blocks in the sketch of the arteries. One can use the coronary artery angiographic drawings for the development of concentration for maximum benefits.
10. The reversal can be judged by various tests and angiography.
11. The best and fastest results are obtained in atherosclerosis when my technique is combined with exercise schedule and dietary advice.
12. Fear Factor: I have found that being diagnosed with CAD comes as a shock to most people. Some of them develop a fear of heart attack and death. Getting rid of the fear is as important for a heart patient as diet and exercise. My technique will provide better exercise tolerance and help in removing this fear. Some people take the help of spirituality to get rid of this fear.

A team of daring stunt performers on a television show, headed by Indian film actor Akshay Kumar, chanted the *Gayatri Mantra* before all dangerous stunts. According to him, "It increases their inner belief and makes them fearless while performing death-defying stunts."[140]

The feeling of isolation can be depressing and stressful at any age. All of us have felt at some point that we are part of something bigger than ourselves. People call it God or Force or Energy, and realising it makes us feel we are not alone and isolated. Dr. Dean Ornish writes in his book *Reversing Heart Disease* that opening your heart to a higher self helps in reversing heart disease, controlling stress, lowering blood pressure, improving performance, having an impact at an emotional and spiritual level, thus healing an auto-immune disease.[141]

On 2nd March, 1991, 49 year old Mr. R.L. Sharma, CEO of a multinational company in New Delhi, was having his lunch in a five-star hotel. He went to the rest room to relieve himself and after returning to his seat, experienced uneasiness in his chest, which in a few minutes turned to pain. He began sweating and became breathless. He was taken to the National Heart Institute, where it was found that he had suffered a massive heart attack. He was kept in the CCIU (Coronary Care Intensive Unit) for two days. He underwent coronary angiography which showed over 90 percent blockage in the main arteries of his heart, with a generalised disease. He was advised to continue medicine and a strict diet regime, with a gradually increasing intensity of exercises. He was refused a CABG due to the generalised nature of the disease. Angioplasty was done and two drug-coated stents were placed in the right coronary artery and left anterior descending artery after dilating the almost closed blocks. He developed hypertension and diabetes also.

The news came as a shock to him. Unmarried and a workaholic, he was a chain smoker, used to rich food and doing irregular light exercises. He was not serious about his health and success in his career had made him arrogant, short-tempered and authoritative. He had not imagined that he could suffer from M.I. it was something that happened to others. He was stunned. He learnt a lesson and gave up smoking, turned vegetarian and started regular exercises.

Mainly, he conquered his fear with the help of meditation and prayers, which cleared the doubts in his mind. He became fearless due to his spirituality. He opened himself to God and started believing that when God was with him, nothing could go wrong. He actually became fearless towards disease as well as death. Now, after 10 years of his massive M.I., he runs on the treadmill for 40 minutes at a speed of 6-10 km/hr at 5-15 degree inclination.

As Dr. Walter Larimore believes, spirituality is a wonder and joy, and should not be left in the clerical closet.[142] Dr. Dale Mathews says that prayer may be a particularly cost-effective as well as efficacious form of treatment.[143]

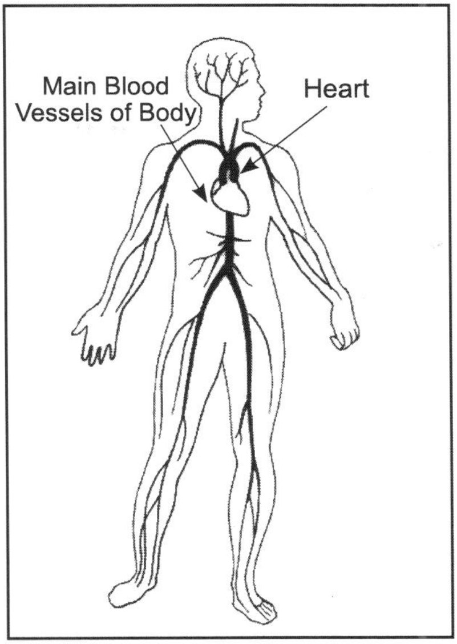

Fig: Blood Circulation of Body

HYPERTENSION

"Our creator has given us five senses to help us survive threats from the external world and a sixth sense, our healing system, to help us survive internal threats. There is much we can do, as individuals, to activate or impede this healing system."

Bernie Siegel, MD,
Paediatric and General Surgeon, USA

- One-third of people affected by hypertension do not know that they have high blood pressure.
- Of those who are aware that they have hypertension, only 50 per cent get treatment.
- Of those who have hypertension, only 25 per cent have their blood pressure under control.
- If hypertension is left untreated, it affects your whole body, particularly the heart, arteries, brain, kidneys and eyes.
- One-third of the population may be salt-sensitive due to high-blood pressure.
- If your blood pressure only increases at the time of checking in at

a hospital and otherwise remains normal, it is called "White coat hypertension". It doesn't require treatment.
- A diet of fruits, vegetables, grains and low-fat dairy products causes considerable reduction in blood pressure.[144]
- Moderately intense activity, like a brisk walk for 30 minutes, improves cardiovascular health and longevity. Mayo Clinic, USA, recommends three 10-minutes of activity at intervals if you don't have time for one 30-minute session. It is equally beneficial.
- If you are overweight and lose 4.5 kilograms, it may reduce borderline hypertension to normal blood pressure.
- If you have high blood pressure and smoke, your risk of death from heart attack is three times higher and from stroke is two times higher than a non-smoker.

Blood pressure is the pressure of blood flowing in the artery, on its walls. "Diastolic pressure greater than 90 mm Hg and Systolic Pressure greater than 140 mm Hg is called hypertension or high blood pressure".

One in every four adults has high blood pressure or hypertension, diagnosed or undiagnosed. It is a life threatening silent killer as it may have few or no symptoms. Hypertension causes heart attack, CVA, kidney failure, blindness and premature death. If untreated, it can shorten your life span by 10-20 years. Many people suffering with hypertension are unaware of this fact, which is why it is called a "silent killer". Ninety per cent of patients of hypertension suffer from primary, essential or idiopathic hypertension, where the cause is not known. Ten per cent of patients of hypertension suffer from secondary or renal hypertension, due to kidney diseases, endocrinal abnormalities or vascular malformations. You can have high blood pressure for years without any symptoms. General symptoms are headache, dizziness, tiredness and palpitation.

WHAT IS THE DEFECT?

Blood pressure depends on the relationship between cardiac output (blood pumped out by the heart) and total arterial resistance (resistance to the flow of blood produced by the walls of arteries). Hypertension occurs either due to a primary increase in cardiac output or an increase in peripheral arterial resistance. Hypertension can cause atherosclerosis by damaging the lining of the arterial wall, depositing plaque and causing obstruction or blocks. Both the high systolic and high diastolic blood pressures cause damage to the lining of the arterial wall. Persistent higher than normal blood pressure can damage internal organs if left untreated. Hypertension is very common in middle-aged and elderly people. A stress filled lifestyle may aggravate the condition. Essential hypertension cannot be cured but controlled. Hypertension can be caused by the following factors:

- Hypertension is a major risk factor for morbidity and mortality due to cardiovascular diseases, stroke and kidney diseases. It is increasing in India due to fast urbanization, changes in lifestyle, diet and stress.
- In India, in the last 30 years, a 30-fold increase in hypertension has occurred among the urban population and a 10-fold increase was noticed in rural areas.[145]
- According to the European Society for Hypertension guidelines, optional BP is defined as <120 mm Hg systolic blood pressure (SBP) and <80 mm Hg diastolic blood pressure (DBP). SBP>140 mm Hg, and DBP>90mm Hg is classified as hypertension in stages 1,2,3.[146]

  The aim is to reduce SBP and DBP below 140/90 mm Hg in hypertensive patients. Patients, with other risk factors like diabetes, cardiovascular and renal diseases, must aim at keeping SBP/DBP below 130/80.
- The Framingham heart study has shown that BP values in 130-139/85-89 mm Hg are associated with a two-fold increase in cardiovascular diseases, compared to a BP value of 120/80 mm Hg.[147]
- JNC-VI and JNC-VII (Joint National Committee on Prevention, Detection, Evaluation and Treatment of High Blood Pressure) guidelines for hypertension and pre-hypertension specifies:

  SBP 120-139/DBP 80-89 mm Hg
  Hypertension above SBP 140/90
  A 12 mm reduction in SBP reduces incidence of stroke by 35-40 per cent, MI by 20-25 per cent, heart failure by 50 per cent and death rate by 13 per cent.[148, 149 & 150]
- In India, cardiovascular diseases caused 2.3 million deaths in the year 1990 and this is expected to double by the year 2020. [151]
- It has been shown that more than 90 per cent of strokes occur in patients with uncontrolled BP.[152]

"A physician is nature's assistant."

Galen,
Greek Physician,
Writer and Philosopher

What are the factors responsible for hypertension?

The following are the common factors that cause hypertension:

1. High pressure: If your heart pumps blood in your arteries at a higher pressure, then more force is exerted on the walls of the arteries, increasing your blood pressure, as occurs in stress and some diseases.
2. Elasticity of the arterial wall: The elasticity of arteries accommodates the blood pumped, maintaining the resistance. When arteries loose elasticity, as in atherosclerosis, they become narrow and resistance of blood flow increases and hypertension develops.
3. High salt intake: Kidneys regulate the water and sodium content of your body. Sodium retains water, so eating more salt accumulates water in the body, leading to high blood pressure.
4. Stress and anxiety: During sleep, both the SBP and DBP are much lower. [153] Some sensors sensitive to blood pressure are situated in the walls of the heart and arteries called baroreceptors. Baroreceptors sense the change in blood pressure and send the information to the brain, which then releases a hormonal adrenaline that contracts the heart and narrows arteries, thus increasing blood pressure and heart rate. It happens during stress and anxiety. Frequent release of adrenaline causes high blood pressure.[154]
5. Environmental factors: A number of environmental factors are involved in the development of hypertension, including obesity, occupation, alcohol intake, family size and crowds.[155, 156]

RISKS OF HYPERTENSION

Hypertension can damage various vital organs of your body.

1. Arteries

   High blood pressure damages the walls of the arteries, leading to:

   - Atherosclerosis
   - Arteriosclerosis
   - Aneurysm

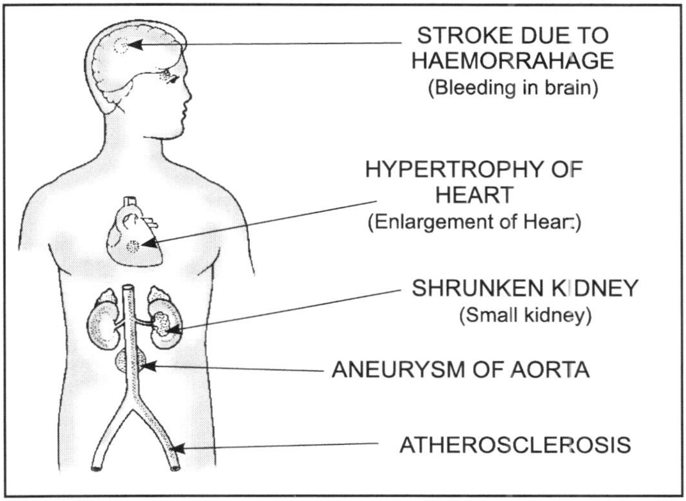

Fig: Organs damaged by Hypertension

2. Heart

   The heart can be damaged due to hypertension, leading to complications.

   CAD (Coronary Artery Disease). The accumulation of plaques leads to a narrowing of the coronary arteries, causing heart attack and heart failure.

3. Brain

   High blood pressure causes brain damage, leading to cerebral attack or stroke, which is either due to a blocked vessel or ruptured vessel of the brain.

4. Kidney

   Hypertension causes narrowing of the blood vessels of the kidneys, causing kidney failure.

5. Eye

   A severe degree of high blood pressure leads to blindness.

Lifestyle changes to prevent and control hypertension:

According to the *Harvard Medical School Guide,* the following steps are recommended to prevent and control hypertension:

- Eat plenty of fruits and vegetables

- Reduce salt intake
- Reduce your weight
- Exercise regularly
- Reduce excessive alcohol consumption
- Stop smoking
- Practice relaxation techniques

Dr. Herbert Benson of Harvard Medical School found that patients remained with significantly reduced blood pressure three to five years after making lifestyle changes that included meditation, group support, diet and exercise.[157]

My technique

This technique prevents chances of developing hypertension and also treats existing hypertension. When blood pressure is controlled, one can reduce the anti-hypertensive drugs after consultation with the physician. The use of this technique, accompanied by lifestyle changes, reduces blood pressure over a period of time.

1. Relax in a comfortable position.
2. Concentrate on your regular breathing.
3. Imagine a picture of your heart and vessels in your mind.
4. Imagine that you are inhaling fresh air and bright and warm light. Your lungs are filled with this air and light. It is spreading through your body. It passes over your heart and different parts of the body making them radiant.
5. Make a mental picture of the heart beating and the blood flowing through the arteries, which narrow at the periphery of the limbs. This causes strain on the heart and arteries. The pressure inside the heart and arteries increases. Now, the light you inhale is concentrated on narrow segments of the arteries in the periphery of your body (limbs). Gradually it goes through narrow segments of arteries, causing relaxation or dilatation. The pressure and strain on the heart and the arteries gradually reduce and now the heart beats regularly, smoothly, rhythmically and without strain. Now, imagine that the vessels are relaxing and are no longer tense, inspite of the heart beating normally. The blood is flowing through the arteries with less resistance as the arteries are relaxed and dilated. Now, you can feel the gradual lowering of

blood pressure. Be relaxed and free from tension.

6. Repeat this process three times.
7. Feel that the arteries and heart are relaxed and no longer suffering from high blood pressure. Your whole body is relaxing, rejuvenating and gradually filling with energy and freshness. Your headache reduces and gradually disappears.
8. Now you are fresh with energy and free from hypertension.
9. Follow this process anytime and at any place.
10. Do this with total involvement and concentration.

On 27th December, 2006, Gaurav Mohle, a 32-year-old successful businessman, collapsed after returning to his office from a meeting, which involved heated discussions and arguments. He was admitted to a nearby hospital. Till then, he had enjoyed good health. He was a non-smoker, had beer at parties, and consumed "gutka" (a mixture of tobacco, betel nut and other chemicals). He occasionally popped a Paracetamol tablet for headache after a whole day's work. His only problem was anger, which could turn him into a raging bull. He would occasionally feel palpitations after an episode of anger.

At the time of admission, his BP was 180/130 mm Hg. with a left ventricular hypertrophy (enlargment of heart). He had never suffered from high BP, according to him, and any occasional check-up had revealed normal BP. He had never undergone a thorough health check. He could not believe his ears when he was told that he had such high BP. The cardiologist asked him why he was risking his health, by burning the candle at both ends. His lipid profile showed high cholesterol, putting him at risk for heart attack. He was prescribed anti-hypertension medicines; for high cholesterol he was given 75mg of aspirin daily, asked to reduce his weight from 70 to 60 kg and told to exercise daily.

He was so shocked that he was willing to try anything to regain his health. I had a few sittings with him and he agreed to my technique along with the treatment advised by the cardiologist. I put him on a vegetarian low-fat diet and asked him to practice my technique twice a day. Initially, I had to sit with him to explain the technique and encourage him. After a few weeks, he became addicted to it as he found himself becoming calmer, less angry and peaceful. His wife and two children were quite happy as his anger episodes reduced in frequency and intensity improving his family life.

*"Love, hope, peace and joy have physiological consequences,
Just as depression and despair."*

Bernie Siegel
Paediatric and General surgeon, USA

Now, after three years of practice (at the time of this book going to press), he has got his life back in control. He exercises regularly and has given up gutka. Anti-hypertension medicines have been reduced to half the dosage by his cardiologist.

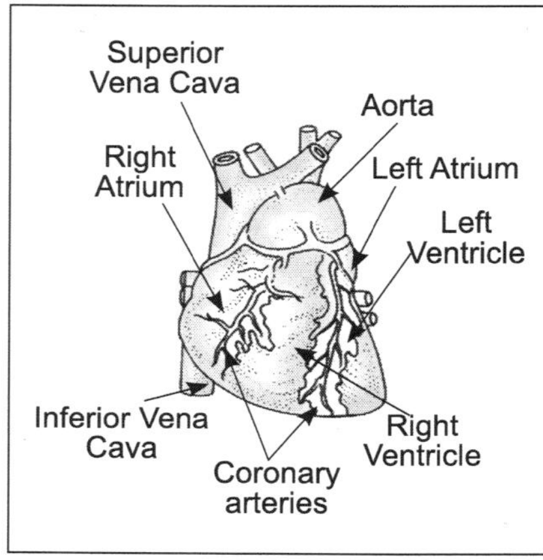

Fig: Parts of the Heart

INSOMNIA AND SLEEP DISORDERS

"The beginning of health is sleep"

Irish proverb

Physiology of sleep

Most people sleep for 7 to 8 hours at a stretch. Normal sleep occurs in several cycles of 70-90 minutes each. At the end of each cycle, you are almost awake. Sleep occurs in REM and NREM (Non-REM) cycles. Dreams occur in REM sleep and NREM is mostly dreamless. Each sleep cycle is divided into four stages.

Stage I

- Light sleep

Stage II

- Intermediate sleep, lasts for approximately 20 minutes

Stage III

- Transitional period between light and deep sleep, lasting 30-40 minutes and is restorative.

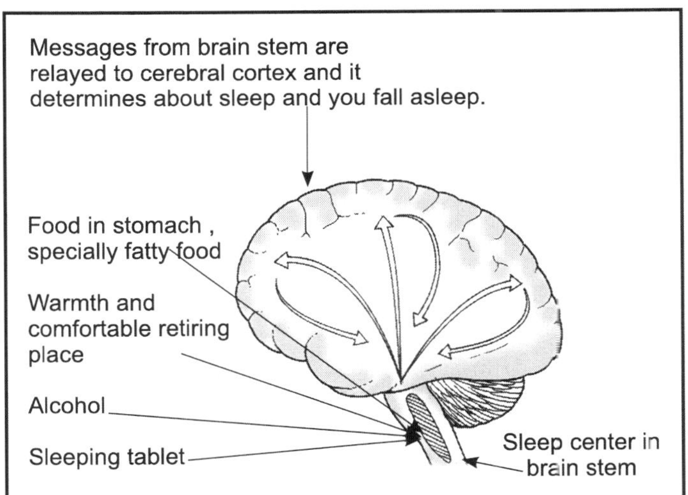

Fig: Factors affecting sleep

Stage IV

- It is deep sleep, Lasts for approximately 30 minutes.

Stage V

- Known as REM sleep. It is the deepest sleep. Most dreams occur during this stage. The body temperature, heartbeat, breathing and blood pressure reduce. Muscles become more relaxed.

Neurophysiology of Insomnia

During sleep, the body rests but the neurons of the brain continue to be alert and send signals. The thalamus, forebrain and reticular formation deal with the generation of sleep and brain stem, reticular formation, the thalamus, sub-thalamus and forebrain are connected to the state of wakefulness. Serotonin is the primary sleep-promoting neurotransmitter. Adrenaline and nor adrenaline are responsible for wakefulness.

Recently, a link between immune function and sleep-wake states have been reported due to the role of "sleep factors"—Interlukin I and Prostaglandin D2 (immunologically active agents).[158, 159]

Insomnia is the most common sleep disorder. It is a symptom and not a disease. More than 50 per cent of the adult population suffers from some type of intermittent sleep disturbance. Fifteen to 20 per cent of adults suffer from chronic sleep disturbances.

The lack of good quality rest is one of the most common causes of susceptibility to illness, and a good night's rest is an effective healing technique that will abort many incipient illnesses. Therefore, improving the quality of rest and sleep should be another priority in a programme aimed at enhancing your healing capacity.[160]

WHAT IS THE DEFECT?

Insomnia is difficulty in initiating or maintaining sleep or perception of poor quality sleep.

Narcolepsy

It is a disorder or ability to sustain wakefulness voluntarily and a disorder of REM sleep.

Cataplexy

It is a feature of narcolepsy, and a sudden weakness or loss of muscle tone without loss of consciousness, often elicited by emotions.

Restless Leg Syndrome (RLS)

A crawling feeling in the calves and feet with an irresistible urge to move the limbs occurs more at night than during daytime. It is temporarily relieved by movement. It increases with insomnia, caffeine, pregnancy, iron deficiency, and five per cent of young people and 10-20 per cent of people above 60 suffer from it. Disturbed sleep is experienced by almost 87 per cent of people.[161]

Sleep Apnoea

It is the cessation of breathing for short periods during sleep. It is due to respiratory passage blockage or an absence of breathing efforts. It is particularly common in overweight and elderly people. 90 per cent of sleep apnoea remains undiagnosed.[162]

Somnambulism (Sleepwalking)

A person suffering from somnambulism may leave the bed, walk, urinate, eat or exit from the house while remaining partially awake. This runs in families and is most common in children aged 6 to 12.[163]

Sleep Terrors

It is a self-limiting condition common in young children. The child suddenly screams and wakes up sweating with tachycardia and hyperventilation.

Sleep Bruxism

The forceful grinding of the teeth during sleep. It occurs during anxiety and tension.

Relaxation skills help in coping with it.[164 & 165]

Enuresis (Bedwetting)

This occurs in young children. Nocturnal enuresis considered normal below the age of six. It usually improves with age.

My Technique

This technique is so powerful that you can ensure a good sleep whenever and wherever you want, even in a crowded place.

1. Relax, let your limbs and head loosen and droop naturally. Take away your control on the limbs and head.
2. Concentrate on your regular breathing.
3. Take a deep breath five times.

4. Now, imagine you are on a peaceful beach by the side of a blue tranquil sea or in a beautiful garden. You can imagine a beautiful and serene place you may have visited in the past.
5. Make a mental picture of yourself walking in the selected spot. Gradually, increase your speed. For a few moments, feel the grass or sand on which you are walking. Now, walk briskly. Experience this for a few moments. Next, start jogging. Feel your feet touching the ground. After some moments of jogging, you are tired, sweating and the muscles in your limbs and back are tired. Feel the jogging, the exertion, sweating, the cool breeze and the fatigue. Feel the walk.
6. Gradually slow down the pace of jogging and walk normally. Next, stop walking and stand still. Now, you are comfortably lying on the ground. Your body is now relaxing. You are breathing slowly and regularly. Try to feel the grass or sand of the ground and the touch of your body on the ground.
7. Feel someone massaging your body, specially the limbs and back, which are tired and aching. Gradually, you are relaxing and enjoying the experience as aches and pains begin to disappear. A fresh, cool breeze is blowing. Feel the wind touching your body and moving your hairs. You are feeling sleepy, your eyes are closing and gradually sleep is setting in. Now, you are sleeping.

What harm can lack of sleep do?

Lack of sleep makes you irritable, lethargic and tired. You cannot concentrate on difficult and complex situations. Studies show that shift workers have higher rates of breast cancer than women who are able to sleep normal hours. Two possible culprits are the hormones melatonin and cortisone. Melatonin is an antioxidant that mops up damaging free radicals, but the body produces less of it when sleep cycles are disrupted. Cortisone, which helps regulate the immune system, may also be compromised by troubled sleep.[166]

A Yale University report says that people who sleep less than six hours a day regularly doubled their risk of diabetes mellitus and those who sleep for more than eight hours triple the risk.[167]

Mr. Suresh Kumar, a 48 year old media personality, wakes up in the morning feeling tired, as if he has not slept at all. He tends to nap during meetings and conversations. He feels tired and suffers from headaches through the day. Sometimes, he wakes up at midnight and cannot go back to sleep again. He was overweight (100 kg). He started practicing this technique to reduce his weight and is now sleeping better though his weight is still 96 kg.

NOTE: To have a good night's sleep with my technique, avoid stimulants which interfere with sleep, like tea, coffee, caffeinated drinks, ephedrine and pseudo ephedrine.

"Sleep my little one, sleep my pretty one, sleep."

Lord Alfred Tennyson

STRESS

"Your age is determined to a surprising degree by your behaviour and attitude, especially the way you handle stress."

Dr. R. Earle and Dr. D. Imrit

Over half the medical schools in the US now include courses on religion, spirituality and health.[168]

"Mental tensions, frustrations, insecurity, aimlessness are some of the most damaging stress factors and psychosomatic studies have shown how they frequently cause migraine, headaches, peptic ulcers, heart attacks, hypertension, mental diseases, suicide, or just hopeless unhappiness."

Hans Selye,
Father of Stress Phenomenon

- Repeated and frequent episodes of anger increase chances of a heart attack.
- Discussing problems with one's life partner relieves stress. 50 per cent of single middle-aged men have a chance of dying within 15 years, compared to 17 per cent for a married man with many friends.
- Tension stresses and depresses the immune system (bone marrow, spleen, thymus and lymph nodes), leading to an increased risk of infection. Cancer is commonly seen in patients with depression but a strong will and desire to survive reduces the risk of relapse. [169] Stress diminishes white blood cell formation and function, and causes the thymus gland to shrink.[170]

An article *"Docs keep the faith"* was published on 1st June, 2008, in

Times Life, Times of India. On 2nd June, 2008, a young girl, Ms Suman Dave, aged 23-24 years, attended my OPD in Apollo Clinic, Gurgaon. She started crying and explained that her father was suffering from cancer of the food pipe (esophagus). Her father was a very jolly and optimistic man, but over the last four to five weeks, had turned depressed and pessimistic. Mr. Dhruve Sahai Dave, aged 68, after reading the Docs keep the faith article became optimistic and started feeling better and hopeful.

I visited his home. He was anaemic, weak and depressed. His voice was very faint, almost a whisper. It was a post-surgery recurrence, involving the larynx. I shook hands with him and held his hands for a few minutes. He required a blood transfusion as his haemoglobin was 6.5 gm (less than half the normal value in an adult). He was depressed and weak and his appetite was reduced as a result of the disease. His family members gathered around him.

He was reluctant to undergo blood transfusion, but we made him understand that it would improve his general well-being and he would be able to eat well, which was essential for recovery and remission.

We told him that we would all pray for his health and he was not alone in his fight against cancer. He would come out a winner. He was later transfused three bottles of blood. His general condition improved, as did his appetite. His depression also reduced.

I have visited him twice later and he looked better and more positive. He is undergoing treatment and accepting the advice of doctors. The prayers and hope provided him and his family the much needed strength and comfort.

Paula Ceccaldi et al write in their book *Stress, the good and bad* that stress may also enhance the progress of cancer or reduce the inhibition of resistance to it. Though cancer is often accompanied by depression, a strong will to live seems to reduce the risk of relapse. Specialists at London Hospital compared survival rates of women treated for breast cancer over five years and found high rates of survival among those who refused to submit to the illness.[169]

- The word stress comes from the Latin word “stringer”, which means to squeeze, clasp or wound. It became “estresse” in French, meaning narrowness or oppression and gave English the word “distress”.
- Hans Selye, “Father of stress”, states that it transforms mental suffering into physical illness, by involving the nervous system and hormones. New researches have demonstrated the importance of

genetic factors in our susceptibilities to stress.

Stress is the main troublemaker of today's life. "Stress is a situation, which produces a negative body response." Though stress is good for the human body if it occurs in small amounts, recurrent heavy stress can lead to psychological problems as well as physical illness.

According to Philip T. Hagan, MD, Mayo Clinic, USA, techniques like guided imagery, meditation, muscle relaxation and relaxed breathing can help in relaxation. It lowers heart rate, blood pressure and muscle tension.[171]

TYPE OF PERSONALITY ASSOCIATED WITH STRESS

A Type C personality is at higher risk of cancer as type A is of heart disease.

A Type B personality is less likely to develop illness.

Type A individuals are emotional and sensitive. Type B are balanced individuals and type C are depressed, introverted and foster negative feelings and attitude.

"Type-A"

This personality is prone to stress. Such people are very sensitive, impatient, ambitious, emotional, aggressive and take up several things at a time. They are hard-working and tend to multitask.

"Type-B"

This personality is balanced, calm, less competitive, easy-going and less prone to stress.

"The most important factor in a disease is it the soil—the human body or the seed—the germ? It is the soil."

Louis Pasteur

Types of Stress

Stress is of two types:

(i) Acute Stress

This is the body's response to imminent danger. It prepares the body for a "fight or flight response" and is specifically harmful to the cardiovascular system.

(ii) Chronic Stress

This is due to constant emotional pressure that weakens the immune system and bones.

False Stress busters

1. Cigarette Smoking:

   Nicotine acts as a tranquiliser but increases heart rate and blood pressure.
2. Caffeine:

   Coffee, tea, cola, etc., stimulate the body and relieve tiredness, but also increase heart rate and blood pressure and cause insomnia.
3. Alcohol:

   It depresses the brain and causes reduced tension and anxiety. However, regular overuse leads to disturbed sleep and depression and causes problems of the liver and heart.

Biochemistry of Stress

The sensory perception of an incident sends signals to the cerebral cortex, which in turn sends signals to the hypothalamus at the brain's base, a centre that controls important body functions. The hypothalamus sends signals to lower centres to alert the body. The sympathetic nervous system sends a message to release adrenaline by the medulla, the central part of the adrenal glands situated above the kidneys and it releases noradrenalin from nerve endings.

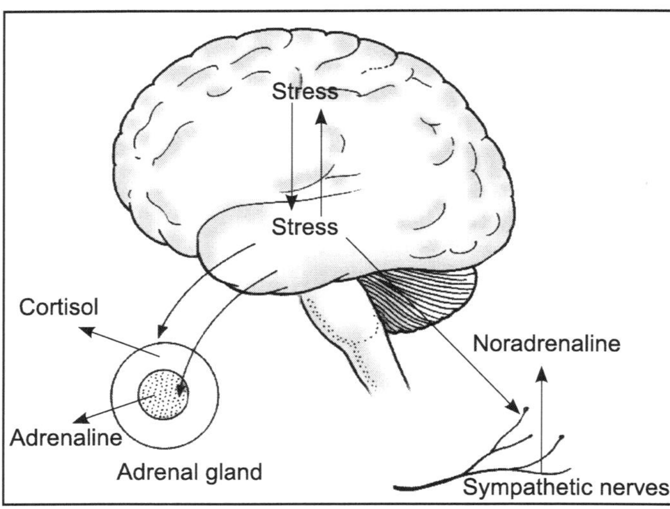

Fig: Physiology & Biochemistry of stress

The corticotrophin releasing factor is released from the hypothalamus and acts on the pituitary gland to release corticotrophin or the Adrenocortico Trophic Hormone (ACTH) to act on the cortex of adrenal gland, the outer part of the adrenal gland, to release glucocortecoids such as cortisol.

Adrenaline, noradrenaline and cortisol are called stress hormones and are the basis of the "fight or flight" response. The pupils of the eyes dilate to allow more light into the eyes for clear vision. The amount of glucose increases in the blood to provide sufficient energy to the muscles and brain. Blood clots minimise bleeding after injury more readily. These hormones act on certain areas of the brain to reassure that the body is fully alert and can face any threat. It also improves decision-making capacity and suppresses actions like sleepiness, sex drive, hunger and sensitivity to pain.

One can control stress by physical activity and movement since neuromuscular activity can release pent up aggressive energy. That is why crying, screaming, shouting and laughing reduce tension, relieve us and restore mental equilibrium.

Recurrent stress or overproduction of stress hormones causes side effects like insomnia, weak memory, anorexia, headache, depression, general weakness, suicidal tendency, panic attacks, menstrual irregularity, impotence, obsessive tendencies, compulsive disorders, etc.

Chronic stress causes a permanent increased production of cortico steroids that affects the hippocampus, leading to impaired memory, which can later cause some nerve cell death in hippocampus, leading to depression.

The brain sends a perception of threat to the hypothalamus, amygdala, pituitary gland and adrenal glands. Now, these parts send hormones and nerve impulses to various parts of the body and prepare it for a "fight or flight" response. The hormone epinephrine (adrenaline) is the main substance behind this response.

The adrenal glands release some extra cortisol, which converts sugars into energy for this function. Nerve cells release nor-epinephrine (noradrenaline) which makes the muscles tense and ready for action. It slows down digestion to avoid waste of energy at this time of crisis.

- It increases heart rate to flow more blood and oxygen into vital organs to deal with the threat.
- Skin arteries constrict to send blood to vital organs than to less important organs.

- Breathing increases and bronchi dilate so that lungs can take more oxygen to prepare the body to run or fight.
- The gastrointestinal tract empties itself to prepare for fight or flight, with least harm to the body. A loaded intestine can soil the abdominal wound if injured.
- The urinary bladder empties itself to avoid injury as a distended bladder is easily injured and with a distended bladder, it is difficult to flight.
- Glycogen converts to glucose in the liver to provide more energy for activities.

When the threat passes, the level of epinephrine and nor-epinephrine drops, but if the stress is repetitive and frequent, it damages the cardiovascular system.

Mother Teresa's work produced a sharp rise in immunoglobulin, especially in people motivated by altruism, that images of love had an effect at the unconscious level.[172]

Physiology of Stress

The symptoms of stress are due to certain hormones called stress hormones.

1. Adrenaline or acute stress hormone:

It produces a "fight of flight" response to acute stress, which causes physiological changes in the body to prepare the body either to fight with the external stimulus or run away. Our metabolism increases to provide more energy. The heart beats faster and the rate of breathing increases to provide blood and more oxygen to body. Digestion diminishes. Muscles of limbs contract to pool blood in vital organs where the requirement goes up in preparation for a fight or flight response.

2. Cortisol or chronic stress hormone:

It is released specially under chronic stress. Chronic stress causes hypertension and coronary arterial blocks. It weakens the immune system, develops osteoporosis and memory disturbances and may cause infertility.

Stress-related problems

Most people develop these problems due to recurrent stress over a period of time:

1. Headache

2. Neck pain
3. Back pain
4. Digestion problems, i.e., increased gas, acidity, belching, abdominal distension, constipation or diarrhoea.
5. Insomnia
6. Eating disorders
7. Drinking disorders
8. Weight gain
9. Weight loss
10. Hypertension
11. Coronary artery disease (P. Chang Patricia, of John Hopkins University, School of Medicine, USA, writes, "Men with highest trends of heart problems had experienced concealed or expressed anger and irritability as young adults.") [173]
12. Irregular menstruation
13. Lack of orgasm
14. Erection problems
15. Depression: For the past 20 years, western medicine in the United States of America has been exploring uncharted territory: The healing power of spirituality. Now, many medical colleges include classes on spirituality as it boosts immune functions and enhances and accelerates the healing process beyond conventional medical treatment. Dr. Puchalski, the founder and director of the George Washington Institute for Spirituality and Health, says, "People who practice spirituality tend to recover from depression a little sooner than those who don't."[174]

Dr. Paul Brand says that the cure for psychosomatic diseases demonstrates the incredible power of the mind to affect the rest of the body. He coined a new word "Pneumapsychosomatic". Pneuma is Greek for spirit, which stands for the spirit or soul body.[175]

16. Suicidal tendencies: According to a survey, conducted on over 543 soldiers of the Indian Army deployed in the LICO (Low Intensity Conflict Operations) Grid, over a hundred of them have attempted suicides since 2002. Military psychologists say prolonged and chronic stress in the counter insurgency areas is a triggering factor.[176]
17. Peptic ulcers in the stomach and duodenum: H. Pylori, a bacterium, is now believed to be responsible for stomach

and duodenal ulcers. However, stress plays a big role in ulcer aetiology also; you can't ignore it due to the evidence of infection with H. Pylori. [177] I was performing an upper gastrointestinal tract endoscopy regularly during my stay at Aden and I noticed a sudden spurt in cases of ulcers during the civil war and post-war period in Aden, during two civil wars in 1986 and 1994. Stomach ulcers have been proved to lead to stomach cancer. I treated my patients with drugs, diet and relaxation techniques like guided visualisation, meditation and prayer.

18. Ageing: Stress causes acceleration of cellular ageing, thereby accelerating the ageing process. Dr. Herbert Benson writes in his book *The Relaxation Response* that this is caused by sympathetic dominance over parasympathetic activities, which leads to faster heart rate, increased blood pressure and prepares us for a fight or flight response. Relaxation events such as meditation and visualisation cause parasympathetic dominance causing slow heart rate and fall in blood pressure. The relaxation response of the body leads to reduction of stress at a cellular level, thereby slowing down the ageing process.[178]

The people of the "Blue Zone" cultures live the longest among humans. Here, people commonly live an active life past the age of 100 years. The world's longest living people reside in Sardinia, Italy, Okinawa, Japan, and Loma Linda, California. Two striking features are noted among them—they follow a plant-based diet and lead a stress-free life.[179]

Ten Commandments to beat stress

1. Set a realistic goal for yourself.
2. Don't remember failure or disappointments.
3. Learn to say "No".
4. Exercise regularly and play games of your liking.
5. Sleep for a full 6-7 hours.
6. Follow a low-fat vegetarian diet. A diet rich in fibre, fruit and fresh vegetables relaxes the mind and body.
7. Be happy and enjoy life.
8. Be positive in your thoughts.
9. Practice a few minutes of meditation, yoga and deep abdominal breathing daily.
10. Open your heart to your partner—discuss every problem.

"In tribulations, immediately draw near God with confidence, and you will receive strength, enlightenment, and instruction."

Saint John of the Cross.

My Technique

It takes up very little time and can be performed at any place and anytime, without any equipment.

1. Lie down on the ground or on a bed. You can perform the technique even sitting in the car, chair or sofa, while waiting for someone or if you have 10 minutes free.
2. Contract the muscles of your limbs and face twice.
3. Picture yourself shouting, getting angry and stressed. You can try and recall any incident when you lost your temper. Make a mental picture of that incident.
4. Relax and make your body loose. Leave your limbs and head loose and free. Do not try to control your limbs and head. Let them fall free.
5. Concentrate on your regular breathing.
6. Now do deep abdominal breathing five times. Inhale slowly, by distending your abdomen and not moving the chest by counting 1,2,3,4. Then, hold your breath and count from 1-16 slowly and exhale by contracting the abdominal muscles and count 1-8.
7. Now imagine yourself gradually relaxing after the bout of anger. Feel your whole body loosening, becoming lighter and relaxed. Feel your anger gradually reducing and disappearing. Your forehead is devoid of wrinkles and tension. The muscles of your neck and face are less tense and relaxed.
8. Now you feel relaxed, fresh and comfortable. You are getting up. Total time taken: 15-20 minutes.

Continuous stress over a long period brings behavioural changes, leading to more stress and suffering for the individual and family. Ara Norenzayam, Associate Professor, Department of Psychology, University of British Columbia, after a three-decade-long research, concluded that "belief in God" encourages people to be helpful, honest and generous, which leads to a happy and stress-free life.

"Imagination may be compared to Adam's dream – He awoke and found it true."

Keats

BENIGN PROSTATIC HYPERTROPHY (BPH)

"Don't give up. Don't lose hope. Don't sell out."

"Superman" Christopher Reeve

Enlargement of the prostate gland is an ageing process in males, just like graying of hair. It is quite a common problem. It starts from 45 years of age and symptoms usually develop between 60 and 65 years. Benign enlargement of the prostate due to age is commonly called Benign Prostatic Hypertrophy (BPH). Researches have suggested, according to Dr. Mehmet Oz of Columbia, Presbyterians Heart Institute, that meditation combined with dietary changes may slow the progression of a tumour in patients with prostate cancer.

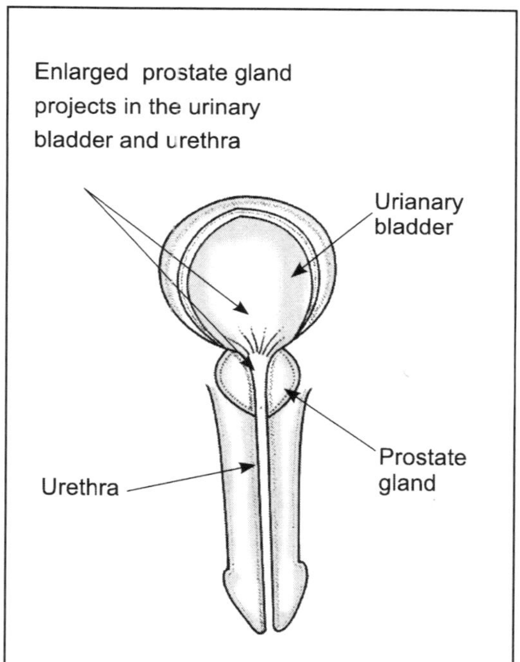

Fig: Urinary bladder, Prostate Gland & Urethra

Dr. Dean Ornish, in April 2003, at a meeting of the American Urologist Association, announced that meditation may slow the advancement of prostate cancer. These patients were also on a diet and practiced yoga.[180]

What is the Defect?

As we age, the level of testosterone (male hormone) falls and the level of Dihydrotestosterone (DHT) in the prostate goes up, which increases the number of prostate cells, resulting in an enlarged prostate gland. Stress can cause increased production of a hormone called prolactin, which can lead to enlargement of the prostate gland. The prostate gland has two zones—the central and peripheral. The central zone is usually responsible for BPH and the peripheral zone is responsible for cancer. BPH starts as a nodule in the central zone and compresses the urethra, causing difficulty in passing urine. It may lead to acute retention of urine.

My Technique

This technique makes the urination easy, without stress, without interruption and with a good stream. While passing urine, hold it for 10 seconds and then again pass and then again hold till you completely empty your bladder. If this technique is practiced regularly with sincerity, the size of the prostate gland is also reduced. If my technique is combined with selected food items in the diet (tomatoes, green tea, pomegranates, soybean, coloured capsicums, blue and violet berries, cranberries), Kegel's exercise and medical treatment, the effect is tremendous.

Soybean contains phytosteroles, which suppress both BPH and cancer of the prostate gland. Saw palmetto, Serenoa repens, is a creeping plant in USA and West Indies, whose dry and ripe fruits are used in BPH and may also help in reducing the size of the prostate gland, if enlarged. It can help in avoiding surgery. Gradually, medical treatment is also reduced and then stopped completely and the person can carry on comfortably with my technique and an effective diet.

1. Relax in any comfortable position that suits you.
2. Concentrate on your regular breathing.
3. Make a mental picture of the prostate gland and bladder.
4. Feel a partial obstruction in the urethra at the site of the prostate gland, which is causing difficulty in passing urine.
5. Now imagine that powerful light rays, like a laser beam, are entering your body from the cosmos, as you inhale. A beam of light falls on your prostate gland. Gradually, the grinding beam of light burns the centre of the prostate (smoke is seen coming out and the size of the prostate gland reduces both from periphery—the zone of cancer—as well as from the centre—the

zone for benign growth). As the laser works, you make a grinding sound of "krrrrrrrrrr... krrrr... krrr...". As the laser works for real, imagine the obstruction in your urinary pathway caused by an enlarged prostate gland also reducing and the path getting dilated. You are passing urine with less discomfort. Gradually, there is full relief. Now, you are devoid of any discomfort and are passing urine in a strong stream, without any obstruction.

6. Do this three times. The technique is best tried in the toilet.
7. Measure your PSA and prostate gland size by Trans Rectal Ultra Sound at an interval of three months.

"Health is harmony, Disease is discord."

Aristotle

WOUND HEALING

"If, you want to succeed, you have to forge new paths and avoid borrowed ones."

John Rockefeller

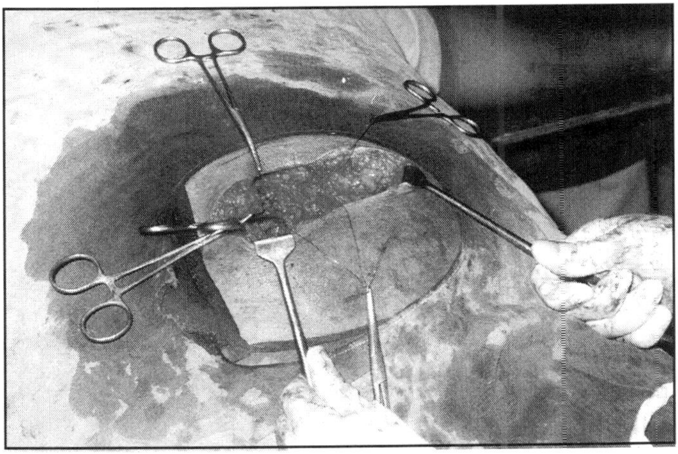

A surgical wound

A quick healing of tidy wounds is called "Healing by First Intention". Slow healing of untidy wounds is called "Healing by Second Intention". I call wound healing of all tidy and untidy wounds assisted by my technique as "Healing by God's Intention".

WHAT IS THE PROCESS OF HEALING WOUNDS?

The healing of a wound starts immediately after its creation (this includes surgical operations) and continues for up to 2-3 months. The wound is first filled up with blood clots. Gradually, the cells migrate and granulation tissue is formed. Cellular and hormonal responses are controlled by the brain. My technique improves healing by stimulating cellular and hormonal responses, while meditation can enhance immune function.[181]

Miss S. L. Cherry, of Switzerland, aged 30, was admitted to Privat Hospital in Gurgaon in July, 2008, with necrotising fasciitis of the left leg and foot. She was flown from Nepal to Gurgaon by air ambulance. On 23rd July, when in Nepal, she experienced pain in her left foot along with oedema and she was admitted to a private hospital there. She developed discolouration in her left foot and the lower part of the left leg. She was operated on 25th July, 2008 in Nepal. Debridement and surgical toilet was done under general anaesthesia and she was shifted to Privat Hospital on 28th July with septicemia and general deterioration. She was febrile with 101° F temperature, her pulse was 98/mt and BP 100/60 mmHg.

There was an infected wound on the dorsum of the left foot, almost covering the whole foot and another on the medial aspect of the left ankle, almost covering the entire medial side. Both wounds were full of pus, with a foul smelling, dirty white discharge. She was in pain. Her white cell count was 19000cells/cumm (almost double than the normal upper limit).

A pus swab taken from the wound showed heavy growth of the deadly bacteria Pseudomonas aeriginosa.

We first did the surgical toilette with debridement under a general anaesthesia on 28th July. As both wounds started oozing blood, their margins were trimmed and irrigation performed with a mixture of povidone-iodine solution and hydrogen peroxide. The wounds were washed with an Oxum solution (oxygen liberating solution) and wrapped with a ribbon gauze soaked in the same solution. She was on I.V. Amoxicillin, Metronidazole and Amikacin. I changed Amoxicillin to Tazobactum and Piperacell in. Metronidazole and Amikacin continued. All antibiotics were given intravenously.

I performed the dressing in the operation room daily. While talking to the patient, I discovered that she had been routinely meditating and praying. I encouraged her. The dressing was done under intravenous sedation as it was a painful process. She and I jointly decided that she would do the visualisation while I did the dressing.

We tried this in the next session and the dressing took place without an IV sedation. Another strange thing occurred when I prescribed Tazobactum and Piperacillin instead of Amoxycillin. I did this before the result of culture sensitivity of pus arrived. The result showed the presence of the bacteria Pseudomonas that responded only to Tazobactum and Piperacillin among the 20 antibiotics tested. Was this a coincidence or a conversation with God, a silent order of the Superpower? This action saved her leg as well as life.

She gradually improved and went to Switzerland with a firmer belief in the practice.

"I would like to know what sort of person has a disease than what sort of disease a person has."

Hippocrates
The Father of medicine

Dr. Paul Brand, Surgeon, writes, "My profession of surgery depends entirely on the body's own healing system. The real direction of prayer for the sick and the suffering should be first to praise God for the wonderful mechanisms of healing and recovery that God has designed and placed in a person's body."[182]

My Technique

1. Relax in a sleeping or seated position.
2. Take a deep breath, five times.
3. Imagine a mental picture of yourself lying down. Visualise the wound caused by a trauma, operation or anything else. Feel the presence of the wound.
4. Imagine a ray of light coming from the cosmos and falling upon your wound. The wound is bathed in the rays of the bright light, which is soothing and comfortable.
5. Now the wound is slowly being filled with a red-coloured tissue, similar to what was present in the wound. The light falling on the wound causes mild irritation. Feel this sensation. Gradually, the wound is filled with normal tissue, starting from the periphery to the centre. The wound fills and gets shallow. The skin gaps reduce. The gap on the skin surface gets gradually covered with fine reddish skin. Gradually, the skin over the wound thickens and becomes darker. Now, it looks similar to the surrounding skin.
6. Feel that there is no pain and feeling left in the wound. It has healed well.
7. Feel the wound covered with normal skin. There is no sign of the wound. The healing is complete.
8. Repeat the process thrice.

"We will either find a way or make one."

Hannibal

IRRITABLE BOWEL SYNDROME (IBS)

"When we are unable to find tranquility within ourselves, it is useless to seek it elsewhere."

Anonymous

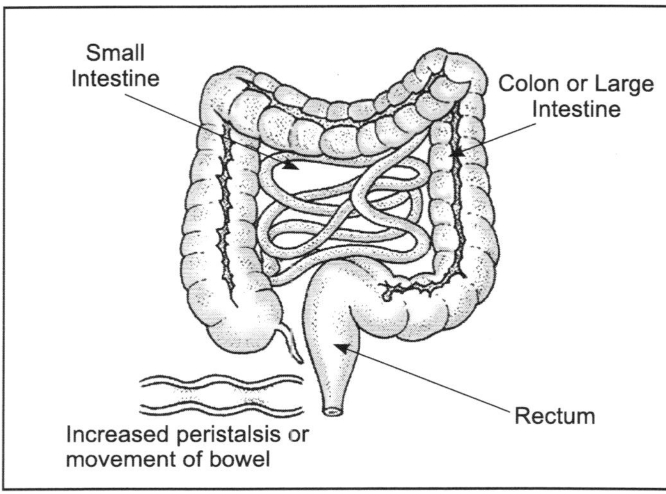

Fig: Irritable Bowel Syndrome

IBS is a combination of abdominal pain, disordered defecation and distension of the abdomen. Young women are commonly affected. It is a functional disorder of the bowel without any anatomical pathology. Twenty per cent of the population suffers from IBS.

IBS is basically a reaction of the intestines to stress. In IBS, the bowel develops abnormal movements at rest and reacts abnormally to the stress. My technique is most effective for IBS, when accompanied by a high-fibre diet.

Visualisation and meditation play a tremendous role in controlling IBS. Medicines can only give symptomatic relief but visualisation and meditation can provide a permanent cure. Meditation soothes irritable bowel disease, reduces the frequency of migraine headaches and enhances immune function.[183]

Many people with IBS have used hypnosis, relaxation therapy and feedback for comfort and to gain better control over their symptoms.

What is the defect?

IBS occurs due to the altered colonic motility at rest and in response to stress. Pain is due to distension or spasm of the intestine. Patients of IBS also suffer from psychological disturbances like depression, obsessive-compulsive disorder, hysteria, etc. A person suffering with IBS may suffer from constipation or diarrhoea.

It is believed that most patients develop symptoms in response to psychological factors. Most people suffering from IBS have the following symptoms:[184]

1. Abdominal pain
2. Abdominal distension
3. Altered defecation like diarrhoea or constipation.
4. Feeling of incomplete evacuation of the bowel.

Associated functional symptoms are dyspepsia, headache, backache, fatigue, disturbed sleep, anxiety, etc.

Stress and depression are often blamed for IBS, but emotions also aggravate the condition. Although no single treatment can eliminate IBS, a simple diet and lifestyle changes can relieve symptoms.[185]

My Technique

Hypnotherapy and visualisation can achieve excellent results in IBS. Patients who believe stress is a contributing factor for their symptoms may be suitable for psychological treatment. Hypnosis has proved beneficial in randomised trials.

1. Relax in a comfortable position and concentrate on your regular breathing.
2. Make a mental picture of your intestines (see text for picture).
3. See yourself in a tense situation. You are very angry and shouting at someone for not following your orders. Now, you are getting abdominal pain, discomfort and distention of abdomen. Try to feel the discomfort. Now, you see yourself lying down at a place that you like the most. You are breathing fresh and brightly lit air.

Feel the freshness and warmth of the bright air. Now, the light is concentrated on your abdomen. Your intestines are moving fast. Gradually, the light has a soothing and calming effect on your brain and abdomen. You are now relaxing and your intestines are gradually reducing their movement and moving at a normal pace. Feel your gut. Experience the feeling. Feel the reduction in discomfort. Your intestines are gradually relaxing and the gas in the intestine is slowly getting absorbed and relieved also.

4. Now, you are feeling relaxed, free of tension and without any discomfort in your mind or abdomen.

"Words can kill as well as heal."

Bernard Lown

GLAUCOMA

"For all the happiness, mankind can gain, is not in pleasure but in freedom from pain."

John Dryden

Glaucoma is the disease of the eyeball when the pressure inside it increases. Usually, glaucoma is a silent disease. It damages the eye without any significant symptoms.

What is the defect?

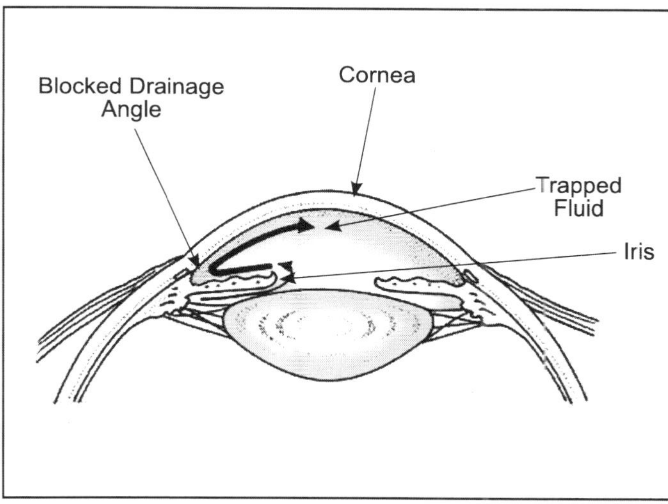

Fig: Mechanism of Glaucoma

Aqueous humour is the fluid in the eyeball. This fluid provides nutrition to the eye structures. In glaucoma, either the production of the fluid is increased or the drainage is reduced, leading to the retention of the fluid, causing increase in the intraocular tension.

My Technique

Lourdes, a shrine in France, is famous for miraculous healing.

Madame Bire was blind due to optic nerve atrophy. After visiting Lourdes, she regained her eyesight. She was later examined by doctors who testified to this. The point is, she was healed by her own subconscious mind and not by the holy water of the shrine.[186]

1. Relax in any comfortable position.
2. Breathe normally.
3. Feel that your eyes are tense with pressure.
4. Imagine your eyes as two spheres, each eye having six red balls representing obstruction (see text for picture).
5. Imagine a ray of light falling on one eye and the other ray of light falling on the other eye. Gradually, the rays are removing the balls causing the blocks of aqueous humour. These obstructing red balls have melted and are falling one by one. Now all balls have fallen and melted. Now your eyeballs are free from the blocks. This happens in both eyeballs, one by one.

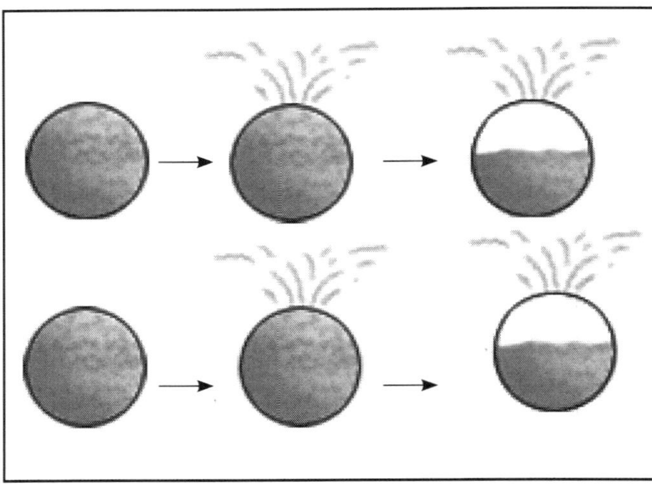

Fig: Dr. Nigam's Technique for Glaucoma

6. Now, your eyes have a free flow of aqueous humour from these holes created by the removal of blocks.
7. Feel the increased flow of aqueous humour in your eyes, which is gradually relieving the tension in the eyeballs.
8. Now you are feeling relaxed, free of tension and headaches.
9. Your eyeballs are now completely free from strain.

"Ignorance is like knowledge, there is no end to it."

Albert Einstein

BACKACHE

"To live long, live slowly."

Cicero

Low backache is a very common problem. In many cases, the defect is not diagnosed. It is quite disturbing and frustrating for the patient as well as the doctor. Some people suffer from low backache for years without any relief and diagnosis.

What is the defect?

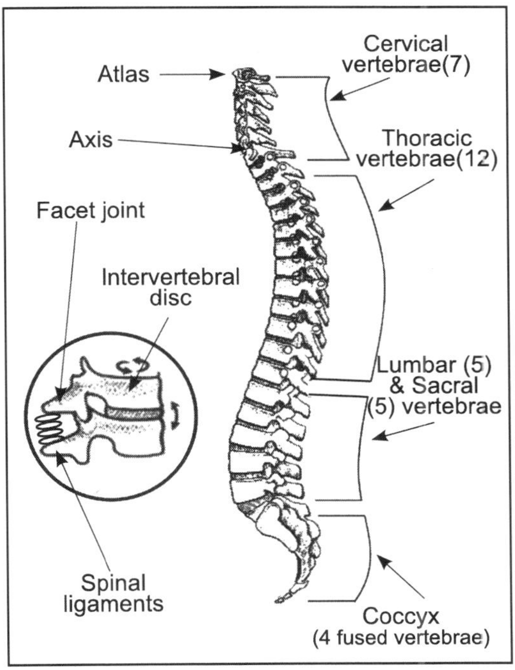

Fig: Anatomy of spine

Backache is a very common problem and almost every individual has back pain at some time in life. It is preventable with a little bit of care.

Your back supports your body and the lower back carries your body's weight. The spine is called the "backbone". It protects the spinal cord and provides attachment for the muscles and ligaments of your back.

The vertebral column or back bone has 33 bones called vertebrae. Seven are neck (cervical) vertebrae, 12 are in thorax (thoracic), five in lower back (lumbar), five in the back of the pelvis (sacrum) and the last four form the tailbone (coccyx). There are shock absorbers or intervertebral discs between each vertebrae to avoid collision during a walking and running. Muscles attached to the vertebrae give support and allow twisting and bending of the trunk. Ageing reduces the spine's flexibility and causes degeneration of the discs. Low backache is usually caused by strain to back muscles or ligaments. The source of low back pain (LBP) includes defects in the spine, vertebral joint, inter-vertebral discs, ligaments and muscles. Injury to ligaments and muscles cause release of histamine, substance 'P' and other chemicals, which cause inflammation and swelling locally. The majority of LBP cases have no history of significant injury or strain but inter-vertebral disc prolapse is a known cause. However, the most common cause of backache is strained back muscles or sprained ligaments caused by overstretching, due to any of the following reasons:

- A sudden awkward movement of the back.
- Injury while playing.
- Lifting of weights.
- Awkward position while sleeping.
- Sitting in a forward bending position for long durations, such as when working on a computer.
- Obesity.
- Stress and strains of day-to-day life.

How to Prevent Backache

1. Exercise regularly to maintain the flexibility of the spine and strengthen your back and abdominal muscles.
2. Continue your usual activities and avoid sudden awkward movements.
3. When lifting weights or heavy objects, avoid sudden jerks and avoid twisting the trunk and keep the back straight.
4. While sleeping, don't sleep on your stomach. When sleeping on your back, keep a pillow under the neck and the knees. Lie on the side with legs drawn up and a pillow between the legs.

My Technique

Meditation can reduce the need for analgesic medication in people with chronic musculoskeletal pain and in those suffering from cancer. [187 & 188]

1. Relax in a comfortable position.
2. Breathe normally.
3. Close your eyes.
4. Concentrate on your regular breathing for a few moments.
5. Do deep abdominal breathing five times.
6. Make a mental picture of your spine.
7. Imagine that the spine is rigid and the muscles around it are in spasm and stiff.
8. Imagine someone massaging your spine from above, downwards. Feel the pressure of fingers over the muscles, by the side of your spine. Try to feel the pressure on the aching muscles.
9. Now, imagine a ray of light falling on your body and gradually concentrating over the spine and slowly moving downwards, relaxing your muscles, ligaments and bones. Relax and feel your pain gradually subsiding.
10. Make a mental picture of yourself getting up and lying down without any pain. Your spine has become more flexible and the rigidity has disappeared.
11. Feel your backbone relaxing.
12. Do it five times.

"A physician is nature's assistant."

Galen

CONSTIPATION

"Nothing will benefit human health and increase the chances for survival of life on earth as much as the evolution to a vegetarian diet."

Albert Einstein

Constipation is the decrease in frequency of stool to less than once in three days or difficulty in defecation. It is the result of wrong food habits and stress.

What is the defect?

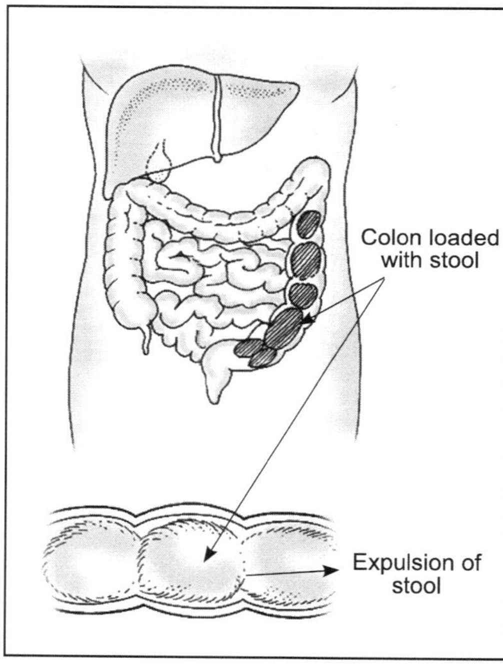

Fig: Constipation

Most cases of constipation are due to altered bowel habits caused by a low roughage diet, inactivity, low consumption of water, inadequate time for defecation, stress, side effects of various diseases, bowel diseases and iron supplements. Food is converted into stool, which exerts distention pressure on the walls of the intestine. The signals pass from the intestine to the brain, which sends commands to the bowel. The peristalsis increases and evacuates the bowel.

Some tips for avoiding constipation

1. Drink 8-10 glasses of water daily.
2. To increase the volume, increase your fibre intake to 25-30 grams including dal and green leafy vegetables. Remember the 10 Ps—peas, paprika (capsicum), papaya, pulses (legumes), prune, peach, pear, pinto beans, peels of orange & lemon and psyllium husk.
3. Don't be in a hurry; give it time.
4. Avoid stress.
5. Avoid refined foods like white bread.
6. Do leg and head raising movements and sun salutation exercises regularly.

My Technique

1. Relax in a comfortable position.
2. Close your eyes.
3. Do deep abdominal breathing five times.
4. Now imagine your large bowel (colon) loaded with faeces.
5. Again, do deep abdominal breathing five times. Each time, visualise that when you inhale air and count from 1 to 4, you distend your abdomen keeping the intestine relaxed. Feel the distension.

When you are contracting your abdominal muscles and exhaling, feel that the abdominal muscles are contracting and pressing your colon. Visualise the faeces inside the colon gradually moving lower. Feel the faeces in your rectum. Feel the pressure and get up and go to the toilet to pass stool.

6. This technique can also be tried while in the toilet.

"Nothing is impossible, for the willing heart."

Thomas Heywood

ULCERATIVE COLITIS

"I think, Therefore I am."

Rene Descartes

Ulcerative colitis is an inflammatory bowel disease. It involves only the colon and not the small intestine. It is common in Western countries and less common in Asian countries though the trend is now increasing. It affects about 10 people in 100,000, and is most common among young adults.

What is the defect?

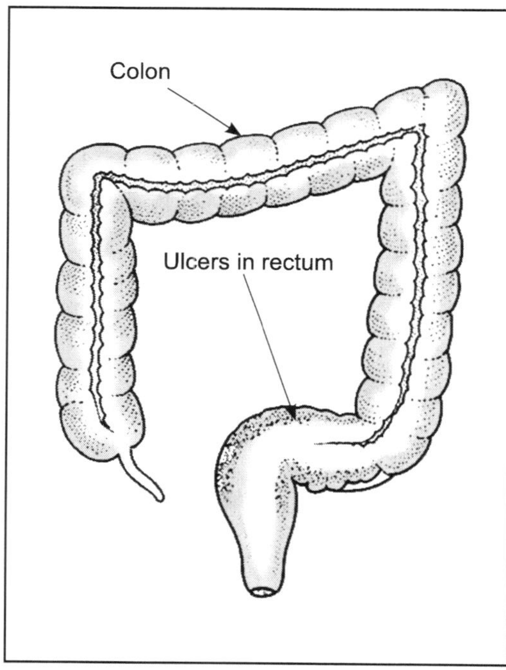

Fig: Ulcerative colitis in colon

This is a chronic inflammatory bowel disease. Dietary and bacterial antigens cause activation of certain cells i.e. macrophages, lymphocytes and polymorphonuclear cells. The release of inflammatory mediators occurs, which leads to the inflammation of the mucus membrane lining the colon, causing small ulcers and abscesses. Some toxic substances are also released which are cytotoxic and cause ulcerations in the mucus membrane of the colon.

This event occurs in normal individuals as well, when exposed to inflammatory insults and is self-limiting in healthy subjects. In genetically predisposed people, dysregulation of these steps leads to chronic inflammatory bowel disease.[189]

What happens

Ulcerative colitis usually exhibits symptoms such as abdominal pain, frequent small loose stools, mucus discharge, rectal bleeding and bloody diarrhoea. Most patients are constitutionally normal.

The attacks are caused by emotional stress, gastroenteritis, Non Steroidal Anti Inflammatory Drug therapy and use of antibiotics. *The New England Journal of Medicine* has reported that it is more common in non-smokers and ex-smokers but not in current smokers.[190] If you work on the premise that ulcerative colitis is psychosomatic, it does not take a great deal of intelligence to surmise that smoking is an effective outlet for stress and that if you shut that outlet, the stress is going to go somewhere else.[191]

Researches conducted in mind and body medicine have shown the mind's influence in healing and repairing surgical wounds. It has been observed by most surgeons that the more a patient displays trust in God and his surgeon, the more uncomplicated healing occurs. I personally feel that appendicectomy or repair of a complicated hernia or removal of a tumour is not the end of treatment. The mind-spirit-body connection must be targeted to achieve curative healing. For example, ulcerative colitis is understood better after an understanding of its psychosomatic nature. Most physicians now include biofeedback and relaxation therapy for ulcerative colitis, along with drug therapy. I regularly treat my patients with guided visualisation, meditation and drugs.

My Technique

- This technique should be done in a quiet room with the lights off. Lying on a carpet on the floor is the best position but it can be done anywhere in any position.
- Get comfortable. Allow your body to relax.
- Contract abdominal muscles by raising both legs straight at the knees. Do it three times.
- Relax

- Do deep abdominal breathing five times, then return to normal breathing.
- Visualise the higher power or God in any form you like to see it clearly.
- Visualise the diagram of the colon (large intestine) as given in the text, with the black spots.
- Feel the discomfort in the abdomen.
- Now feel that the higher power is gradually touching and caressing your abdomen. His hand is moving in a downward motion.
- Feel the hand of God burning away the disease (black spots) with a strong light which is gradually turning it from black to pink. Now there is no black, diseased area.
- Feel the healthy colon. Now, the feeling of discomfort has disappeared. Feel relaxed and healthy. Repeat it three times.

"Happiness lies, first of all in health."

George William Curtis

MIGRAINE

"The pain of the mind is worse than the pain of body."

Syrus

"98 per cent of the population has suffered from an ordinary headache at some point in life. Meditation can reduce the frequency of migraine headaches. Many sufferers of migraine say they successfully foil headaches by using non-pharmacological methods, such as yoga, meditation and biofeedback."

A to Z Health Guide

Migraine is a triad of paroxysmal headaches (bouts of headache) associated with nausea and/or vomiting along with an aura of focal neurological events, usually visual.

Common headache does not possess an aura.

It is common in women.

- The aura is in the form of jagged lines and shining lights seen just before the attack of migraine.

What is the defect?

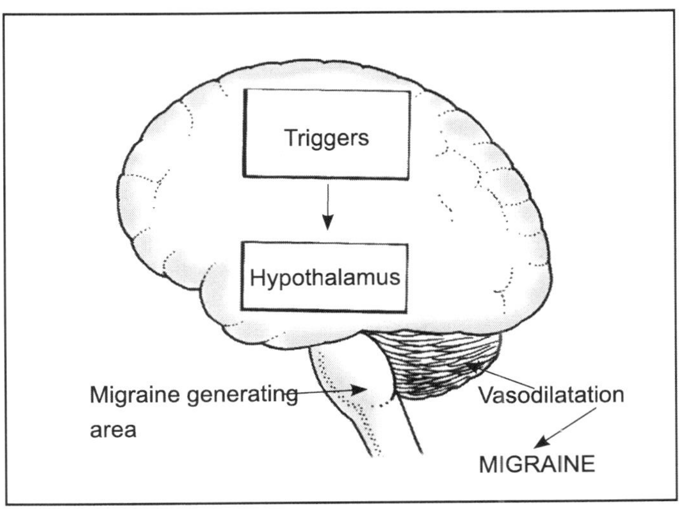

Fig: Mechanism of Migraine

TRIGGERS[stress, insomnia, allergy, menstruation, coffee, alcohol, weather changes,] ⟶ HYPOTHALAMUS ⟶[MIGRAINE GENERATING AREA OF BRAIN] ⟶ VASODILATATION ⟶ MIGRAINE

A migraine is thought to be caused by vasodilatation of extracranial vessels. Its triggers are stress, insomnia, allergy, menstruation, coffee, alcohol, weather changes, etc.

Most triggers act upon the hypothalamus that sends signals to the migraine generating area of the brain stem, which has trigeminal nerve fibres. These cause vasodilatation of vessels in the duramater (covering of the brain). The blood vessels are surrounded by pain sensitive nerve fibres, which convey a throbbing headache.

The trigemimal nerve (5th craneal nerve) is the main nerve conveying pain.

What happens

A migraine is a one-sided headache, a throbbing pain that lasts for four hours to 2-3 days and worsens with movement. Usually, it is accompanied by nausea and vomitting and can be aggravated by noise and light. It is usually triggered by stress.

My Technique

These days, doctors also know that migraine is a neurological problem and not a vascular one. Thus, relaxation techniques are included in the repertoire of treatment for migraine.

- Sit comfortably or lie down and relax, try to lose control of the limbs and muscles of your body.
- Take five deep abdominal breaths and then breathe normally.
- Try to focus on emotions and the factors causing stress.

Concentrate just on feeling the cause, do not be judgmental.

- Imagine the face of your loved one, perhaps your mother, child, wife or God, or anyone who is caring and compassionate.
- See yourself talking calmly and happily to the image you have selected and promise him or her that you will not be disturbed by factors causing stress. Repeat this three times.
- Feel yourself relaxing and de-stressing.
- You can practice this as soon as a migraine's aura begins.

Faith in God can relieve pain, as confirmed by Oxford University scientists. Using the latest brain scanning techniques, they confirmed that faith in God reduces the feeling of pain by 12 per cent.[192]

"Seek not outside yourself, heaven is within."

Mary Lou Cook

DEPRESSION

"He is not elated by good fortune or depressed by bad. His mind is established in God, and he is free from delusion."

Bhagwad Gita

Nearly one-fourth of the population has experienced a moderate degree of depression in their lifetime. Depression indicates a relation between the mind and body, as it affects the physical being also. Depression is a common cause of suicide and an under-diagnosed sickness. It has been seen that people who are depressed after MI die sooner than those who are not.[193]

What is the defect?

People, who are depressed, have less amounts of the neurotransmitter serotonin required for activation of the next brain cell. This imbalance doesn't activate other brain cells and depression occurs. Depression may be major, a bipolar disorder or seasonal. Bipolar disorders have alternate periods of depression and hyperactivity and uncontrolled elation (mania). It was earlier called manic depression or manic depressive disorder.[194]

The common causes of depression are:

- Genetic
- Infection
- Hormonal changes in life, i.e. pregnancy and menopause.
- Bereavement
- Stress and anxiety
- Marital disharmony
- Insomnia
- Diet or sensitivity to certain foods, aspartame, deficiency of vitamin B1, B6, C and red wine (the tyramin in it causes depression).
- Chronic pain
- Terminal sicknesses
- Serotonin reducing factors; i.e., alcohol, smoking, diabetes and hypoglycemia.

What happens

- Loss of power, energy and weakness
- Weight gain or loss due to changes in appetite
- No interest in life, friends, family and sex

- Insomnia
- Irritability and mood swings
- Pains, headache and backache
- Suicidal tendencies

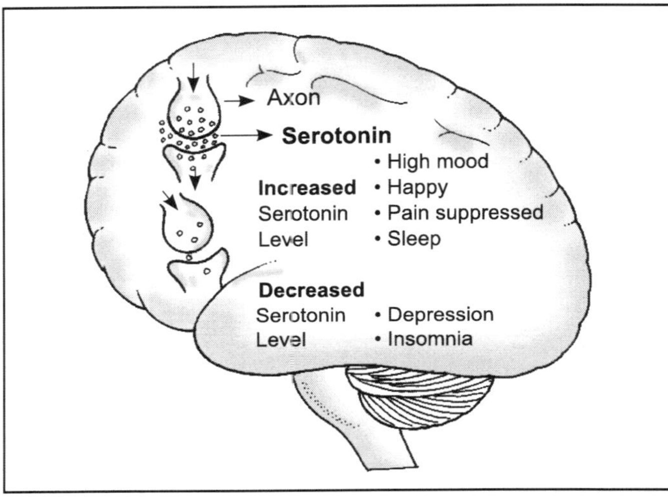

Fig: Physiology of Depression

My Technique

Eat plenty of fruits and green vegetables. Take vitamin B-complex, vitamin C, magnesium, zinc and essential fatty acid supplements to deal with depression

- Relax on the floor, a carpet or on the bed.
- Breathe normally, concentrate on your breathing and then do deep abdominal breathing for a few minutes.
- Now, visualise yourself lying down or in a seated position, but looking depressed. Gradually, try to remember images of happy moments from your life or when you achieved some success. Concentrate on each aspect of this event. Repeat this picture three times and concentrate on the event. See yourself smiling, laughing and happy.
- Now repeat to yourself, "I am not depressed, I am happy, I shall win the situation". Repeat three times.
- Now feel happy and satisfied.

"What's the use of worrying? It never was worthwhile, so pack up your troubles in your old kit boy, And smile, smile, smile."

George Asaf

TUMOUR AND MALIGNANCY

"The possession of knowledge doesn't kill the sense of wonder and mystery. There is always more to mystery."

Anais Nin

"You cannot teach man anything. You can only help him turn to find it within himself."

Galileo

"Cancer appears when the immune system becomes suppressed. Whatever upsets the brain's control of the immune system will foster malignancy. The state of the mind has an immediate and direct effect on the state of our body. Emotions and imagery get our minds and bodies to communicate with each other through CNS. Why do tumours sometimes regress when patients are convinced that an orthodox treatment—hypnosis, diet, prayer, meditation—is going to work?"

Bernie Siegel, MD

"Here is some good news: Your genes are not your fate... It's based on our latest research showing that you can actually change how your genes are expressed—Just by changing what you eat and how you live... in general, turning on (upregulating) the good genes and turning off (down regulating) the harmful ones."

Dean Ornish, MD
The Spectrum

A cancer is an uncontrolled growth that damages surrounding tissues and may spread to surrounding areas and also to other parts of the body. Cancer or a malignant tumour can be defined as, "A localised growth or tumour, caused by an abnormal and uncontrolled reproduction of cells that invade the surrounding tissues. It can spread to other parts of the body if left untreated." [195]

The cells multiply uncontrollably because the normal regulating mechanism of cell division is damaged. Faulty genes may be inherited or caused by carcinogens (agents that cause cancer) or the ageing process. A tumour is a mass of cells that results from an uncontrolled multiplication.

A tumour can be benign or malignant. A benign tumour does not spread to surrounding tissues or other parts of the body. A malignant tumour that spreads to surrounding tissues and other parts of the body is also known as cancer.

The cancer cell is an abnormal cell, which divides excessively and in an uncontrolled fashion, without performing its normal function.

How cancer begins

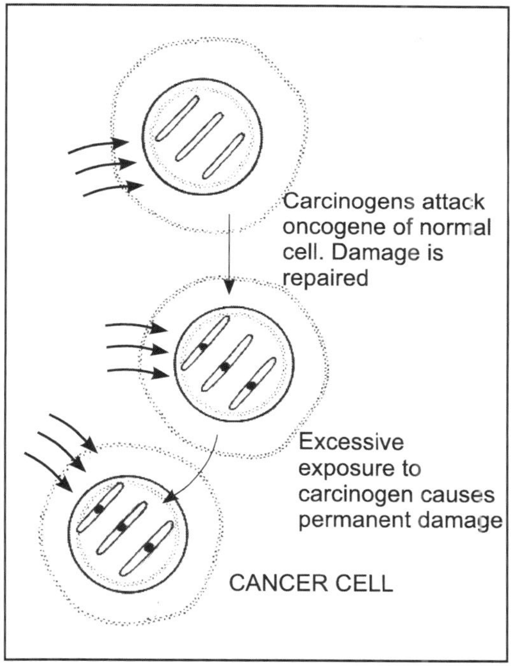

Fig: Development of cancer

Cancer causing substances are called carcinogens. Carcinogens damage genes, which are termed "oncogenes". Most of these damaged genes are repaired, but those which cannot be repaired, because of regular and repeated exposure to carcinogens, begin to function abnormally. They turn cancerous and multiply to form a malignant tumour. It takes just one cell to undergo cancerous changes and form a tumour.

Three important things appear in cancer:

1. Oncogene, which causes cells to multiply, is stimulated to do so.
2. The tumour suppressor gene, which depresses and controls cell multiplication.
3. Telomerase is an important enzyme. Telomere is a small spindle-shaped structure that holds the chromosomes of the cell together.

The telomere shortens each time the cell divides. When it becomes very short, the cell dies. Telomerase does not allow the telomere to shorten, so the cell becomes immortal.

How cancer spreads to other parts

The spread of a cancerous tumour to other parts of the body is called "metastasis". The initial tumour is known as the "primary tumour". Those that develop at other sites are called "secondary tumours" or "metastases".

Tumours spread in two ways:

(i) By lymph: cancer cells enter a lymph vessel and then travel with it.

(ii) By blood: some cancer cells spread by entering the blood stream and reach the liver, lungs, bones and brain.

The origin, development and spread of cancer is closely connected with the three main systems of the body, i.e., the immune, endocrine and central nervous system. Oncologist O. Carl Simonton studied the relation of cancer with psychological factors and stress, revealing the connection between cancer and these three body systems. He realised and made the medical fraternity realise the advances made in theology, psychology as well as holistic medicine regarding malignancy. He published his findings that out of 159 patients of cancer, who were not expected to live more than one year, 19 per cent of patients got rid of their cancer completely and that the disease was regressing in 22 per cent. Those who succumbed to cancer had, on an average, doubled the expected survival time. He was the first Western doctor to use imagery techniques for cancer. If a "miracle" like permanent remission of cancer happens once, it is valid and must not be dismissed as a fluke. If one patient can do it, there is no reason why others cannot.[196, 197]

The positive placebo effect requires high trust in the treatment and the clinician, along with an intense desire to be cured. Psychiatrist Jerome Frank of Johns Hopkins University, USA, found that patients full of optimism and faith in their doctor before the operation, healed faster. If the doctor has hope in his patient, the healing process can start even before treatment does.

Dean Ornish writes in his book "*Spectrum*" that the progression of early stage prostate cancer may be slowed, stopped or perhaps even reversed… any type of cancer may be modified just by changing what we eat and how we live.

Carl Jung, psychotherapist, wrote in his bestseller *Modern Man in Search of a Soul* about doctors, that they must first change themselves and learn the ways of positive thinking and lifestyle changes before then they can preach. He writes, "The physician must overcome these resistances himself, for who can educate others while he himself is uneducated? Who can enlighten his fellows while still being in the dark about himself?"[198]

The Harvard Medical School Family Health Guide states that some studies have found that therapies aimed at reducing stress may boost the function of certain immune system cells.

Studies have confirmed that depression, grievous loss, divorce and childhood crises depresses the immune system, lowers the efficacy of the body's disease fighting killer T-cells and may increase the incidence of cancer and other catastrophic illnesses. [199] Stress, especially chronic stress, is associated with cancer. Type C personality individuals are introvert, depressed and known to have higher risk of cancer. Having a strong will to live seems to reduce the risk of relapse, so writes C. Paula et al, in her book "*Stress:The Good and the Bad*".

Prayer is talking, meditation is listening. Western science has only just began to study the effects of meditation and visualisation on diseases. Alberto Villoldo of San Francisco State College showed that regular meditation and self-healing visualisation improved WBC response and immune system functioning.[200]

Simonton developed an imagery technique for cancer, which is mentioned in the book "*Imagery of Cancer*", like the patient drawing a diagram of the disease that shows the WBC eliminating the cancer.[201]

I, too, use similar techniques by asking the patient to imagine a mental picture of the illness in the body and then destroy it with their immune cells and antibodies.

My Technique

- Sit comfortably or relax in any position that you find comfortable.
- Try to lose control of your body, let the muscles relax and let the limbs and head fall.
- Take five deep abdominal breaths and then breathe normally.
- Now make a mental picture of your body and the disease in it (cancer). (Refer to the diagram for the organ, make an area of cancer over it using black ink or a sketch pen.)

- While you are breathing in, feel you are inhaling bright light coming from infinity. As the light spreads to all parts of your body, the cancerous area remains black but the rest of the body shines with the light.
- Gradually, feel that the light you inhale has rounded, small, white, opaque particles or cells of the immune system. These cells are spreading to all parts of your body. Now, these cells are attacking the cancer (black area) and bombarding it. Gradually, the black area is reducing in size and disappearing. Now, there is no black area or cancer left in your body. Feel healthy without the cancer.
- Repeat three times in your heart: "Now the healing process has started in every cell of my body. My whole body is healing. I will be 100 percent healthy and free of cancer."

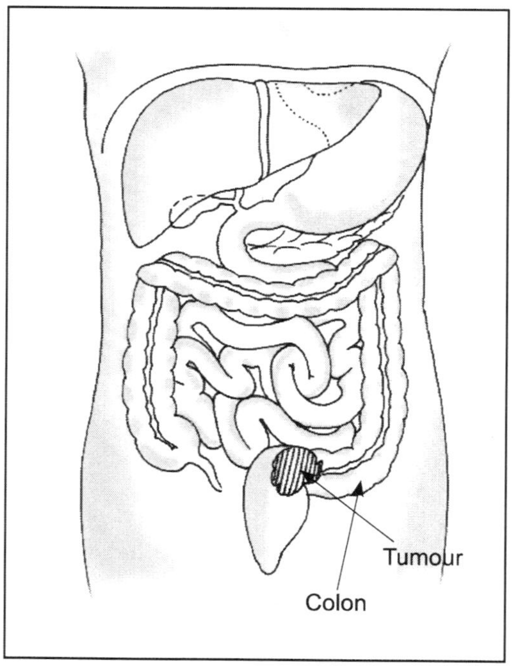

Fig: Cancer of Colon

Your conscious mind is the builder of your body, but you cannot consciously perceive or hear that inner silent process. Begin now to take care of your conscious mind, knowing in your heart and soul that your subconscious mind is always expressing, reproducing and manifesting in accordance with your thoughts.[137]

"The human spirit is stronger, than anything that happens to it."

C.C. Scott

5

VIEWS OF MEDICAL WORLD ABOUT HEALTH, MEDICINE AND SPIRITUALITY

"We still do not know one-thousandth of one percent that nature has evoked to us."

Albert Einstein

Bernie Segal, MD, Connecticut, USA, author of the bestseller *"Love, Medicine and Miracles"* communicated that he knows several patients who prayed or left their troubles to God and healed their cancers.

Larry Dossey, MD, Dallas, Texas, USA, author of *"Healing Words and The Power of Premonitions"* writes, "Scientific evidence has confirmed the contribution of spirituality and prayer to health and longevity. No longer should people believe they have to choose between 'the scientific' and 'the spiritual', for these domains can come together in a beautiful complementarity."

Harold G. Koenig, MD, Professor of Psychiatry & Behavioural Sciences, Duke University Medical Center, Durham, North Carolina, USA believes that prayer and a strong faith in God are the keys to our healing the world.

Dr. Jas Katariya, MD, Chief Anaesthesiologist, Artemis Health Institute, Gurgaon, India feels that "medicine is not really a job, it is a way of life. We are constantly surrounded by many instances of suffering, intractable pain and death. It is at those times that the spirituality that we develop comes to our rescue. Spirituality is the anchor that holds us down in the stormy sea of life. I have worked hard to incorporate these beliefs in my everyday life and practice. In our hospital at dawn and dusk, chants and prayers are played through the PA system, every single day. There are numerous times I have felt my prayers have actually been heard".

Dr. H.M. Chawla, MD, Ex-Associate Professor, Department of Psychiatry, AIIMS, New Delhi accepts that life and death are not in our hands. Patients with serious problems survive as patients with trivial sicknesses succumb to death.

Dr. (Col) B. Kalra, renowned Senior Cardiologist, Gurgaon, says that as a cardiologist I feel that without Gods help a massive heart attack patient can not survive inspite of advancement in technology.

Dr. Ashok Wali, Senior Consultant Anaesthesiologist says that in anaesthesia teachings it is always taught how to put patients to sleep for surgical procedures and no book ever mentions how to wake them up. So we put them to sleep and it is almighty God who wakes them up.

Dr. Ashok Raina, Honorary Ophthalmologist to Honourable Vice President of India, feels we can not work without the blessings of God as we operate but He gives eyesight.

Dr. Prem Chand, Senior Orthopaedic Consultant and Joint Replacement Surgeon, Apollo Clinic, Gurgaon, believes in spirituality and feels that it can't be explained in words. Miracles do happen and happen frequently.

Retired Air Commodore VSM and ENT Surgeon Dr. Lalit Kochar feels that a miracle is not a rare phenomenon, especially in the battlefield.

Dr. Devi Shetty, a renowned Cardiac Surgeon, says, "I strongly believe in the presence of God. If you dissect the body and figure out what was there before and what has gone away, it makes all the difference between life and death. We have no explanation, since everything that is supposed to be inside the body is inside it even after death. Before I start an operation, I pray to God and do the operation in his name. Success and failure is not because of me."

Dr. Parveen Bhatia, Chairman Minimal Access & Bariatric Surgery, SGRH, New Delhi and Director, Global Hospital and Endosurgery Institute, New Delhi, believes that the surgeon is one who thinks of God most often as he is aware that post-operative healing is not in his hands.

Prof. Mahesh C Misra, Prof. and Head of Minimal Access Surgery (Laparoscopic), AIIMS, Head of Trauma Centre, New Delhi, believes that we cannot treat the patient without God's help. Sometimes, patients, after a serious trauma, don't come to hospital in the "golden hour" or reach hours later but are still saved, making one wonder where the catch is. There is a superpower who helps at these critical moments.

Dr. Sandip Mukerjee, ex-Honorary Surgeon to the President of India and a renowned expert, says a surgeon's reputation depends upon the healing and success of his operations and that is in the hands of God. How can anyone explain why a dying patient survives and a surviving patient dies? In a long career of surgery, one feels on certain occasions that there is something that happens beyond the understanding of medicine.

A renowned Neurosurgeon, Prof V. S. Mehta, Director of Neurosurgery, Paras Hospitals and President of Neurological Society of India and South Asian Associations of Neurosurgeons, believes that God helps in the outcome of surgeries. He says, "Every surgeon prays, some pray regularly before an operation for his patients and others when complications develop. If a surgeon says he doesn't pray, then he is either too bold or hiding it as a weakness."

Prof J. P. Wali, former Professor of Medicine, All India Institute of Medical Sciences, New Delhi, and the Chairman of the Rational Independent Ethics Committee, AIIMS, says that "experience in medicine makes you believe that there is a superpower or force which keeps the universe running smoothly and maintains its balance. We may not see the force or God, but circumstances and feelings definitely indicate the presence of God".

Dr. Kushagra Katariya, Cardio Thoracic Surgeon and CEO of Artemis Health Institute, plays shlokas and bhajans in the operation theatre and has a space for prayers of every religion in the hospital.

Dr. Ashok Vaid, Padma Shree awardee and a renowned Oncologist, believes that the response to chemotherapy and remission depends upon the Almighty. He has seen and treated thousands of cancer patients from all over the world and has seen and felt the association of spirituality and medicine intimately.

Dr. Sumita Mullick, Ex HOD, Paediatric surgery, Safdarjung Hospital, New Delhi, prays before, during and after every operation and feels the presence of God while operating little angels.

Dr. Lalit Verma, Senior anaesthesiologist at Apollo, Gurgaon, who was an hostage in IC 814 which was taken to Kandhar, Afghanistan, in 1999, had felt the power of God from very close as he surrendered to God and not to hijackers. Throughout the captivity period, he was busy boosting the morale of co-passengers smilingly and treating them with whatever was available. He is a strong believer of God and his Faith has increased after this episode. He has otherwise also felt the God's help on number of occasions in operation theatre giving anaesthesia to patients. He feels "We are the tools, He is the operator"

Dr. S.P. Yadav, Senior Urologist, feels that there is definitely a power helping you in desperate situation. Prayer works and we feel presence of Force or God quite often.

Dr. Prabhakar, Consultant, Internal Medicine, Private Hospital, Gurgaon feels that "almighty dictates the outcome of an operation or a treatment while we take the credit".

"The most sacred place is not the church, the mosque or the temple, It's the temple of the body. That's where the spirit lives."

Susan Taylor

6

EPILOGUE

"Ask and it shall be given to you; Seek and ye shall find, Knock and it shall be opened unto you."

Mathew; VII

In the western world, people tried to keep faith and medicine separate, but now the new world order is trying to connect the two. Some Western medical practitioners perceived the trend as a threat to scientific practices. The medical fraternity that held this view was hell-bent on "excluding God from medical practice". They never gave any thought to the medical benefits of spirituality. For the last two decades, various studies have been published with evidence about the health and medical benefits of faith and spirituality.

More and more members of the medical community are expressing their views and experiences with their patients on the positive effects of faith, spirituality, prayer and mind-body practices on healing and health.

A new branch of medicine, Neurotheology, is increasingly promoting the role of functional MRI and other neuroimaging techniques in understanding the bridge between science and God. Various polls have indicated that 70-80 per cent of the population believes in praying for the sick and shows faith in spiritualism and its relation to healing and health. How can we ignore the faith of such a big portion of the public without further investigating this field?

Another argument from believers that cannot be ignored is economic benefits. The cost of today's medical treatment, particularly of surgical intervention is sky-rocketing. It is becoming unbearable without the help of medical insurance companies. The spiritual approach is cheaper and without the side effects of medical treatment. This further helps in promoting distance healing and intercessory prayers. Dr. Larry Dossey, a proponent of spiritual healing, says "the most important discoveries of the next 50 years are likely to be ones of which we cannot even conceive of."

The state of mind changes the state of the body—this is a known phenomenon today, so why not explore this field and reap its benefits for the human race?

"One generation's miracle may be another's scientific fact."

Bernie Siegel, MD
Peadiatric & General Surgeon

"The compassionate mind is like an elixir, it is capable of transforming bad situations into beneficial ones."

His Holiness Dalai Lama

BOOKS RECOMMENDED FOR FURTHER READING

1. H.G. Koenig, M. E. McCullough, and D. B. Larson, *Handbook of Religion and Health,* New York: Oxford University Press, 2001.
2. D. A. Matthews and C. Clark, *The Faith Factor,* New York: Viking, 1998.
3. Cissi Williams, *An A to Z Guide to Holistic Healing: The Well-Being Handbook*, Jaico, 2008.
4. Deepak Chopra and David Simon, *Freedom*, Jaico, 2008.
5. Steve Parker, *The Human Body Book*, Dorling Kindersley Limited, 2007.
6. Anthony L. Komaroff, *The Harvard Medical School Family Health Guide*, Cassell, 2003.
7. Richard Dawkins, *The God Delusion*, Black Swan, 2006.
8. Andrew Weil, *Healthy Aging: A Life long Guide to Your Well Being,* Anchor, 2005.
9. Atul Gawande, *Complications: Notes From The Life of a Young Surgeon*, Penguin, 2002.
10. Philip T. Hagen, *Mayo Clinic Guide to Self-Care*, Orient Paperbacks, 2001.
11. Dalai Lama, *The Art of Happiness,* London: Hodder and Stoughton, 1999.
12. Neale Donald Walsch, *Conversations with God,* London: Hodder and Stoughton, 1997.
13. *Dorland's Illustrated Medical Dictionary*, 30th Edition, Saunders, 2003.
14. Ashok,Dilwali. *Bhagvad Gita – An essence,*
15. Madonna Gauding, *The Meditation Bible: The definitive guide to Meditations for Every Purpose*, Octopus, 2005.
16. How to Know God, The Soul's Journey into the Mystery of Mysteries, Deepak Chopra, Random House, 2000.
17. Deepak Chopra, *Ageless Body, Timeless Mind: A Practical Alternative to Growing Old*, Random House, 1993.

18. Louise Hay, *The power is Within You*, London: Eden Grove, 1991.

19. Louise Hay, *You Can Heal your life*, London: Eden Grove Editions, 1988.

20. Debbie Shapiro, *The Body Mind Work Book*, Element Books Ltd, 1990.

21. Herbert Benson, *The Mind-Body Effect*, New York: Simon and Schuster, 1979

22. Norman Cousins, *Anatomy of an Illness as Perceived by the Patient*, New York: Norton, 1979.

23. Elida Evans, *A Psychological Study of Cancer*, Dodd, New York, Mead, 1926.

24. James L Fosshage, and Paul Olsen, *Healing: Implications for Psychotherapy*, New York: *Human Sciences Press*, 1978.

25. Viktor Frankl, *Man's Search for Meaning*, New York: Pocket Books, 1959.

26. Judith Glassman, *The Cancer Survivors: And How They Did it*, New York: Doubleday, 1983.

27. Thomas A Harris, *I'm Ok – You're Ok: A practical Guide to Transactional Analysis*, New York: Harper and Row, 1969.

28. Gerald Jampolsky, *Teach Only Love: The Seven Principles of Attitudinal Healing*, New York: Bantam, 1983.

29. Carl G Jung, *Modern Man in Search of a Soul*, New York: Harcourt Brace Jovanovich, 1955.

30. Elisabeth Kiibler-Ross, *On Death and Dying*, New York: Macmillan, 1969.

31. Harold S Kushner, *When Bad Things Happen to Good People*, New York: Schocken, 1981.

32. Howard Lewis and Martha E. Lewis, *Psychosomatics: How Your Emotions Can Damage Your Health*, New York: Viking, 1972.

33. Steven Locke and Mady Hornig-Rohan, *Mind and Immunity*, New York: Institute for the Advancement of Health, 1983.

34. Hans Selye, *The Stress of Life*, New York: 2nd ed. McGraw-Hill, 1978.

35. O. Carl Simonton, Stephanie Matthews-Simonton and James Creighton. *Getting Well Again*, New York: J. P. Tarcher, Los Angeles: 1978.

36. Aleksandr Solzhenitsyn, *Cancer Ward*, Farrar, Straus and Giroux, 1969.

37. Eknath Easwaran, Living Thoughts of Great people, Jaico, 2004.

38. Bernie Siegel: Love, Medicine and Miracles, Arrow Books

39. Larry Dossey: Healing Words: The power of Prayer and The Practice of Medicine, Harper, 1993.

REFERENCES

1. *Journal of Internal Medicine,* Times of India. June 24, 2005, p 17.
2. Richard Sloan P, *Blind Faith, The Unholy Alliance of Religion and Medicine,* StMartin's Press, 2006, p 4
3. O. Hallesby Prayer, Augsburg Publishing, 1975, pp 16-17.
4. Richard P Sloan, Blind Faith, *Blind Faith, The Unholy Alliance of Religion and Medicine,* St Martin's Press, 2006, pp 5- 6.
5. Richard Swinburne, *Science and Theology News,* 7 April, 2006.
6. Richard Dawkins, *The God Delusion,* 2006, p 90.
7. R Swinburne, *Is there a God,* Oxford University Press, 1996.
8. R Swinburne, *The Existence of God,* Oxford University Press, 2004.
9. Richard Dawkins, *The God Delusion,* Black Swan, 2006, p 33.
10. W. S. Harris et al, *A Randomized Controlled Trial of the Effects of Remote, Intercessary Prayer on Ooutcomes of Patients Admitted to the Coronary Care it,* Archives of Internal Medicine, 159, 1999, pp 2273-78.
11. Jermias J, *The Prayers of Jesus,* Naperville, 1976, p 78.
12. Hillesum E, *An Interrupted life,* pp 180-260.
13. A. Newberg etal, *Cerebral Bloodflow During Meditation Prayer: Preliminary findings and methodological Issues, Perceptual and Motor Skills,* 97,(2), 2003, pp 625-30.
14. Why not T, *Body, Soul and Mind Over Matter,* Sunday Times of India, New Delhi, September 7, 2008, p 25.
15. Mother Teresa; Everything starts from Prayer, white cloud press, 1998, p 35.
16. Weekly soul hits, mind over matter, Sunday times of India, New Delhi, Sunday August 3, 2008, p 27.
17. Dawkins R: The God delusion, Black Swan, 2006, p 52.
18. Shelton Ken K.; Personal Excellence, Jaico, 2007, p 73-74.
19. Koeing, H. G. "Religion, spirituality and medicine", Southern Medical Journal, 2004

20. O. Hallesby Prayer, Augsburg Publishing, 1975, pp 16-17.

21. Hindustan Times, New Delhi, July 8, 2008, p 20, London July, 7.

22. Benson H. etal, study of therapeutic effects of intercessory prayer (STEP) in cardiac bypass patients, American Heart journal , 151:4, 2006, p 934-42.

23. Ornish D; Dr. Dean Ornish's program for reversal of heart disease, Ballantine ,1992.

24. Herschel A J; I asked for wonder, Crossroads 2000, p 18.

25. Siegel B, *Love, Medicine and Miracles*, Arrow Books, 1988 p 178.

26. Byrd R, *Positive Therapeutic effects: Harris etal, Randomized controlled Trial, Dusek etal, study of the therapeutic effects.*

27. *Most in US Believe in Guardian Angels*, Times Global, Times of India, Sept' 20, 2008, p 19.

28. AB Astrow, C M Puchalski and D P Sulmary; Religion, Spirituality and Health Care; social, Ethical and Practical Considerations, American Journal of Medicine, 110(4) 2001, p 284.

29. D. E. King and B. Bushwik; Beliefs and Attitudes of Hospital Patients About Faith, Healing and Prayer, Journal of family practice, 39 (1994), pp 349-52.

30. May G. C; Addiction and Grace, San Francisco, Harper San Francisco, 1988, p 1.

31. Hindustan Times, New Delhi, July 8, 2008, p 20, London July, 7.

32. Mueller, P. S. et al "Religious involvement, spirituality and medicine", Mayo clinic proceedings, Dec'2001.

33. Byrd R; Positive Therapeutic effects: Harris etal, Randomized controlled Trial, Dusek etal, study of the Therapeutic effects.

34. R. C. Byrd; Positive Therapeutic effects of Intercessory Prayer in a coronary care unit population, Southern Medical Journal, 81 (1988), pp 826-829.

35. Dossey L; Prayer and Medical Science, Archives of Internal Medicine, 160(12) 2000, p 1736.

36. Dr. David Servan-Schreiber, "The Instinct to Heal," February 2004.

37. Gregg Jacobs, The Ancestral Mind.

38. J Borg etal; The Serotonin system and Spiritual Experiences, American Journal of Psychiatry, 160(11), 2003, pp 1965-69

39. D. E. King and B. Bushwik; Beliefs and Attitudes of Hospital Patients About Faith, Healing and Prayer, Journal of family practice, 39 (1994), pp 349-52.

40. A Newberg and E d' aquili; why God won't Go away, New York, Ballantine Books, 2001, p 168-69.

41. Siegel B, *Love, Medicine and Miracles*, Arrow Books, 1988, p 67.

42. Sawyer R. K., Explaining creativity; The science of Human innovation, Oxford.

43. Murphy J; (2001), The power of your subconscious mind, Bantam Books, p 44.

44. Yancey P; Prayer does it make any difference?, Hodder, 2008, p 244

45. Dr. Brewer S; Natural Health Guru, DBP, 2008, p 156.

46. Dr. Brewer S; Natural Health Guru, DBP, 2008, p 157.

47. Dr. Brewer S; Natural Health Guru, DBP, 2008, p 159.

48. Dr. Brewer S; Natural Health Guru, DBP, 2008, p 45.

49. Consumer Reports Guide of Diet, Health and fitness, 2005, p-143.

50. A to Z Health Guide; TIME 2004, p 96.

51. Peter Albright, complimentary therapies; A Marshall Health Guide, 1979, p p 151-152.

52. Myra Huth, Assistant Vice President of center for Professional Excellence Research at Cincinnati Children's Hospital, Medical Center, Cencinnati, Ohio, USA. April 2007, Journal of Pediatric Nursing.

53. Dan Quayle ; The American family: discovering the values that make us strong".

54. Buttrick G; Prayer, pp 114-115.

55. Shanker Raghuraman, Times insight group, *A survey of Religiosity in India, Times – TNS India Survey*, Sunday Times of India, New Delhi, November 26, 2006, pp 22-24.

56. Yancey P; Prayer, Does it make any difference?, Hodder, 2008, p 14.

57. Murphy J; (2001) The power of your subconscious mind, Bantam Books, p 79.

58. Mind over matter, Sunday Times, Oct'5, 2008, p 27.

59. Health chronicle, Hindustan times, July 17-30, 2008, p 4, www.myhealthguardian.com

60. Health chronicle, Hindustan Times, 17-30 July 2008, p 4, www.myhealthguardian.com

61. Times Life, Times of India, June' 1, 2008, p 1.

62. Hindustan Times, New Delhi, Saturday, July' 18, 2008, p 3.

63. Herbert Benson MD, Your maximum Mind (New York: Times books, 1990), pp 1-2.

64. Laubach F; Man of Prayer, 1990, p 45.

65. Times Trends, Times of India , Wednesday, AVG 20, 2008.

66. News week, November 17, 2003, p 44.

67. M W Krucoff etal; Integrative Noetic Therapies as Adjuncts to Percutaneous Intervention During Unstable Coronary Syndromes : Monitoring and Actualization of Noetic Training (MANTRA) Feasibility Pilot, "American Heart Journal, 142(5) (2001); p 761.

68. Stephen R Covey, *The Habits of Highly Effective People*, Pocket Books, 1999, p 319.

69. Andrew Weil, *Healthy Aging for Enhancement of Health and Well-Being*, Anchor Book, 2005, p 294.

70. L Dossey, *Prayer and Medical Science: A Commentary on Prayer Study by Harries etal and a Response to Critics,* Archives of Internal Medicine, 160(12) 2000, p 1736.

71. F. Luskin; Review of effects of spiritual factors on Mortality and morbidity with a focus on cardiovascular and pulmonary disease, Journal of cardiopulmonary Rehabilitation, 20(1), 2000, pp 8-15.

72. Arthur Block; Murphy's Law, Doctors, Price stern Sloan, 200, p 9.

73. Siegel B, *Love, Medicine and Miracles*, Arrow Books, 1988, pp 176- 77

74. Chopra D, Simon D, *Freedom: Meditations to Counter Stress A Complete Detoxification Plan. Techniques to Redirect Cravings*, 2008, pp 59-60

75. A. Newberg etal, *Cerebral Blood flow During Meditation Prayer: Preliminary Findings and Methodological Issues, Perceptual and Motor Skills*, 97,(2), 2003, pp 625-30.

76. W. Lee Cowden et al, *Longevity: Alternative Medicine Definitive Guide*, Magna Graphics (India) Limited, 2002, pp 173.

77. Peter Harrison, *A Complete Guide to Discovering Meditation*, Caxton, 2001, p 77.

79. Paula Ceccaldi et al, *Stress: The Good and The Bad*, Beacon, 2001, p 125.

78. *A to Z Health Guide*, Time, 2004, p 96.

80. Dr. Dean Ornish's Program for Reversing Heart Disease, Ballantine Books, 1990.

81. Ornish D, Healthy Life Style ups Enzymes Slows Aging Process, Times Trends, The Times of India, New Delhi, Sept'17, 2008, p 35.

82. Meditation slows AIDS progression, Times Trends, The Times of India,

New Delhi, Saturday, July 26, 2008, p 21.

83. Dossey L, *Cancer Seems Almost to be an Occupational Hazard of Sainthood; Meaning in Medicine*, Bantam, 1991, p 209.

84. Dossey, L; Beneficial effects of prayer on health: Healing words: The power of prayer and the practice of medicine, Harper, 1993.

85. Mayo Clinic guide, to self-care, 3rd edition, 2001, p 285.

86. Harmaon Amy; When faith and science clash in US schools, Times Global, The Time of India, New Delhi; Aug' 27, 2008, p 32.

87. Mayo Clinic on Digestive Health; p 105.

88. Dr. Brewer S; Natural Health Guru, DBP, 2008, p 92.

89. Koenig H G; The Healing power of faith, Simon and Schuster, 1999, p 9.

90. R. K. Wallace et al, *Physiological Effects of Transcendental Meditation, Science* 167 (1970), p 1751-1754.

91. R.W. Cranson et al, *Transcendental Meditation and Improved Performance on Intelligence – Related Measures. A longitudinal Study, Personality and Individual Differences*, 12 (1991), pp 1105-1116.

92. Stuart Rothenberg MD, director, Transcendental meditation program for south Florida; tm. Org.

93. Dorland's Illustrated Medical Dictionary, Saunders, Third Edition, International Edition, 2003, p 908.

94. Dr. Herbert Benson, *The Relaxation Response, Harward Medical School Family Health Guide*, 2003, p 90.

95. Yancey P, *Prayer Does It Make any Difference*, Hodder, 2008, pp 249.

96. Myra Huth, April 2007, Journal of Pediatric Nursing.

97. Ken Shelton, *Personal Excellence*, Jaico, 2007, pp 73-74.

98. J Achterberg, *Ritual: The Foundation for Transpersonal Medicine*, Revision, 14;3, 992, pp 158-164

99. Murphy J, *The Power of Your Subconscious Mind*, Bantam Books, 2001, p 96.

100. Catherine Shainberg, *Kabbalah and the Power of Dreaming: Awakening the Visionary Life*, Inner Traditions, pp 02- 05.

101. Tiburon CA, *Alternative Medicine: The Definitive Guide,* Future Medicine Publishing, 1995, p 245.

102. Weil A; Healthy aging, A life long guide to your well being, Anchor Books, 2005, pp 264-265.

103. Martin E. P. Seligman, Learned Optimism New York, Alfred A Knopf,

1971.

104. R Killner et al., *Changes in Chronic Nightmares After One Session of Desinsitization or Rehearsal Instructions*, American Journal of Psychiatry, 149:5 May 1992, pp 659-63.

105. Davies, N. J. H., and Cashman, J. N., Lee's Synopsis of Anaesthesia, 13th edition, Elsevier, 2006, p 838.

106. Actberg, J., "Ritual: The Foundation for Transpersonal Medicine: Revision, 14:3, 1992, pp 158-64.

107. Lone, Siegel B., Medicine and Miracles. Arrow Books, 1988, p 171.

108. Hindustan Times, New Delhi, July 8, 2008, p 20.

109. Yancey P., Prayer: Does it make any difference?, Hodder, 2008, pp 215-21

110. www.hindustantimes.com

111. C. S., Lewis, Miracles, New York, McMillan Co., 1947, p 187.

112. 'Pain, Present, Past and Future', Ronald Melzack; Canadian Journal of Experimental Physiology, 47, 1993 pp 615-29.

113. Harrison's Principles of Internal Medicine, Volume I, 15th Edition; p 76.

114. McLatchie, G. R., et al., Pain relief after abdominal surgery, Oxford hand book of clinical surgery, Publisher, 1994, p 130.

115. Komaroff, Anthony L., The Harvard Medical School Family Health Guide, 2003, pp 382-83.

116. Neale Donald Walsch, Conversations with GOD, Hodder and Stoughton, 1997, p 11.

117. Roland, Paul, How to Meditate, Octopus Publicising group, 2005, p 20.

118. Why some one can feel your pain, Times Trends, Times of India, New Delhi, 2007, June 18, p 21.

119. Dorland's Illustrated Medical Dictionary, 30th Edition, Elsevier, 2003, p 818.

120. A., Carrel, Prayer and Modern Man, More House-Gotham, 1948, pp 42-43.

121. Matthews, D. A. and Larson, D. B., *Faith and Medicine: Reconciling the Twin Traditions of Healing*, Mind/Body Medicine 2, 1997, pp 3-6.

122. Kumar V., Abbas AK, Fausto N., Robbins and Cotran Pathologic basis of disease, Saunders, 7th Edition, 2005, p-88.

123. Goss R.J., Regeneration versus repair. In Cohen I K, Diegelman RF, Lindball W J (eds): Wound healing. Biochemical and Clinical Aspects, Philadelphia, W B Saunders, 1992, pp 26-39.

124. Life, The Universe and Every Thing Hindustan Times, Oct'6, 2008, p 21.

125. Ornish D; Dr. Dean Ornish's Programme for Reversing Heart Disease, Ballantine Books, 1996, pp 10.

126. Murphy J, The power of your subconscious mind, Bantam Books, 2001, pp 74-93.

127. Peter Albright, *A Marshall Health Guide, complimentary therapies*, Marshall, 1997, p 151.

128. Mc Avoy, B. R, *Death after bereavement*, B. M. J., 1986, p 293.

129. Mc Avoy, B. R, *Death After Bereavement*, B. M. J., 1986, p 835.

130. Matthews, D.A., McCullough M. E., D. B. Larson, H. G. Koenig, J. P. Swyers, and M. G. Milano, "Religious Commitment and Health Status, "Archives of Family Medicine 7 ,1998, p 123.

131. Koenig, H. G., "Religion, Spirituality, and Medicine: Application to Clinical Practice," JAMA 284, 2000, p 1708.

132. Mueller, P. S., Plevak, D. J., and Rummans, T. A., "Religious Involvement, Spirituality, and Medicine: Implications for Clinical Practice," Mayo Clinic Proceedings 76 (12), 2001, p 1226.

133. Matthews et al: "Religious Commitment and Health status," Archives of Family Medicine 7 ,1998, pp 118-24.

134. Gawande, Atul, Better, A surgeons notes on Performance, Penguin Book, 2007, p 191.

135. Barnes VA, Davis, HC. etal, Impact of meditation on Resting and Ambulatory blood pressure and heart rate in youth, psychosomatic medicine, 66, 2004, pp 909-14.

136. Hill M, Weber R, and Werner S; The heart mind connection, Behavioral healthcare, 26, 2006, pp 30-32.

137. Weil, Andrew, Spontaneous Healing, Ballantine Books, 1995, p 100

138. Ornish, Dean, Dr. Dean Ornish's Program for Reversing Heart Disease, Ballantine Books, 1996.

139. Barnes VA, Davis , HC. etal, Impact of meditation on Resting and Ambulatory blood pressure and heart rate in youth, psychosomatic medicine, 66, 2004, pp 909-14.

140. Delhi Times, The Times of India, July 20, 2008, p 14.

141. Ornish D, Dr. Dean Ornish's program for reversal of heart disease, Ballantine, 1992.

142. Larimore, W. L., "Providing Basic Spiritual Care for Patients: Should It Be the Exclusive Domain of Pastoral Professionals? American Family

Physician 63 (1), 2001, p 40.

143. Matthews, D. A., Larson, D. B., and Barry, C., The Faith Factor: An Annoted Bibliography of Clinical Research on Spiritual Subject (Rockville, Md.: National Institute of Healthcare Research, 1993), introduction (unpaginated).

144. Sheldon G. Sheps, Mayo clinic on High blood pressure, Orient paper back, 1999, pp 77-78.

145. Das S.K. , Sanyal K, Basu A-Study of Urban community Survey in India. Growing trend of high prevalence of hypertension in a developing country. Int. J. Med. Sci 2005, 2: pp 70-8.

146. European Society of Hypertension, European Society of Cardiology Guidelines Committee, 2003- European Society of Hypertension, European Society of Cardiology Guidelines for the management of arterial hypertension, J. Hypertension 2003, 21: pp 1011- 53.

147. Vasan RS, Larson MG, Leip EP- Assessment of frequency of progression to hypertension in non hypertensionsive participants in the Framingham Heart study. A cohort study, lancet 2001; 358: pp 1682- 6.

148. He J. Whelton P.K. – Elevated systolic blood pressure and risk of cardiovascular and renal disease: Overview of evidence from observational epidemiologic studies and randomized controlled trials. Am Heart J 1999; pp 138 : 211-9.

149. Fuster V etal; Pathogenesis of coronary disease: The biological role of risk factors. J Am coll Cardiol, 1996, pp 27:964.

150. Ogden L G, He J, Lydick E,Whelton PK: Long- term absolute benefit of lowering blood pressure in hypertension patients according to the JNC VI risk stratification. Hypertension, 2000, 35: pp 539- 43.

151. Gupta RJ: Trends in hypertension epidemiology in India. Hum Hypertension, 2004, 18: pp 73-8.

152. Lic, Engstrom G, Hedbald G, Janzon L: Blood pressure control and risk of stroke. Stroke 2005, pp 36:725-30.

153. Steve Parker, The Human Body Book, Dorling Kindereley, 2007, p 127.

154. National Institute of health, The sixth report of the joint National committee on prevention, detection, evaluation and treatment of high blood pressure, 1997.

155. rahulsingh@hindustantimes.com

156. Gordon H Williams, Hypertension Vascular disease, Harrison's principle of Internal Medicine, Vol-I, 15th Edit, P-1415

157. Benson H, McCallie D P; Angina Pectoris and the placebo effect", N Engl. J. Med, 1979, 300:pp 1424-29.

158. Scammell TE: The neurobiology, diagnosis, and treatment of narcolepsy. Ann Neural 53: p 154.

159. Scammell TE: The neurobiology, diagnosis, and treatment of narcolepsy. Ann Neural, 2003, 53: p.

160. Weil, Andrew, Spontaneous Healing, Ballantine Book, 1995, p 237.

161. Roth, T.A., L Merlotti & SA Burton et al: Narcolepsy. 3rd international symposium proceedings, Chicago, Matrix communication, 1989.

162. Flemons WW: Clinical practice, Obstructive sleep apnoea, N- Engl J. Med:, 2002, 347:pp 498.

163. National sleep Foundation, 1522k street NW, suite 500, Washington, DC 2005.

164. Guide to Diet , Health and Fitness, Time incorporation, 2005, p 107.

165. Indian sleep Disorders Association, Dept of Pulmonary and sleep medicine, casualty Block, Safdarjang Hospital, New Delhi.

166. A TO Z Health Guide, TIME, Time Book, 2004, p 35.

167. Norman Vincent Peale: The positive way to change your life, vermilion, London 1998, p 87.

168. J.S. Levin, Larson, D. B. and Puchalski, C. M. "Religion and Spirituality in Medicine: Research and Education," JAMA 278, 1997, pp 792-93.

169. Ceccaldi P, Diricq A, Bagieu C; Stress the good and the bad, Beacon, 2000, p 38.

170. Irvin M. etal; Biol. Psych. 27, 1990, pp 22-30.

171. Philip T Hagen: Mayo clinic guide to self care, third edition, 2004, p-236.

172. Seegel B, Love, medicine and miracles, Arow Books, 1988, p 183.

173. Patricia, P. C., Archive of internal medicine, 2002.

174. Sunday Times, Times of India, July 20, 2008, p 27.

175. Brand P, Healing, port land, 1984.

176. Delhi Times, Times of India, Aug 30, 2007, p 5.

177. Mon Maney 'T', Ulcer as an infections disease, Annals of Medicine, Sept, 1993.

178. Benson, Herbert, the relaxation response (New York: Harper Torch, 1976

179. Health Capsule, Leizure, Delhi Times, Times of India, Sept 25, 2008, p 4

180. A to Z Health Guide – Time 2004, p 96.

181. Davidson, R. J., Kabbat- Zinn J. etal; Alterations in Brain and Immune function produced by mindfulness meditation, psychosomatic medicine, 65, 2004, pp 909-14.

182. Yancey P; Prayer- Does it make any difference, Hodder, 2008, pp 254- 255.

183. Keefer, L and E. B. Blanchard; A one-year follow-up of relaxation response, meditation as a treatment for irritable bowel syndrome; Behavior research and therapy 40, 2002, pp 541- 46.

184. Haslett C, Chilvers ER, Boon NA, Colledge NR; Davidson's Principles and Practice of Medicine, 19th Edition, Churchill Livingston, 2002, pp 817- 818.

185. Hagen P. T., Mayo Clinic guide to self care, 3rd Edition, Oriental paper. 2001, p 77.

186. Murphy J., The Power of your subconscious mind, Banton Books, 2001, p 45.

187. Creamer P, Singh C. C etal; Sustained improvement produced by nonpharmacologic intervention in fibromyalgia: Results of a Pilot study, Arthritis care research, 13, 2000, pp 198-204.

188. OTT MJ, Norris R and Lad Bauer-Wu S. M; Mindfulness meditation for oncology patients: A discussion and critical review, Integrative cancer therapies, 5, 2006, pp 98-108.

189. Palmer K. R., Penman ID, Peterson Brown S; Inflammatory bowel disease, Davidson's Principles and Practice of Medicine, Churchill Livingstone, 2002, p 809.

190. E. J. Boyko, etal; Risk of ulcerative colitis among former and current cigarette smokers, New England Journal of medicine, 1987, pp 707-10.

191. Andrew Weil; spontaneous Healing, Ballantine Books, 1995, p 113.

192. Faith is God can relieve pain; Times Trends, Terms of India, Sept'29, 2008, p 17.

193. L Loyd G. G., Sharpe MC; Medical Psychiatry, Davidson Principles and practice of medicine, 19th Edition, 2002, pp 262.

194. Komaroff A L; Stuttaford T; The Harward Medical School Family Health Guide, 2003, pp 395-401.

195. Parker S, The Human body Book, Dorling Kindersley, 2007, p 239.

196. Siegel, B, Love, Medicine and miracles, Arrow Books, 1988, p 18-20.

197. Simonton O etal, Getting well Again, J.P. Tarcher, Los Angels, 1978.

198. Jung C G, Modern Man in search of a soul, 1955.

199. Siegel, B; (1988), Love, Medicine and miracles, Arrow Books, p 67-75.

200. Siegel, B; (1988), Love, Medicine and miracles, Arrow Books, p 152.

201. Achter berg J.Lawlis G F, Imagery of disease, 1978.

202. Calaprice A; The New Quotable Einstein, Princeton Univeristy Press, 2005.

GLOSSARY

Aerobic exercises:

Exercise designed to increase oxygen consumption by the body to improve functioning of the cardiovascular and respiratory systems.

Amaterasu:

Ancient sun goddess of Japan's Shinto religion, born from the left eye of Izanagi.

Amputation:

The surgical removal of a limb or any other part of the body.

Anaemia:

A decrease in the body's haemoglobin (oxygen carrying component of red blood cells).

Angina Pectoris:

Chest pain, which occurs when the heart's demand for blood is more than its supply.

Antibiotic:

A substance that can destroy or inhibit the growth of bacteria and some other organisms that cause disease.

Appendicectomy:

Removal of the appendix through surgery.

Arrhythmia:

An abnormal rhythm of the heartbeat.

Atherosclerosis:

A disease of the arteries in which a build up of a tissue called plaque on the wall of the artery narrows it and reduces blood flow.

Autoimmune response:

A reaction of the body against its own tissues, which are treated as foreign substances.

Autopsy:

Postmortem examination of a body.

Bacteria:

Tiny, single-celled organisms that can cause disease.

Benign:

A harmless tumour, which is not cancerous.

Brain stem:

The part of the brain that connects the brain with the spinal cord. It consists of the medulla oblongata, pons and the midbrain and controls movements, sensations and reflex actions.

Cancer:

Abnormal growth of cells resulting in tumours that may spread to other parts of the body.

Cardiac arrest:

The cessation of pumping when the heart stops beating completely.

CCU:

Caronary Care Unit.

Cerebrovascular accident (stroke or apoplexy):

Sudden attack of weakness or paralysis due to the interruption of blood flow to the brain. It could be due to blood clotting in the artery of the brain or a haemorrhage.

Cholecystectomy:

Removal of the gall bladder through surgery.

Cognition:

A process of knowing, which includes perceiving, recognising, conceiving and reasoning.

Colon:

Part of the large intestine.

CT:

Computed Tomography.

Defibrillation:

Administration of a controlled electric shock to restore normal heart rhythm.

DIC:

Disseminated Intravascular Coagulation, serious bleeding disorder.

DNA:

Deoxyribonucleic acid, a complex organic compound that helps the formation of genes, found in all living beings.

Ejection fraction:

The proportion of blood ejected during each heartbeat.

Endoscopy:

Process of looking into a body cavity or organ through a flexible tube with a light.

Evisceration:

Removal of viscera from its cavity.

Oestrogen:

A female hormone.

Femoral Hernia:

Protrusion of a loop of intestine or part of an organ through the femoral canal (an opening in the groin).

Fibrillation:

A rapid and chaotic beating of individual heart muscle fibres, which may lead to inability of the heart to pump blood.

Free radical:

An atom carrying an unpspaired electron, which is highly reactive and unstable.

Haemorrhage:

Bleeding from a damaged blood vessel.

Heparin:

A substance with anticoagulating properties.

Hippocampus:

Part of the brain that deals with processing memory and emotions.

Hormone:

Chemical substance, formed by one part of the body which travels to another to initiate action. Hormones regulate physiological activities.

Immunity:

The body's resistance to infection and disease.

Infarct:

A part of the tissue or organ that has died due to interrupted blood supply.

Infection:

The invasion of the body by harmful organisms such as bacteria that cause disease.

Inflammation:

A condition characterised by swelling, heat, redness, and pain. The body's reaction to injury or infection.

Intestinal Obstruction:

Blocking or clogging of intestinal lumen causing hindrance to the passage of the intestinal contents.

Ischaemia:

An inadequate flow of blood to a part of the body, caused by a blockage in the blood vessel.

Kabbalah:

Hebrew word, meaning to receive the communication between God and Moses. A form of Jewish mysticism.

Kurukshetra:

The place where the battle of Mahabharata was fought.

Laparoscopy:

Examination of the interior of the abdomen using a laparoscope (endoscope).

Malignant:

A tumour that can invade adjacent tissue and spread to other sites in the body.

Malignancy:

Cancer.

Metastasis:

The spread of a malignant tumour from its original site to other parts of body. Usually, cells from a tumour travel through the blood or lymph stream.

Myocardial infarction (MI):

Death of a portion of the heart muscle, following interruption of its blood supply.

Necrosis:

Cell death.

Nirvana:

End of suffering and desire, which leads to peace and liberation from the cycle of birth, death and rebirth.

Noetic:

Pertaining to the intellect or cognition.

Pancreatitis:

Inflammation of the pancreas, caused by autodigestion of the pancreas by its own enzymes. Common causes are alcoholism or a biliary tract disease.

Placebo:

A substance that should have no effect on the body. In some instances, it can relieve symptoms because the patient believes it can.

PSA:

Prostatic Specific Antigen, a tumour marker to detect cancer of the prostate gland.

Psychogenic:

Pertaining to symptoms and illnesses that begin in the mind rather than in the body.

Psychosomatic:

Pertaining to symptoms and illnesses that involve both the mind and the body, such as IBS (Irritable Bowel Syndrome).

Pulmonary embolism:

Obstruction of the pulmonary artery or one of its branches by blood clots.

Sedative:

A drug that has a calming effect and relieves anxiety and tension.

Septicaemia:

A condition in which disease causing organisms have spread to the blood stream due to an infection in any part of body.

Serotonin:

A neurotransmitter.

Side effect:

An unwanted reaction caused by a medication or treatment.

Spider Woman:

Native American goddess, who holds everybody and everything in her web.

Spleen:

A solid organ in the abdominal cavity. Acts as reservoir of blood, disintegrates red blood cells and also produces blood cells.

Strangulated Hernia:

Compromise of the blood supply of the hernial content, leading to gangrene.

T- Cell:

A white blood cell, which is part of the body's immune system and is produced by the bone marrow.

Tachycardia:

An increase in the heart rate above normal.

Tumour:

A new growth of tissue in which multiplication of cells is uncontrolled and progressive. Also called neoplasm.

Index

Scientific evidence has confirmed the contribution of spirituality and prayer to health and longevity. No longer should people choose between 'the scientific' and 'the spiritual', for these domains can come together in a beautiful complementarity. Dr. Vinod Nigam's splendid book shows how. This book is a window onto the medicine of the future: the union of the body, mind, and spirit—and intellect, intuition, and inner knowing.

Larry Dossey, MD
Author of *Healing Words and the Power of Premonitions*,
Dallas, Texas, U S A

I am impressed by this book. Treat yourself to marvelous adventure and inspirational experience by reading this book.

Harold G. Koenig, MD
Author of the bestseller *The Healing Power of Faith*
North Carolina, USA

...You sound like me. I know several patients who prayed or left their troubles to God and healed their cancers.

Bernie Siegel, MD,
Author of the bestseller *Love, Medicine and Miracles*
New Haven, Connecticut, USA

Prayer has tremendous power to heal. Dr. V.K. Nigam, a surgeon, prays to alleviate his patient's sufferings and cure them of chronic illnesses. In *40 Minutes with God*, he shares his meditation techniques and shows how spirituality can breach the boundaries that limit traditional medicine. He does not rely on his skills with the scalpel alone, he prays for his patients. He is one of the few Indian doctors who has a medical technique patent to his name, that is "Window Operation" for Hydrocele.

The Times of India

Dr. Vinod Kumar Nigam, a laparoscopic surgeon, prays for his patients for forty minutes every morning and has found it quite fruitful. He is not alone as researchers substantiate the belief that prayers possess miraculous powers.

Hindustan Times

40 Minutes with God is an extremely well-written book. I feel that spirituality is very supportive to the patient's needs, the results are encouraging to the people. When you have a medical problem yourself and there is not much hope, then reading this gives encouragement to you both physically and mentally. The present day realization that the scientific medicine and religious beliefs are both required together in unison for treatment and cure of the sickness, they are not against each other.

Mr. Robert G. Harrison
The Asswin Project in India
(U.K. Registred NGO)
For Welfare of Animals

40 Minutes with God in a simple manner advocates the theory of spirituality as an aid to modern medical science. Dr. Nigam's effort is to spread the knowledge that science and spirituality go together and are complementary and medical practitioners need to use both in their treatment.

Vasant Sathe
Former Union Minister

40 Minutes with God is an outstanding book about health and spirituality. It deals well with healing and spirituality. We, Arabs, as Muslims are God-fearing and believe in healing with God's blessing. Prayers to God, we believe, are always answered. This book, I am sure will put confidence in people and patients and will help in healing and recovery.

Dr. Ahmed Salem Al-Wahishi, Ph. D
Ambassador (Retd.), Chief Relation Officer,
Arab League, in New Delhi

40 Minutes with God is the most valuable research work of Dr. Nigam. He has proved, through real case histories, how science and spirituality complement each other. The book carefully and creatively presents techniques, developed by Dr Nigam for health and healing, that anyone can use for treatment of certain acute and chronic diseases. *40 Minutes With God* is not yet another simple advisory but a self-help book. Read on to find a real connection between the body, mind and spirituality.

Dr. K.B.L. Mathur
Former Economic Advisor
Government of India